# This is Love

## Jeremy Jaeger

For you

# Prelude

## before

"You want some bananabread?" he asks. She's sitting on the kitchen counter, shakes her head no. He moves around her, close to her, slicing the bread, reaching for the butter. "You sure? My mom made it and sent it to me under the care and protection of the US Postal Service, and it's preeetty goo-ood." She smiles, shakes her head again. "I don't want anything to eat," she says. He looks at her, shrugs. "Okay, sewt urseff," he mumbles through an oversized mouthful. She laughs a little and dips her head, looks down at her swinging legs.

He's happy. Happy to have someone in his house to offer something to, happy that he doesn't care whether or not she takes it. The night started with Kevin and Joseph, and some girl who was with them, at Takara's. A party from the get-go: waves of edamame and tempura and sushi and sake, gales of laughter. They leave the restaurant and the girl waves goodbye, he and Kevin and Joseph look at each other: what next? The Galaxy, for karaoke? Splendid idea, hrrm, capital notion old

2

fellow, hrrm hrrm. Why are you talking in a bad British accent? Shut up, you.

The blood is warm, the night is young. In the car someone calls Tess, Joseph's ex. The two of them are on good terms, and Tess is fun, and maybe she'll bring someone.

He's sitting at the table, sipping a cocktail, browsing the song catalog. Hey!, he hears Kevin say. He looks up and here comes Tess, smiling and waving. She sits down along with Isobel, the friend she's brought. Ole! Drinks clink together, to the good times. He feels happy, in star-alignment, knows he is filled with the light tonight. Drinks get drunk, songs get sung. Tess is complaining about her too-girly little pink shirt, somehow moments later he's wearing it and she's giddy with laughter.

Later than that he's dancing with Isobel, and inside himself he realizes this is exactly how it's supposed to be when a boy and a girl are dancing together; realizes with delight that this feeling of cooperatively-motivated movements is the reason why people dance in pairs.

The party moves from the bar to his house, begins to sift away, to wind down. Kevin and Joseph are going to go home, Tess and Isobel are going to sleep here in his bed, and he's going to sleep on the couch. But he's busy with something, puttering away at some task, when he looks up and Joseph and Tess and Kevin are gone; gone, and not coming back. Shortly thereafter he finds himself in the kitchen, happy with a mouthful of his mother's bananabread and a quiet, slim, dark-haired girl he met a few hours ago now sitting on his kitchen counter, smiling as she looks down and her legs swing to and fro.

"You look a lil' sleepy," he says. "It's pretty late," she says, nodding. "Well," he says, "let's get you to bed."

Two lamps, one sitting on the desk next to the bed, another standing in the corner, next to an aging brown recliner. The lampshades mute the incandescence, glow, make the light quiet. Soft rugs on the tile floor, posters on the walls; books and cd's fill the bookcase, stand here and there in piles. He hands her a pair of pajama pants and an old t-shirt, stands there looking innocent until she laughs and motions impatiently for him to turn around. He busies himself with the stereo, hears the sound of clothes falling softly to the floor, of bedsheets being drawn back.

The cd he's chosen is Air's *Moon Safari*. It starts with water sounds, a hidden stream flowing over rocks, around the roots of night-trees that reach up to a sky full of watching stars. He turns, she is sitting in the bed; propped against the pillows, covers drawn up to her waist, hands folded in her lap. Wearing his t-shirt, watching him.

"I see you like comic books," she says quietly, pointing to the bookshelves behind him. "No," he says, "I *love* comic books." A half-smile crosses her face, she nods. "Me too," she says. He turns back to the bookshelf, selects a few favorites, goes to the bed and sits down next to her. Well, this is by so-and-so, it's about such-and-such, the story is fine mostly I like the artwork, and here's this one, it's pretty great, it takes place in...

The nighttime forest around them, the stars above. He feels it moving within him, feels it drawing them together, as their lips meet he feels how it is a part of the flow.

Moon safari, stardust memories. Kissing is a flame,

a wake-up call. Who is this, what is this. New questions. Mouths come apart to talk, to ask each other who they are.

Some kind of reticence in her eyes. "So where's your girlfriend?" she asks. Taken aback, he shakes his head. "I don't have a girlfriend," he says. "I'm not…like that. How could I be here with you if I had a girlfriend? If I did, this obviously would be a crappy thing to do to her, to cheat like this. But it wouldn't be a very nice thing to do to you, either. That's not…I'm just not built that way." She's quiet, looking back at him.

She turns onto her side, towards the wall, nestles into the pillow. "I'm tired. Your bed's comfortable," she says, in a voice that says, I don't want to talk anymore. He looks down at her for a moment, at this slim, dark-haired cipher lying next to him. "Okay," he says. "Let's go to sleep then." He lets his arm rest across her body; lies there wondering, listening to her measured breathing for awhile before sleep takes him away.

Sometime later she wakes. She turns, watches him as he sleeps. The lamp in the corner is still on, and her eyes travel across all that it illuminates around her; this room full of memories, of a color and kind of life she has never known. She will tell him this, much later. How she looked at him, lying there so close. How she wanted him to wake, and also not to wake; afraid that if he did, she would find that it was only some dream that she was dreaming.

Morning light. Knocking on the bedroom door. It's Joseph and Tess, apparently Tess and Isobel have to be somewhere. Come on, Joseph says to him, we'll get breakfast after we drop them off.

It's a short drive to their apartment. He sits in the back seat with Isobel, unsure what to say. The goodbye is strange; something about the way she moves, the way she won't quite look at him. A little bit later, asking Joseph questions, he finds out that Tess and Isobel are currently on their way to the bus station to pick up Isobel's arriving boyfriend.

When he gets home he walks into his room, stands there for awhile. He picks up the pillow she slept on, brings it to his face; his eyes close as he breathes the ghost of her into his body. He sits down at the desk, picks up a pen and fills an empty page with the way he feels. Sweet melancholy, gratitude at having been so open; a heart that empathizes with her, that is glad to be alive in this world full of strange, tender, fragile creatures.


Much later, he will tell her about this single page; she will ask for it, and read it, and fold it into a small square which she will keep in her wallet for a very long time.


A week goes by, and another. Busy with his life, thoughts of Isobel come and quickly go. He remembers the conversation, the look in her eyes; wonders what the night might've cost her, hopes she is okay.

Out at night, headed to some bar with several people. Just beyond the edge of his awareness is the idea that she might be there too.

Colored lights. Loud, crowded. He doesn't really

know these people, they're Kevin and Joseph's friends. Two of the girls are flirting with him, poorly, falling flat. He smiles politely, says something banal, looks around as he sips his gin and tonic. Tess, laughing. Behind her Isobel. As their eyes meet he feels it. A sense of focusing, a shift in the quality of the night.

They find each other at the bar. A brief island-time together in which neither really knows what to say, but it doesn't matter. The friends and acquaintances eclipse the moment, swirl them back up and apart. Later in a group, on the crowded dance floor, he maneuvers his way to her and notices that same feeling as they dance; together, briefly, that body-harmony he'd felt before. Other forces swirl them apart again, and by the next time he looks for her she's gone.

Later that week something bends him out of shape. An inconsequential event that shouldn't matter but it does; triggers somehow a flow of anger and sadness, and the fact that he knows it shouldn't matter makes it worse, a what's-wrong-with-me cycle of recriminations. He thinks of going out and getting drunk. Instead finds himself calling Isobel on the phone.

"How are you," she says. He can hear the curiosity in her voice.

"Um, not great, actually. I was thinking about going out alone and getting drunk...alternatively, though, maybe you want to watch a movie."

"I don't think you should go get drunk, that doesn't sound like a good idea. I like movies. I can't stay up late, I have to go to work early in the morning, but I think you should come over."

"Okay. Cool. I'll see you in a little bit then." He sits there for a moment after hanging up. Noticing that the anger and sadness are gone now; that he is calm, is himself again.

"So you don't really live here?"

"No.  I moved here for work and rented a room in somebody's house.  But he turned out to be crazy, so I had to get out.  I'm just staying here with Tess until I can find another place."

"Crazy, huh?"

"…Yeah.  I don't really want to talk about it," she says quietly.

"Okay.  Me neither," he says after a moment.  She looks up, gives him a small, grateful smile.  "What movies did you bring?" she asks, reaching for the stack of videos on the coffee table.

They watch *Waiting for Guffman*, sitting on the sofa a few inches apart.  Halfway through she takes the half-mattress that's standing rolled up in the corner and lays it out on the floor.  Have to get up early she says, going to lie down.  If I fall asleep you should keep watching though, it's okay.

Before long she is fast asleep.  He watches the movie, at intervals watches her.  Some kind of distance in who she is, even while sleeping some way in which she guards herself.  Who are you.

When he goes he leaves the stack of rented movies on the coffee table, a reason to come back.

Two days later.  They are sitting on the sofa again.  Late afternoon sunlight slants through the blinds, generating a stillness.  The stream of conversational distractions has dried up, dwindled away to nothing.  Locked inside himself; he looks down into his empty hands, feels the pressure mounting. Do something. She's waiting for me, what's wrong with me…Jesus Christ, do something…do something!

He moves with sudden awkward force, pushing his body towards her body, his mouth towards her mouth. Her hands come up, against him, push him back down.

"No," she says. "No, not like this."

In a swirl of confusion he stares back at her. Blinks, swallows. "Because…because you're with someone?"

She sighs, shakes her head. "Yes. Yes, I'm in a relationship. A relationship that's been dying for some time now. That I haven't been able to leave." Her hands press against him as she talks, her voice carries the wonder of disbelief. "You…this gorgeous boy comes out of nowhere. All that part of me wants to do right now is tear your clothes off. But you were right, what you said to me that first night. I don't want this, don't want it with you to be like this."

He sits without moving. Feels her hands resting on his chest, her eyes watching him. Time passes. The bars of sunlight and shadow on the wall deepen, slowly, as the sun dips downward in the sky.

"Can we still keep seeing each other," he says finally.

"Of course. Of course we can. But it can't be anything more than this until…until I can figure out what to do." He looks up, sees her anxious face, her eyes a question. He has no name for this feeling, this sense of stillness deep within.

"I have to go," he says, rising. He sees the sack of groceries they bought earlier sitting on the kitchen table, as though from sometime long ago remembers they're supposed to make dinner here tonight. "I won't be gone long. Something I forgot at home."

He drives. Her words echo, unfold. A seed, invisible in the dark earth of his body, starting now to open.

He goes into his room, closes the door; moves surely, purposefully, following some nameless instinct, a secret programmed sequence that has finally received its activation code. He puts Neutral Milk Hotel's *In the Aeroplane Over the Sea* into the stereo, presses Play and lies down on the bed. Why that, he wonders dimly, and as it begins he realizes clearly that for all the times he has listened to this, it is something right now that he has never heard before.

He lies alone in that sudden, secret garden. Vines grow along the walls, dark violet and blood-red flowers, golden shadows and streaks of silver light that swoop, fall through the air.

What is this asks his silent voice, and at the same time the answer comes: This is who you are.

# after

I awoke into darkness.

It stayed that way for a long time. Days, months, years; how long it lasted, I don't know. In the absence of light, there was no way to mark the passage of time.

While the darkness lasted I lay without moving, feeling my body bring itself together again. The broken pieces shifting about finding where they belonged, stitching themselves back into place. In the darkness around me I heard, or felt, things moving sometimes. Observers of the process, perhaps; or perhaps parts of my body, finding their way back to me in the dark. I don't know. Whatever it might've been, nothing was ever said, nothing was ever spoken.

Eventually the darkness began to recede, slowly. As it did I found myself able to move: first a finger only, after awhile I was able to lift my arm. Finally I was able to sit up, to stand, to move about and see what was around me.

But I found myself to be incoherent, weak. Lost in a world full of ghosts and shadows. The only thing I could grasp was a delicate fragment, the broken shard of a memory. I held that fragment as I slept one night, and as I slept I had a dream. I dreamed of the discovery of a heart: of its landscape, its form and dimension; of discovering a heart's true, secret power. And when I woke, still holding that fragment in my hands, I saw that I had to follow it, to find where it came from; that it was the only way I might ever find my way back out of here again.

I know I can't stay here, in this shadow world, any longer. I can feel myself dying here, slowly but surely, and I know that the only way out is for me to tell this story, to follow where it leads. If I could tell you where it's going to go I would, believe me; but I can't, I wish I could but I can't, I'm sorry.

I don't know how I got here; my memory is broken into bits and pieces. It is probably going to be a difficult journey, for me and for you as well, until I can start to put those bits and pieces together into something that makes sense. And I can't make you any promises. Instead, all I can do…all I can do is ask you to please trust me. Please. I swear that I will not lie to you. I swear that for what I cannot tell you now, there is a reason. And I swear above all else, that by the end you will know everything, that there will be nothing left to hide, no more secrets. But for now, please: I need you to please just trust me.

# I

## the thing behind her eyes

An answer.

This is who you are.

As he drives he sees it in the panorama of ocean rolling away on the left, rolling away to the far-off horizon and rising into the darkening sky. The waves unfurl themselves, fall back again, crash down upon the shore and die there, over and over. I fought with you once, he remembers. With your endlessly repeating mystery, your utter dominance. Heavily drunk and with a sudden storm in his heart, he'd stumbled out alone into the water one night; swore into the darkness, kicked wildly into the waves as they broke against him, beat the water with his fists. He found himself standing there, in water up to his knees, his mind empty. I am the ocean, said the ocean. Why are you so angry, fighting a thing you cannot fight. I am the ocean, and I always will be.

He remembers all this as the road turns away, winds through town. The sudden understanding, the acceptance. How he'd fought with an infinitely patient god who had only waited for him to look up, to see. He parks the car alongside the curb, gets out. Opens the gate, closes it behind him; turns, sees, a short distance, no more than twenty feet away, the front door to the nondescript, bungalow-style apartment she lives in. As he crosses that short distance he feels the clear difference within; that it is not the same door he walked out of, only an hour ago; that who he was, then, is no longer who he is now.

The evening passes; calm, easy. Enough has been said: a line drawn, an agreed-upon boundary they won't cross. They know where they stand now in relation to one another, and they move that way as they make dinner, as they sit together and eat. From time to time their eyes meet, rest there until he smiles, or she smiles, and looks away again. Quiet, easy. The simple feeling of having arrived somewhere together is enough.

They are clearing up, washing dishes, putting things away. Noises outside. A car door slams shut. Raised voices, coming nearer, growing. The front door bangs open and Tess careens into the room, followed closely by her boyfriend Bobby.

Immediately the atmosphere changes. Dark clouds on the near horizon, a gathering storm. In what seems like no time at all he finds his body tense, his mind on full alert as he tries to understand what is suddenly happening.

Tess and Bobby are drunk, fighting. A strange, loose, dangerous kind of fighting, from behind masks and with hidden knives. Bursts of sharp-edged laughter, wild movements. What flashes through him is the realization that he and Isobel are somehow involved, that there are unknown forces at play here that have swept them up into this brewing conflagration.

Isobel's eyes are cast down. She sits at the table, still as a stone, her face pale and drawn. He looks at her and sees that she is shutting down. Fading. He can't explain why but knows it is serious, can feel the danger.

He doesn't understand. He doesn't have time to try. He rises, sword drawn, acts and reacts: moderating, soothing, asserting principles. Puts himself between Isobel and the battle, but Tess and Bobby want something, need something, there will be no peace given for nothing tonight. Finally Bobby puts his offer on the table. Four little white pills. MDMA, he says. Ecstasy, one for each of us. Take it, and then everything will be fine.

The room passes into stillness. The still, quiet eye of the storm. He feels the three of them watching him, waiting.

He knows what this is, what this little white pill will do to him if he takes it inside himself. How it opens the floodgates of emotion. Dismisses locks, doors. Ignores lines, boundaries.

The three of them, this is what they all want. Isobel will barely look at him. In her face he sees that she knows she cannot ask this of him, but is asking it all the same.

He could just leave, he knows this. Could just turn and walk out the door right now. But he also knows something bad will happen here, will happen to her, if he goes.

He knows this is not what he wants to do, to take this little white pill. That in doing so he will be walking into a country he can't control.

But he is not afraid. He looks at Isobel, sitting there pale and silent. Understands the choice he is making, as he picks the little white pill up from the table, puts it into his mouth and swallows it down.

Bobby claps him on the back, Tess claps her hands and hoots. Bobby, Tess and Isobel each take one of the little white pills as he sits down in a chair, across the table from Isobel. Without saying anything she looks at him, and in her eyes he sees disbelief mixed with gratitude, hope mingling with fear. He nods, barely, says nothing. Tess and Bobby cavorting now, the hostility draining quickly away. He sits quietly, waiting for the invisible wave that is now racing towards the shore.


Memories are falling from the sky like snowflakes. Ornate, tangible, they collect in his lap; he picks them up, turns them over, astonished at how beautiful they are, how they resonate within his body. A rush of wind through all the leaves, they tremble as the great trunk itself bends, sways.

He is sitting on the sofa, someone taps him on the shoulder. He looks up, Isobel smiles, a dream smile; she takes a video from the stack on the coffee table, waves it in the air, laughs gently at his confusion. You rented this, she says, you said you hadn't seen it since you were a child. I think now is a good time, she says as she slips the video into the player.

Click, whirrr. Whoosh...and he is lost, awash in a blaze of sound and light, of memory. The giant robots battling amongst the stars, the child within him crying out, soaring. Ohmygod, Transformers he says, holding his head between his hands; Isobel laughs, pleased, Yeah I thought you might like this right now, she says. Oh my god I used to love this so much he says, his hands holding his head, his face as he tries to contain himself, tries to contain the pure wonder of the awoken child within. Isobel claps her hands and laughs as he squirms, pushes himself into the sofa, his body shivering with an almost terrible joy.

Somebody plops down next to him, talking, laughing. Here mate, says Bobby's Cockney-accented voice. Bobby presses something into his hand, he looks down, sees he's holding a phone. It's my brother, all the way across the pond. Say hello!

He barely knows Bobby, certainly doesn't know his brother. It doesn't matter, it's a human voice, a collection of infinite possibility. Good things tumble out of the phone into his ear, more good things roll back out of his mouth. Connection, across thousands of miles of space and time. Connecting drives his body up, in an arc towards the stars.

Time disappears, drifts away. The apartment is darker, the TV off. Tess and Bobby are gone, he doesn't know where and doesn't care.

He closes his eyes. Crystalline embers glow within, burn with a soft, sweet radiance, burn in pulsing slow waves. He feels Isobel's body come next to him, come so close. Together, alone now. Where is the line. Hold fast to the boundary.

He feels the people he loves forming out of the darkness, filling the room. Watchful silhouettes, emanating care for him and who he is. He breathes in, riding the wave, searching for the words.

Friends…it's such a little word, he says. To just say friends is too small, too little for something that is so much…

Tell me, says Isobel, softly. Her hands come to rest on his shoulder, fingertips on his arm. Tell me where you come from.

Oh god…Amber and Tiffany, just to see them. To watch them, how two friends can make a whole. They sat with me when I was lost and they mapped the possible world, wondering at all the things I could do, at all the places I could go. Voices that built my heart, my home. Tyler and I were the Masked Lovers, were gargoyles perched on fenceposts waiting to spring…game after game, we made them up over and over. Leandro and Jamie, I can tell them anything, on the same page always. Jamie said Is there a miniature version of you I can carry around in my pocket…

He speaks their names and they coalesce, outlines in the darkness watching; a silent, focusing power. Angels, he whispers. My life is filled with extraordinary angels…

I need…I need to touch you, says Isobel. Can you lie down. Can you take off your shirt and lie down.

Eyes closed, body pressed against the carpeted floor. He feels her hands grasp his neck, his shoulders. Her fingertips tracing fire-lines down the skin of his back. He feels her hands and fingers say the words she cannot speak, saying thank you; saying How and Who and Thank You, over and over again.


Morning the next day. Late morning, close to noon. The two of them are in a restaurant, having breakfast. The busy air of weekend brunch moves around them, doesn't touch them, as though they are in some space beneath this bustling world's notice.

Isobel takes a small, timid bite of food. After a moment puts her fork on the table, looks down at her plate.

"You're not eating very much."

She nods, barely. "I'm not that hungry." She says this and looks up at him then and her eyes are full of questions she can't find the words to ask, full of things she can't name.

And as he looks he sees something else, looking out. Sees something behind her eyes staring back at him. She turns, looks away, looks down into her plate again.

He opens his mouth, closes it again without saying anything. He knows they walked through some kind of fire last night, and it has changed them.

Beneath this bustling world's notice. It is so new. Down in the formless dark it turns, barely even knowing yet that it is something that can turn, can move. It moves, between them, and they feel it and they know they feel it.

She looks up at him, the thing behind her eyes looks up at him. It stares out at him, and from within himself he feels something rise to meet its gaze.


The days pass, growing longer; winter fading, bending quietly into spring. Day by day they grow closer, he and Isobel; as the world around them slowly, inexorably changes, so does the world within.

He knocks on the door, hears her footsteps approaching. The handle turns, the door opens and she is standing there. Always with the same, almost unnoticeable smile at the corners of her mouth, in her face the same gladness, at seeing him on her doorstep, that she tries to but cannot quite suppress.

The boundary stays firm. The promise to wait is like a sacrament they practice each evening; the way they move, the way they sit together, inches apart. The air that stays between their bodies is a talisman, they feel how it binds them together more powerfully than could anything else. Sometimes Tess is there too, sometimes not. Less so, almost never Bobby. Regardless there is no return of that gathered darkness, the storm of that night has disappeared with no visible trace.

But he does not forget. The door closes behind him and he stands still, alone with himself; looks up into the dark sky, breathes in the cool night air. He sees how it is a place in which to become lost, just as clearly sees that is the one thing he cannot do, cannot lose himself. He remembers what he saw within her, and as time passes the things she cannot say begin to show themselves; cracks in Isobel's quiet demeanor manifest as ghosts, as rays of light and dark shadows.

A late dinner, in a nearly empty, brightly-lit chinese restaurant. The waitress takes their order, walks away.

"Would you like some tea miss?" he says, reaching for the teapot. Isobel nods, briefly, bird-like, as he fills her cup. He drinks and she sits unmoving, looking down at her lap, her arms at her sides as though bound there by some invisible force.

"What do you think about that tiger?" he asks, trying again, gesturing towards the painting across the room. "Looks to me like he's hungry. You think tigers are into chinese food?"

She looks up, then; not at the tiger, not at anything, her eyes wide, moving back and forth across the room. Looks down into her lap, caught somewhere, trapped by something he can't see. She looks up at him, helpless, struck dumb by whatever spirit has suddenly, out of nowhere possessed her.

"Hey," he says. "It's okay," he says, finding the words, feeling his way through this moment. "We don't have to talk. Sometimes people talk just to talk, we don't need to do that. I don't need that. I'm happy just to be here with you." Her eyes are wide and bright, her mouth makes tiny movements, her body locked in the struggle, he sees, to accept that he is here, that he is with her, that he wants to be here with her. The thing behind her eyes stares out at him, trying to see him and remain hidden at the same time.

"Who wants to talk, not me," he says. He leans forward slightly, cocks his head to the side, smiles. "Words are for birds, that's what I say." Emotion fills her face, happiness fighting its way across a battlefield, taking over. She looks around, back down again. Her body quivers.

Two nights later he pulls up alongside the curb, sees Isobel sitting on the step outside her door, hunched over. She walks to the car with her head down, gets in without saying a word, without looking at him. Her aspect is dark, crowded with shadows.

Where do you want to go?

I don't know.

Are you hungry? Have you eaten?

I don't...I can't...

She is slumped against the door, pinned down by something. He doesn't know what; can't see it, can only see what it's doing to her. Can only see the sad exhaustion of a battle being fought in some invisible country.

He drives. He turns the music up and drives, carrying them with speed out of town and into the deep night. She bends toward him, wraps around his arm; he feels it when she starts crying and knows, instinctively, there is nothing he can do or say. He lets her need break against his body like waves upon the shore, his eyes on the road, his questions drifting in the outer darkness. Minutes pass, the trembling of her body against him begins to subside, to pass into stillness. He turns around and drives back towards home.

Later that week he calls her in the afternoon to tell her he won't be coming over, that he's going to stay at school to attend an event, a talk being given later that night. But it turns out to be shorter than he anticipated, so on his way home he stops by anyway.

The surprise, of seeing him when she was expecting not to see him, sends Isobel to the moon. She squirms on the sofa next to him; grabs his arm, giggles and covers her face with her hands. "Look at you!" exclaims Tess, laughing. Isobel burrows further into the cushions, helpless. She can barely look at him. Each time she does she re-collapses, each time her eyes re-assert that he's there she's a bird flying around the room, like a child whose body speaks the joy her mind can't capture, can't express.

He sits bemused, in mild wonderment; happy in the moment to have become her playground, her favorite climbing tree. Tess laughs, and he smiles, teases gently as Isobel squirms, struggles to contain herself.

But deeper within, in his own recesses he is quiet. Too many questions and too few answers. He sees clearly that he is the source of what is happening within her, and he feels its gravity. In the places within him beneath what she yet touches, he is still, and quiet.

## 3 women

So.  So, then.

As I said, I don't know where, or to what, this is all going to lead.  As such, I'm unsure of how to move, in which direction.  But I've got to just take a deep breath, I think, and start walking forward.

A heart.  That dream, that's my starting point; what told me that I didn't belong here, that I came from somewhere else.  What is a heart.  What is the landscape of a heart, this container of a mysterious Something: a force that draws, compels, attracts.

But what is that, what is this force-thing called attraction?  Given a specific instance it's possible to enumerate a list of components, to cite the qualities of specific circumstance; what I mean is that a list of reasons can be found, often, to account for any specific attraction's existence.

But there is also always this level of irreducibility; this kind of acquiescence to the fact that our expressive tools are too limited to accurately depict these greater forces, to discover their true names.

Still, though; still, I have to try. This place that I am in, as much as I don't know what it is or how I came to be here, I do know that I can't stay here any longer; I can feel it…shrinking, darkening, I don't know exactly how to put it, but I can feel it changing around me. I know the margin for error is slim, but I also know that I am working against time. So I can't worry about what I can do or can't do, I just have to try.

My fragmented memory is a ghost town; an abandoned house, an overgrown and long-untended garden. But as I move through it there are things I remember, or at least think I remember. Objects, images that provoke strong feelings. Not just feelings, one particular feeling. Distinct in the singular nature of its pursuit, of its power and influence; its ability to wrest control of the whole of my being and drive my life accordingly. Searching, constantly searching, cataloguing possible repositories for its need, opportunities to perform its single function. A vast warehouse filled with names, faces, postures; boxes of things they said or didn't say, crates full of curves and skirts, of eyes that never even saw me.

Names. Dedicated rooms, almost like temples. When the feeling's constant, ongoing analyses discovered a set of parameters that required attention, a vivid engagement. What might they have to say, what might they remember? What might they be able to tell me about where I come from and who I am? The names form themselves within me, the syllables take shape inside my mouth: Jill Page. Dawn. Sumiko…

The feeling rises, I realize something is about to happen. I breathe in, deeply, and the strong feeling within is carried along with the breath as I let it back out, leaves my body and gives shape to the surrounding

25

world.

There's a stage, a kind of small theater. Footsteps. My heart is beating faster suddenly. Footsteps, approaching…

(There's a round wooden table, upon which sit: a glass pitcher filled with lemonade; three glasses; and a silver tray with small cakes and cookies. There are three wooden chairs around the table, padded with velveteen, dark purple velveteen. The chairs have armrests. The scene is framed in a pool of warm light, beyond which there is darkness. Three women, three young women, emerge from the darkness. They seat themselves in the chairs, which are evenly spaced around the table. They regard each other in silence, and then turn at the sound of approaching footsteps. A man, an older man in formal serving attire, black-tailed coat and white bow tie, white-gloved hands emerging from his sleeves. His graying hair is slicked back from his balding forehead; his carriage, his appearance is impeccable. He carries a tray upon which there are three small porcelain dishes, three silver forks, and three white linen napkins. He places one of each of these, in turn, before the three young women. He then sets the tray on the table and reaches for the pitcher and the three glasses, filling each with lemonade and, again, places a glass in front of each of the young women. Finally he produces from his coat pocket three tea candles and an old-fashioned silver lighter, arranges the candles in symmetry near the center of the table and lights each one, before retrieving the tray, bowing slightly, and taking his leave. As the sound of his receding footsteps fades, the three young women visibly relax, to varying degrees. They exchange glances, of a what-was-that-all-about nature. One of them shakes her head, smiling. She has light brown hair that falls in curling waves to her shoulders and kind, friendly eyes.)

JILL PAGE: He always made me laugh. That was the first thing, probably. He made me laugh, made everyone laugh. But it wasn't just that he made me laugh it was that...(she hesitates, looks up thoughtfully)...it was that he was never mean. He wasn't trying to impress anybody. He made me laugh, all of us laugh, just because he could. Because it was more fun that way.

(The other two young women look at her as she's talking. One of them has short, dark hair that frames her face. Her expression has been serious, almost solemn, but she smiles slightly as Jill Page finishes speaking and looks up at them. She speaks, now, and her voice is soft but clear; the intonations are bell-like and purposeful.)

DAWN: How did the two of you meet? How did you know him?

JILL PAGE: Oh, gosh. Well, it was a long time ago. It was at a summer camp, I think it was called a "High Adventure" camp, or something like that; rock-climbing, river-rafting, that kind of thing. But it was a small group, I don't think there were more than twenty-five of us. And we had this crazy, crazy weather all week, thunderstorms, hail and lightning, even a couple funnel clouds that appeared at one point, just very dramatic weather. And it was serious, you know, because we'd be out somewhere and suddenly these dark clouds would appear, and it's dangerous to be out in the wilderness in weather like that. I remember, we were out on this overnight trip, hiking to this spot where we're going to set up our tents and spend the night. And halfway there this storm sets in, with lightning, so we have to take our backpacks with the metal frames off, because the metal could attract lightning, and then we had to spread out on the hill away from any trees, and away from each other because, at least supposedly, our collected body heat if we were all huddled together could attract lightning too; but, so anyway, there we all are, spread out on this hillside, sitting hunched-up with our ponchos pulled down over our knees in the rain, and then it starts hailing! We're cold and wet and now we're getting pelted with little pieces of ice, it's miserable. Or, at least, it should've been. But he's sitting there yelling, shouting at the weather, these funny, ridiculous things, I don't even remember what but he's literally shouting at the weather. And then, and then he starts singing "You Are My Sunshine" at the top of his voice. And I, all of us, we just couldn't help but be lifted up into that. And I start singing it, and Hope, his sister, she's at the camp as well, and she starts singing it too. And pretty soon the storm breaks, and the sun comes out, but Hope and I can't stop singing. There's just something so silly about it, so silly and fun; she and I just keep singing that song and laughing. Anyhow, that's what the whole week was like, this string of unforeseen circumstances and broken plans that could've ruined the whole camp, but instead had this effect of bonding us, knitting all of us as a group close together. It was...the whole thing was kind of magic, really. And he was a big part of keeping us all aware of...of the possible spirit, I guess is maybe a way of saying it. Anyway. That's how I met him.

DAWN: So you know Hope?

JILL PAGE: Well, yes, but not very well. She and

I became friends that week, but never really after. They lived far away from me; I don't know if I ever saw Hope again, actually. Why do you ask?

DAWN: That's how I met him. I was friends with Hope, we went to the same small college. It was our junior year, in the fall. She and I had become close, kind of suddenly...we kind of had a crush on each other?...I mean it was innocent, but serious too. I'd written a poem about her that was actually published in the school's newspaper. Disguised, it wasn't called "An Ode to Hope" or anything like that, but she knew what it was. And then he came to visit her, and it was...(she pauses, searching for the words)...wonderful, and confusing. (She looks up at Jill Page, who nods.)

JILL PAGE: I can imagine. What did you do?

DAWN: I...(looks down, shakes her head)...what happened between he and I was special. It was a discovery of something...beautiful, honestly. The morning he left, it was early and I was asleep. He woke me up, and it was such a wonderful thing to wake up into, to wake up into remembering, you know: You, oh yes you, I've just discovered you. But you're leaving, too. It felt like being cheated. I remember holding him and saying so (her soft voice settles clearly on each word): It feels like I'm being cheated right now. (She is quiet for awhile.) Afterwards it was just too much. We talked on the phone, he wrote me these long letters that I read and re-read. But it made my relationship with Hope awkward, and we had a pretty small circle of friends; and besides, he wasn't there, and he wasn't going to be there. As much as it was beautiful, it was hard, it was just too hard. He came...he came to see me over Christmas, several weeks later. I was home and he came and stayed with me and my family. And he was won-

29

derful, really, my family loved him. And part of it was very sweet, part of me loved him being there. But I couldn't, I knew the whole time that I couldn't. He could tell, he didn't push, he just kept being so good and sweet. But he was sad, and it grew. In the end we sat across from each other, with this sadness between us. I wanted to reach out to him, but I would've had to go into that sadness to reach him, and I knew I couldn't do that.

JILL PAGE (gently): But it's a beautiful story.

(Dawn nods, smiles.)

DAWN: Yeah. That was the difference between us, I think. I think that to him the sadness was different. He knew we lived far apart, it wasn't that he tried to ignore that reality, or pretend that it wasn't difficult. But the sadness was beautiful to him, I think. He was willing to live with it because he could see its beauty.

JILL PAGE: And you couldn't? I don't think that what happened between the two of you would've happened if you couldn't see it too. I mean, wasn't that probably the strongest part of the attraction? Discovering someone else who could see things that way too?

(They look at each other intently for several seconds, and something unspoken passes between them. Dawn smiles and nods, once.)

JILL PAGE (speaking slowly): But for you, the greater part was the difficulty. And for him, the greater part was the beauty.

DAWN: Was it the same thing between he and you, then?

JILL PAGE (shaking her head): No. Maybe in part, but no. We were very young, too young for that kind of experience, that kind of emotion. It was about discovering somebody, like it was for you too, but more

30

about discovering something.    Realizing that...that there were people out there who you could discover; realizing, with each other, what it's like to be involved in a real, mutual attraction.   It ended because we were young, not because it was hard or sad.    It was always...nice to think about him.

(Jill Page and Dawn look at each other for awhile with satisfaction, and then at the same time, as though remembering that she is there, they turn to the third young woman.   She receives their attention, looking back at each of them in turn, with no discernible change in expression.  Her face, her eyes are silent, say nothing. She is sitting back in her chair, arms folded across her chest.  Dawn and Jill Page exchange a glance.  The third young woman makes a sound, suddenly, of clear irritation, bending forward as she does so.  Her elbows come to rest on the tabletop, her fingertips pressed against her temples.)

SUMIKO (in a barely audible voice): So...annoying.

(She sits up.  Her full lips are compressed in a tight line, the ellipses of her dark Japanese eyes flash with anger as she looks back at Jill Page and Dawn.)

SUMIKO: This is ridiculous.  This whole thing-- (she gestures at the table, the general scene)--is ridiculous.  It's vain and egotistical, and besides it's just pointless.  If he wants to keep drowning himself in his memories then fine, whatever, but leave me out of it.  I don't think he's funny, or sweet, I think he's a foolish child. Do you hear me?

(She looks up into the darkness, scowling).

SUMIKO:   Just because they're willing to play along with your stupid game doesn't mean I'm going to do it too!

31

(She folds her arms tightly across her chest again, glaring at Jill Page and Dawn.)

SUMIKO: Why are you doing this? Why are you letting him do this?

JILL PAGE: Well...because I agreed to. We all did. We chose to enter into his life, to become a part of him. This is a part of that agreement, and I think...I think you already know that, don't you?

DAWN (hesitantly): I'd like to know why...what makes you so angry.

(Sumiko shakes her head, looking down. She bends forward slightly, presses her palms against her eyes. She takes a deep breath, exhales. Reaches for the glass of lemonade and takes a drink. She looks into the distance, focusing. She shakes her head again, sighs.)

SUMIKO: You don't understand. You don't understand because you knew him before. Because when you knew him, he hadn't met her yet, none of that had happened yet. But I only knew him after.

(She is quiet, studying her folded hands. She looks up, at each of them in turn, before she begins to speak again.)

SUMIKO: While each of you were talking, I got angrier and angrier. Because I knew who you were talking about, I knew that person. But he was an illusion. He kept insisting that he was real, that I should believe in him. But then he would just disappear again. I tried to make him stay. I tried everything. I supported, cajoled, pushed, provoked. I threatened. I cried. None of it worked. None of it was enough. He kept turning into a shadow, right before my eyes...

JILL PAGE (quietly): You loved him.

SUMIKO: No. You don't understand.

(Her voice becomes brittle, hard.)

32

SUMIKO: How can you love a ghost? He was gone. There was no one there to love anymore.

(Jill Page looks at Sumiko, who is sitting with her arms folded tight again, a hard, unyielding posture. Everything is silent as the two young women look at each other, and Jill Page's face gradually takes on a more serious, even somber character.)

JILL PAGE (quietly): I'm not ready to...to agree with what you're saying. But I know...I think I know what you're talking about.

(She looks down, concentrating on her thoughts).

JILL PAGE: I did see him again, once, more recently. It had been years since we'd spoken, even, and he just appeared out of nowhere. We were living only a couple hours apart, and after a few emails back-and-forth he came down to see me. I had no idea what to expect, but I was single at the time, and the idea of seeing him again was somewhat exciting. Like I said before, he was always nice to remember. I was a little nervous, but more excited. And we ended up having a really nice time. Really nice. We went out for dinner, and then somewhere else for a couple drinks, and just kept talking. He was engaging and funny, he was a really good listener and had all these interesting things to say...it started to feel kind of magical, to be re-connecting so easily, after so many years in-between. And then...

(She pauses, her aspect narrowing with focus.)

JILL PAGE:...I never understood this, afterwards, but--(she glances up at Sumiko, for a moment)--but maybe I do now. We got back to my house, late. The plan was already for him to stay the night, I'd made up a bed on the couch. What I mean is, getting into the house together was easy. But then...well, we're sitting on my bed.  And it's gone.  The magical thing is just...gone. And it's not me, nothing has changed inside of me. But the person sitting next to me is—the person I've spent the last few hours with has vanished somewhere. And this other person just sits there not saying a word, and after a little bit just stands up, says "goodnight" and walks away.  I didn't understand it at all, I had no idea what to think.  It felt...it wasn't pleasant.  It was so confused. And it wasn't a nice feeling.

(Jill Page is looking at Sumiko as she says these last words.  Sumiko says nothing.  The emotion that pours from her glittering eyes fills the space, causes the light to dim, the darkness to grow closer around them. The silence is a palpable entity, a weight bearing down, daring them to speak now.  Dawn closes her eyes and inhales, deeply; she shakes her head with a deliberate slowness as she lets the breath back out.  Her eyes open. Her soft voice reaches out, renders visible figures of purpose and meaning in the air.)

DAWN:  No.  The worst thing is only the worst thing.  Even the very worst thing of all is still nothing more than something to be afraid of.  And he is afraid, yes.  He is terrified.  No, neither one of you knows where he goes when he disappears.  I don't know either. But I do know that he is still there.  He is still inside, somewhere.

(She looks at Sumiko, now, into her eyes, into those pools of ice and anger.  She speaks again, and the quiet bell-tones of her voice come to rest as if at twilight on the branches of trees.)

DAWN:  I would be angry.  If I had come as close as you did I would try to erase him as you do.  But if he is a ghost then your memories of him will become a ghost, and then that ghost will live in you.  I don't know what path he's on, but I know he chose it. And I think he knows that he has to walk it alone.

(Slow tears slide down Sumiko's face. Her body trembles.)

SUMIKO (quiet, just above a whisper): Yes, it was real. And it was strong, and beautiful. But I had to let it go, I had to move on. I couldn't trust him, couldn't wait to find out if he could figure it out or not. And the fact that the three of us are here, like this...what does that tell you?

(This time it's sadness. This time it's sadness that curls around the three young women in the silence, that hangs like still vines. Ever so slowly the light dims, or they begin to fade. At the last something snaps, like the shutter of a camera, and then the darkness swallows everything.)


I'm...I don't...that's not what I...those women, the things they said...

I'm sitting in the empty theater, staring dumbly at the dark stage. Something is happening in my mind, I —it's too soon, it's...Jesus Christ, what's happening? The deep shadows on the stage are increasing, thickening, starting to take some kind of shape, I—my god, what's happening. The darkness is not just darkness, it is forming tendrils, fingers, slowly reaching out...and as if from very far away something is rising in my mind...

I get up, stumbling, backing away, turning, walking fast away. Damnit, goddamnit. Not too fast. Keep your head down. Go, anywhere, get away from here. My footsteps quicken, I'm running now, my god what happened...

## the right way

Slate gray and violet clouds billow across the western horizon, single bright stars pierce the indiscernible twilight sky above as they walk down the street, slowly. Isobel's hands are jammed into the pockets of her jacket.

"He's coming," she says. "The day after tomorrow."

"I know. I didn't forget." He glances over at her, unsure of what he can or should say. "What are you going to do?..."

"What I have to do. What I already should have done. I'm going to end it." Her voice is a monotone. She looks at him, forces a sad, tired smile.

At the gate she stops, turns to him. "He'll be here for three days. I have to do this alone. I'll call you when he's gone...when it's over."

"Okay."

They stand for a few moments longer in silence. She takes a deep breath, as though bracing herself, and turns abruptly away.

He watches her walk to the front door and go

inside, she doesn't turn, doesn't look back.

Three days, he thinks to himself as he drives away. Three days. Okay.

Friends of his are in town, have come to visit him. The three days are full of laughter and warm light. Beer in hand, he stands in the shallow water with his jeans rolled above his knees, watching the sun set slowly, slowly.

He's gone, her voice says through the phone. He's gone, it's done, she says. It's over.

The three of them sit at a small table. His friend Jack is still here, leaves tomorrow. The bar is filled with dim, red light, noises of conversations, laughter, some music through the stereo system. There are dark circles around Isobel's eyes. I want to come, she'd said. I want to meet your friend. But she is obviously exhausted, and he watches her carefully.

It is somewhat awkward, at first. But as they talk and drink it starts as a trickle, and gradually begins to flow. Isobel and Jack are talking to each other now, a connection emerging. He watches them, realizes he was worried as he feels that worry begin to dissipate. Relax, he thinks. Drink, relax. It's going to be okay.

Time passes, empty glasses begin to clutter the tabletop. Well into it now. Raised voices, expressively exaggerated movements, giggling. Time to leave this bar? But we need more to drink, don't we!

Walking down the street to the liquor store, his spirit begins to float, and he doesn't notice. Doesn't notice, doesn't see. Doesn't see what she's doing with the bottle of liquor they buy. Floating above some-where, he doesn't see the swift convergence of deep shadows, the sudden rush of dark waters.

And then her body isn't working right anymore. She's on the ground, laughing in a way that he doesn't understand, an empty laughter. He is trying to hold her up and it is like trying to hold a broken thing and she begins to retch as it comes out of her, comes out of the mouth of her broken body. He is carrying her to the car, calling Tess as he drives, Isobel slumped over in her seat unconscious and the world a sudden animal chaos, a rushing torrent all around him.

He carries Isobel into the apartment as Tess opens the front door, lays her down. Her face is ghost white, her body shivering, shaking. Something at a high pitch races up inside, spreads against the inside of his skull and flares outwards as he stands above her, watching the body she has fled from convulsing on the floor.

Baby, poor baby, Tess coos softly. She kneels at Isobel's side, smoothing her hair, wiping her face with a towel, ministering to her with a calmness that he sees, registers, latches onto like a frightened child. Tess looks up at him, realizes. She's done this before, Tess says. She'll be fine, Tess says, assures him in a gentle voice. Take off her socks and shoes, rub her feet. We need to get her warm again.

Her feet are so cold. Ice against his fingers, against the life in his hands. Animal anxiety pours into him, painting everything white, blank and white. He presses her feet in his hands as the minutes pass, as the spas-modic trembling of her body withers beneath the blan-kets Tess has wrapped her in, withers and finally sub-sides away.

She'll be okay, Tess says. I'll watch her. Come, put

her in my bed for the night.

He picks Isobel up, cradling her unconscious body in his arms as he carries her into the darkened bedroom, lays her down on the bed. He stands for a long moment, watching her chest rise and fall, her breathing quiet now.

I'll take care of her, Tess says, a hand on his shoulder.

Okay, he says. Thank you. Mind and body empty he turns, walks back out the front door.


He drops Jack off at the airport in the afternoon. What happened, Jack had asked him. I don't know, he'd replied. But he knows that answer is only partly true. As he drives back into town he finds himself wondering, almost in passing, if Isobel made it through the night. He wants to dismiss the thought as silly, overly dramatic. People drink too much and get sick, he's made that mistake himself more times than he cares to remember. But the thought stays, and he knows that there was no mistake in what she did last night. She was so…so far gone. Like she was trying… to go somewhere.

He knocks. Footsteps within. The handle turns, the door opens. When he sees her, standing there, he feels the truth of it as the part of him that was preparing for something else dissolves quietly away.

Her face is a silent admission, a helpless kind of apology. The thing behind her eyes stares out at him, openly now.

He moves, speaks carefully. Careful to be with her, here and now. Careful to stay slightly apart.

"What happened?"

"…He punched a hole in the wall. Then later he apologized and fixed it. He went to the hardware store and bought what he needed and fixed it. He left. I sat for awhile. I called you. And then I…and then I tried to forget."

They sit together on the sofa, just as they have been for the last few weeks. For the first time without anything to say, for the first time in real silence.

He spends the next few days alone, working. Schoolwork that's almost due, a research paper applying the principles of semiotics to a study of Japanese comic books. It's engaging, he is absorbed with it; reading and writing, discovering ideas and struggling to articulate them. At the same time he's generating a transfer application, to a school in another state with a program that he knows would be a very good fit for him.

It all reminds him that he has goals and ambitions. That he has a life which has steadily gained momentum over the last year, a life in which purpose has grown stronger, in which vision has begun to clarify.

Isobel moves in the background of these thoughts, a silent shadow. He feels something like a question, within him, that he can't grasp, can't articulate.

He finishes the application, mails it off. Puts the finishing touches on the paper and turns it in. The quarter is over, spring break has arrived. He's getting on a plane tomorrow, flying to Iowa to spend the week with his sister. It's a morning flight. Isobel's car-pool to work leaves early, goes by the airport, so he is spending the night with her, catching a ride in the morning.

They have dinner, watch a movie. For the first time they find conversation together dropping into awkward lulls, stilted pauses. Neither can find or name the silent elephant in the room: that there are no more obstacles, no more clear reasons to not move across the space that sits between them. Nothing, any longer, standing in the way.

Lying in her bed, unsleeping, he stares up into the darkness. The air is still, heavy like a blanket. She moves, suddenly, her mouth comes onto his with a desperation, a near-panic. It breathes words into him, finally. "No," he says, as his hands take hold of her, hold her firmly, gently away.

"No," he says again. "It's not that time. If we're going to do this, it's not going to be a thing that fumbles in the dark, that doesn't know itself; a thing that doesn't know what it's doing. We have been careful. We have waited this long for it to be the right time. We can wait a little longer." He speaks the words and feels it as they enter her, dispel her body's tension, a mechanism of release. Her head comes to rest against his shoulder, her hand across his chest.

"I'm afraid." Her voice is a small thing, barely audible. "Afraid you won't come back. Afraid you'll never be here again."

"That can't be the reason. If we do something because we're afraid then it will be wrong. The one and only thing we know is that we want to do things the right way. Right?" She says nothing, presses closer; close enough that he can feel the bird of her heart, its wings beating softly against his chest. "I know that you're scared...I don't know what's going to happen. But I know that we've found the right way so far, and that we need to keep believing in that. It's the only thing that's important. It's the only thing that really matters."

She is silent, holds him tight. He can feel her acquiescence, the trust she is placing within him. He lies for awhile, looking up into the answerless dark, before closing his eyes.

**iowa**

The darkness. That woman's tears, her anger, the things she said…and then that—that thing. That darkness, that *thing* in the darkness.

I thought—I don't know what I thought. That this would be—I want to say easier, but that sounds stupid as soon as I say it. It certainly doesn't feel anything like easy anymore, if it ever did. It feels scary now, and dangerous. My broken memory feels like a minefield. But what's worse, is that I'm not even sure it's actually *my* memory anymore.

I remember those women, yes. But at the same time I feel like I don't; feel like what I'm remembering actually happened to someone else. And the way they talked about me…the way Sumiko seemed to know that I was out there somewhere, listening. I call this place a shadow world, but that's only because I don't know what else to call it. Clearly it's more than that, clearly there is more going on here. Because I called those women. They didn't just come of their own accord, I didn't realize it at the time but I do now: they

43

came because I called them.

And that—that thing, that shadow-thing. I don't know what else to call it, either. Part of me wants to say that I'm just making it up, that there was nothing actually there...but the fear I felt was very real, too real to try and ignore. And maybe the shadow-thing came because I called it, too.

I have to be careful. All I have to go on at this point is instinct. There's nothing else; no maps, no signs telling me where to go. But what happened back there frightened me, enough that I ran from it, without paying any attention to where I was going. I have to tread more carefully now.

This place seems safe enough. I ran until I couldn't run anymore, stopped to catch my breath finally; bent over, hands on my knees, breathing hard. When I looked up I saw that I was in some kind of tunnel, or hallway; things are always shifting here, in ways that make it hard at times to call something one thing or another. There was a light, a room, I walked towards it. It seems safe enough in here. But something about it... something about it makes me slightly uneasy, too.

There's a desk, a lamp sitting on the desk. The lampshade is a paper cylinder, patterned in thin vertical stripes of black and age-yellowed orange. A small, stuffed tiger is affixed to the lamp's base. The tiger is sitting upright, cartoonishly; he has gold buttons for eyes and is wearing an orange necktie. Various trinkets, scraps of paper, odds and ends litter the desk's surface, a couple of framed photographs. In a cleared space, framed in the lamp's pool of light, there is a pad of lined yellow paper filled with writing.

It's all vaguely familiar; the lamp, especially, resonates with some old memory-chord. But the pad of paper, the writing, is what's making me uneasy.

I don't know why. It's obvious that I'm supposed to read it. Obvious enough that I can feel it pulling me in, almost.

But as much as a part of me is saying don't, it doesn't matter. I have to be careful but I have to take risks, as well. Time is no longer on my side; I have to find my way out of here, I can't turn back now.

A folding chair is pushed back slightly from the desk, waiting for me. I stand for a moment longer, staring down at the simultaneously angular and loopy, precise handwriting that fills the page. I sit down, and begin to read.

*With hindsight, as the years go by, one can look and see that certain moments were Moments: crossroads in one's life, major turning points. On the threshold of those moments, however, that kind of vision is difficult to attain. And no, I don't remember having a specific, articulated knowledge as I flew towards Iowa; don't remember anything like saying, to myself, that this was the time in which I would decide one thing or the other.*

*But I know that I knew it in my body, that it wasn't just a trip somewhere and back again. Ever since the transformative experience I termed my Epiphany; ever since that early morning as the sun rose, years before, when I'd found myself, astonished, crying tears of joy, alone beneath a suddenly beautiful sky; ever since then, I'd been fighting to believe in a certain kind of life and living; had been trying to get somewhere, but without ever really knowing where it was, or even with any sure sense of moving in the right direction. What I mean is that my entire life had become this single, directed movement towards a "something" that gave no easy evidence of itself, that I had to just keep hoping* was actually real; and, unsurprisingly, much of that time gave way to moments of anger as to whether I was just deluding myself, and currents of deep melancholy over what seemed like the possibility that I would discover myself and my work as empty; that I was simply extending myself towards an illusion, an unreachable dream.

And then, without warning, I had now come inside of it and it had come inside of me; completely new and yet completely familiar, this clear sense of arriving at a long-sought destination, and finding that it was everything I had been searching for, that it was home; this sense of being whole. But even so, the fact remained that I lived in a body whose long and direct experience had been in that never-forgotten shadow of fundamental doubt. And that doubt echoed, that long experience left me still afraid.

I think watching Isobel try and drink herself to death shook me into remembering the fear; that confrontation with how serious and real the darkness inside of her was, shook my faith in the young reality of what was happening inside of me. And in Iowa, a space apart from her and alone, I had to look at everything, and really whether I wanted to or not; in that space, away from her, with the knowledge that there were no longer any obstacles between us.

I'd visited Hope several times while she'd been in school there, and as such it had become a specific body of experience. A small college in a small town, surrounded by farm fields. Hope had founded herself within a smaller community there, a tightly-knit group of friends whose sense of bonding was intensified by their isolation from the larger world. Being there with her, amongst them, always felt vividly honest, alive and real; stirred strong feelings, created strong memories.

It had also been the source of the most intense emotion

I'd felt in the direct experience of another person, a friend of my sister's named Dawn. One year ago, far away from her, with no other resolution in sight of what had become a confusing and isolated sadness, I had made a decision to quit trying, to move on, and in a poem one night I had written Dawn out of my body. If we had talked at all in the subsequent year, it had been only once or twice, and it had been very simple and essentially about nothing. She and Hope had remained close friends, in fact now lived together, and knowing that I was going to see her again now was another question mark, provoked a mixture of emotions that were hard to name.

I'm not sure what to say, now, these years later, about what that week in Iowa was like. I mean, I had a really wonderful time, felt good and clear; but there was a strange extra weight, a feeling in the back of my body that seemed to stay just beyond identifiable reach. Part of it was that Hope was graduating later that spring, and as such it was the last time we'd be able to spend together in that place. Part of it was seeing Dawn; being in the same room again, spending time with her alone, together. Re-connecting without re-kindling, the pleasant discovery of being able to find the intimacy without the intensity. It became a comfort to hold her, to feel her in my arms, a sense of relief that affirmed the change that had taken place within me.

But it was a resolution in regards to the past only, told me nothing about the future that lay directly ahead. There were a couple of times during the week when I took Hope's car and drove alone into the woods a short distance away from town. I'd park and walk between the bare trees under the grey and overcast sky, or I'd sit and watch the wide and quiet, slow-moving river. Isobel seemed very small and far away; but at the same time there was that extra something, that melancholy, that strange weight, a feeling I didn't *know and couldn't name.*

*At the end of the week I called her to tell her when I'd be flying in the next day, since she and Tess were picking me up at the airport. I remember sitting in the stairwell to call her, just outside the door of Hope's second-floor apartment, on the old carpeted stairs next to the wooden bannister; remember the way it felt to momentarily isolate myself and reach back towards the place that, all week, had felt very far away. A bare and surface recognition that I was going back, but all the same a clear one. I don't remember what Hope and I might've talked about that night, later; but I remember feeling quiet, feeling like I didn't know what to say.*

*I had a three-hour layover at the Chicago airport between connecting flights; this time, with only myself, in this place between places. I wandered around the airport, feeling the lost feeling of so many people hurrying in transit. Later, I sat near the window and watched the moving world outside, and I listened through my headphones to a band called Saturnine, music that was sad and lovely. I thought about Dawn, and I thought about Isobel; I cried a little, without understanding why I was crying. I felt like that place felt, only a space through which things were passing to get from one place to another.*

*There were no answers in that anonymous passageway. I heard it sing but my body remained silent; the last of my tears were gone, and without knowing what I had left I got on the plane that would take me back to where she was waiting.*

I sit. Staring at those last words as they echo in my empty skull. My heart is beating like a drum, a madness. Things are starting to crawl up from somewhere, whispering, smoke curls from tiny fires that burst into sudden life at the edges of my mind. I knock the chair over as I stand up, still staring at the paper, as the words themselves peel away from the page, hover in the air. Run, says the voice inside. Into the darkness I run, feeling myself disappear, feeling the desk and the lamp and the paper and the words, feeling all of it disappear behind me.

# paralyzed

There's the bump and jerk as the jet hits the runway, the shuddering rattle as tremendous opposing forces battle for control. The noise diminishes, the drama dies away as the airplane slows, rolling sedately across the tarmac to the gate. It gives him nothing; the sense of arrival changes nothing inside.

Through the jetway tunnel and out into the airport, walking forward, getting closer and closer and still he has no idea why; no idea at all of what it is, exactly, that he's coming closer and closer to, and there she is. Twenty yards ahead, walking towards him. He stops, realizes she hasn't seen him yet. She's looking down, walking fast, and he stands there waiting as she approaches and...passes right by. He sees her face, sees the unmasked quality of how excited she is to be walking towards whatever it is she's walking towards, and he says nothing. She passes him with an eager, hurried stride and a face aglow and he says nothing at all.

Tess laughs. Walking towards him she calls out to Isobel, laughing, and her laughter gives him an action to hide within, a mask. Isobel turns back and sees him, sees that she walked right by him as he stood there. She tries to assemble composure, to rein her feeling in but she can't, not really, the excitement keeps poking through, bubbling over. He sees this; feels it come into him and disappear. Tess's laughter is his disguise as they walk.

They came in his car. He gets behind the wheel, drives them back up over the mountains and down into town. He follows the obvious steps, makes the necessary motions. Physical hunger, the body needs food. The three of them go out for dinner. They order, they eat, they talk. All necessary motions, he has no difficulty playing along. He drives them back to their apartment, pulls up alongside the curb. I'm pretty tired, he says. Been flying all day. Tess and Isobel get out of the car. Isobel looks at him; the emptiness puts a smile on his face, produces a brief nod. She shuts the door, sealing him off within his solitude.

His foot depresses the brake. His hand closes around the shift-lever, sliding it from Park into Drive.

As the car eases forward something begins to stir within him.

What am I doing, he thinks. What am I doing. His hands on the steering wheel, eyes on the road. The night-world swims by, headlights flash past. He feels it growing from within, an implacable, unstoppable force, a feeling like the rising sun.

Down the road alongside the moonlit ocean and the piles of silver-laced waves that catch the moonlight and they are slowing down, down. Within his body it is rising, faster now, breaking into strands that separate and separate again, threading through him and taking over, beginning to ring out. His hands begin to tremble on the steering wheel, the stars are falling, everything inside of him is falling, his whole body is trembling, is shaking as though it's going to break apart, the world blurs as his eyes fill with tears and he swerves, the tires skid in the dirt and gravel as he comes to an abrupt, sudden stop on the side of the road.

His fumbling fingers find and turn the key, the engine dies, like a rag doll his body slumps back against the seat, trembling, shaking. The tears are flowing freely now, overflowing, running down across his face. Within his body is a raging flood, unlike anything he has ever known. He can't move, can't think, a massive, invisible weight is pinning him to the ground. His home is only a hundred, perhaps two hundred yards further up the road. I can't make it, he thinks, realizes dimly with a kind of shock. My god, I can't…I can't get any farther away. I can't go any further away from her.

Minutes pass. He sits in the car seat like a broken statue, deep within the storm of his paralyzed body; trying to understand what is happening to him, and knowing exactly what is happening at the same time. Deep down inside. Inside the quiet sphere that rests, untouched within the center of this raging flood, this fury. He makes a decision that will determine the course of the rest of his life.

His arm moves. His hand closes around the phone. He looks down, presses the buttons; puts the phone to his ear, waiting for her voice. He knows what he will ask. He knows what she will answer. As the phone begins to ring the force releases him, finally, the emotions begin to sift away. His body is his own again. He breathes in deeply, waiting.

"Hello," she says.

"Hello. Do you want to come over and stay the

night with me." She is silent for a moment.
"Yes."

## destroy

I am…deep inside, somewhere. Far away, some-where deep down. Far away from the sound and the light, from the things that burn and the things that are broken.

I think maybe; maybe I could, with a very little effort, just merge with this. Could become just nothing. That all I have to do is…let go.

But I can't. Something within me stubbornly refus-es, holds on tight.

Why. Why is this happening to me. Terrified by words on pages, by the voices of ghosts, by fragments of memory I can't even recognize. Broken into pieces and left behind…who did this to me. Who made me this way.

Without warning I feel it welling up, a dark flower-ing; a building anger, a dark spirit filled with power. My power. Who made me this way. I stand, rising up, higher and higher, feel it burning, smoldering in my clenched fists. There will be no more giving way, no more respect given for nothing. No more sacrifice, no more lying at your feet in a pool of my own blood on the floor. The anger is a rushing, rising river, the dam shatters, the power is mine and a scream, a long howl of rage erupts from within me as I lash out.

It sweeps the moon and stars from the sky, blackens the sun. Cities burn. Dreams wither and die, hearts are crushed; all the precious, beautiful things are smashed and broken, left in tiny unrecoverable pieces, smashed into broken dust. Vengeance that I know is mine to take, that fills me with its tremendous, world-changing force and vision. A vision that burns bright, a dark fire in my eyes, forever…

I can't. My god, I want it; as badly, I think, as I've ever wanted anything. But I can't; broken memory or no, I know enough to know that I can't. It's a trick, a baited hook; an emptiness that eats away from the inside, until there is nothing left anymore. Pain cries tears in a dark garden, hatred grows up from that dark earth. Righteous or no, vengeance is not what I want. What I want is to leave this place, and vengeance won't take me away from here.

Bits of memory rise up from the fog and shadows. Drinking, laughing. A bottle of something. Drinking, more and more, trying to drown something alone. Driving, swerving into sudden chaos, running away, hiding in the dark…waking into pain, and then memory, and then panic…and then sudden quiet light, clarity. Grace. Silence.

It is only fragments, from where I don't know, but it's enough. What I need, what I want, is clarity; light and clarity.

Only fragments, but enough to know. Whatever this place is, I have chosen it. The things I can't remember, the memory I have lost, must be some kind of bargain; something I had to give up, in order to be able to come here, to enter into this.

The anger is still there; I can feel it like some kind of animal within me. A force, a dangerous weapon. But I can't wield it without knowing why, without knowing where it comes from.

I don't understand the things I'm encountering here, the fear and terror they provoke. But I have to keep trying. So much, obviously, that I still don't know.

But I can't just keep hiding, can't just keep running away anymore.

I have to start trying to take control.

# kid a

"What do you want to do?" she asks. She's sitting on his bed, already in a t-shirt and pajama pants.

"I just want to lie down. I am...it's been a long day. I'm worn out." He doesn't tell her what happened. Doesn't say: Look, I just experienced a kind of emotional paralysis and physical breakdown unlike anything I've ever felt before. His face, his body tell the story for him; he hears the change in the sound of his own voice, sees it reflected in the subdued intensity in her eyes.

"Maybe I should put some music on...I think that sounds nice right now."

"Okay," she says quietly, pulling back the covers and getting into bed.

The pools of lamplight draw clear silhouettes, cast soft shadows. He moves around the room, looking for what he wants; finds himself taking it all in as he does so. The aging brown recliner that sat in his parents' home years and years ago, the shelves lined with books that changed his life, with music that gave him new emotions; the posters on the walls, the photographs, windows into memory. The lamp on the desk, the little tiger with the necktie, that's been with him for as long as he can remember. A curated expression of what has brought him to this point: he sees without surprise that it is all in the right place, that everything in here has meaning.

He picks up a cd lying on top of a small stack of books on the little table next to the recliner. Something he hasn't listened to yet, still wrapped in cellophane, an album by Radiohead called *Kid A*. He turns it over in his hands, realizes it's what he wants, that it's what he was looking for. He doesn't know how he knows this, but that sort of question doesn't matter any longer.

Maybe it's just that he knows that nothing in the room's collection of memories can do this; that he needs to hear something he's never heard before.

He tears off the cellophane, puts the cd into the stereo: the tray whirrs out, whirrs back in. He picks up the stereo's remote control from the desktop, presses Play.

He slides into bed. Feels the slow breath leave his body as his head comes to rest on the pillow. He finds her eyes, staring back at him. As the song begins, rising quietly into the night, the rest of the world fades away.

It is the moment. The waited-for, arrived at moment. The music sings it, somehow the music knows it and sings it into the room. Sings cities of pain and hope, dreams that live and die in starlight. Deep green vines, dark beautiful flowers. The music sings, the angel voice swims softly around the rhythm that is a heartbeat. He feels the ghosts as they rise from the shadows. As she stares into him he can see them, all his ghosts; fears he has never spoken aloud, dreams he has locked within himself; secrets of pride and shame and joy. They rise before him, silently all around him, rendered visible by the way she stares at him: as though she has never in all her life till now seen a true thing. Somehow the music sings it, the angel voice rising, his heart begins to ache, to burn in rhythm with the beauty. His eyelids slide shut, cover his burning heart; no longer able to bear her astonished eyes staring so deeply into the secrets of his body.

The last of the distance between them dissolves as her lips meet his. Time echoes, disappears. A kiss that is a resolute and tender stillness, a lasting peace, the fire in his heart becomes a candle flame in the darkness. His hands find her face, his body unfolds in slow motion; a kiss that is everything he has ever waited for, the softest, sweetest thing he has ever known.

He moves and she moves as it begins to flow, to swim between them; becomes a struggle, a hungry animal in the night as the feeling in bodies surges, straining for release. It rises, soars into him, an electric strength takes over and the kiss is the sudden birth of a world: commanding him, demanding everything all at once, his tongue lost so deep within her mouth that it feels as though they are fighting to swallow each other whole…

…They tear apart, at what seems like the last possible moment; gasping for breath, hearts hammering. He is shocked by its power, its violence. That was just—just a kiss; how can there be so much…*feeling*, within a single kiss…what is this, my god what is this. He opens his mouth as he looks back at her, and nothing comes out; he finds no words, nothing to speak, to say.

Isobel is staring into him, her eyes wide, searching, in a way that no one and nothing has ever stared into him before. Alone within his own body, he begins to feel it. Pain, as the truth in her eyes travels its course, as the violence of the kiss reaches within, as some collection of things inside him begins to crumble, to break down. He rolls onto his back, his eyes close as he surrenders, as the tears begin to run slowly down his face.

He feels her hand, moving in the air over his body, searching. Feels it as it stops, hovers just above his chest.

You are...you are so beautiful, she whispers. He feels her hand, somehow touching without touching, a final ghost hovering in the air over his heart. I mean... your face, your body, all of you, yes. But...but inside you, you have this...this *light*, she breathes. You have this...this light, *inside of you.*

The invisible structures, the now-useless architecture within him begins to shatter now, to fall apart; old, brittle, her breath brings it all tumbling, crumbling to the ground.

Something...something is—breaking...inside of me, he says; his voice catches, trembles with the effort. And it—hurts. It's...breaking apart, and it hurts...but it's something that *needs* to break. It's something that's been waiting to break...has been waiting, for a very long time.

His eyes open, and he sees her; her eyes wide and filled to the brim with wonder, filled with ancient words and secret names. His hands come to her face, she bends to him as he brings her down, mouths come together and again the kiss is a long, shattering intensity, a feeling-thing that ripples a series of explosions across his inner sky. They fight with desire, break away to breathe, to see it, to feel it. The music hums, vibrates, the angel voice that sings the night, the silent ghosts, the dark flowers; a thing that carries them on gentle waters as they stare into each other beneath the stars.

## violated

I am looking for that room. I've been walking for hours, searching for that room with the desk and the lamp, trying to find it again.

I stop, tired and frustrated. I could walk for forever in here and still never find it. What is it I'm trying to find, exactly? Not just a room somewhere; something I...ran from. Something of which I'm afraid.

I close my eyes, remembering. Remembering fear; remembering what frightened me. I concentrate, and feel it taking shape, feel it as it emerges up ahead of me. And at the same moment I feel the presence of Something else, and my heart begins to race as my eyes snap open.

At the far end of the hallway or tunnel I'm in I can see the room, see the lamp and the desk within. But standing between me and the room is a dark shape, a figure made of shadows. I can feel its pure malevolence reaching out, its hunger to drive ice and shadows into my bones.

Fear rises, soft cold fingers pressing at my throat.

Run, says the animal voice inside. Turn and run.

But I can't. I know there is no other way around, no other way forward. I breathe deep, looking at the shadow figure; feel the dark waves of its hatred wash over me, fight down my body's command to turn and run away. Focus, concentrate…inside I notice something: a glimmer of light, some bare sliver of memory. A thing behind her eyes, tears like rain, a blood-red ruby light hovering above still waters…

I stare into the dark pools of its shadow eyes, shadows begin to swim through the air, I clutch the sliver of memory like a prayer and I brace for the shock of contact as I feel the darkness close itself around me.


Alone. Helpless and alone. A black sadness, creeping, clawing its way in. I wrap myself around the ball of light, the ruby star, and it burns through me. The claws recoil, the darkness disperses, draws back and away.

I am standing on a desolate gray plain. The shadow figure stands before me, at the edge of a dead forest sweeping to the far horizons. Waiting.

*Why are you here*, I ask without speaking.

*To violate you.* The figure's voice is a toneless whisper, a wind in my mind.

*Why.*

*Why. There is no reason. Why. Because I am a thing that violates.*

*Where did you come from.*

*From hate. From fear. From a need to corrupt, to violate.*

*You are not a real thing. You are a thing that needs to be desired to be real, and I do not desire you.*

*Come to me and see if I am real.*

*I do not believe in you.*
*Come to me and see if I need you to believe.*
*Will you let me go on.*
*No. I will violate you.*

A cold wind rises, the shadow-thing stands at the edge of the dead forest, unmoving. I stare at it, into its dark eyes, searching for the way...

*You are here because I concentrated on fear.*
*Yes.*
*Because I called you.*
*Yes.*
*Then you know why I am here, why I have come to this place.*
*Yes.*
*Then you know that I do not yet have what you truly want. That if you wait, you will find me again. You will find me again, and when you do I will have what you want, will have the thing that will feed your true hunger.*

Silence. The figure stands motionless. I feel it reaching out, the shadows blacken with sudden power, a wave of ice passes through me and I gasp, stumble to my knees.

*I will violate you.*


And it is gone.

"It"? What is "it"? Where am I?

I'm in some kind of passageway. At the end of it I can see the room, with the desk and the lamp.

I'm on my knees, for some reason. I stand, blink. What happened just now? I feel something like a breath of cold wind across the back of my neck. I turn, but the passageway is empty.

Something happened. I know something just happened. But...I shake my head. It doesn't matter. Whatever it was, it doesn't matter right now. I take a deep breath, exhale slowly, and walk forward into the room.

The same vague sense of familiarity. But different this time. The apprehensiveness, the anxiety is gone. Because I have been here already? Everything is as I left it; the chair lies on its side, even, where I knocked it over to the floor.

Because I need this. Because I know that I need this. I pick the chair off the floor, set it upright before the desk; stand there for a moment, looking down at the pad filled with words. I sit, crossing my forearms on the desktop, bending over the pages, and begin to read.

*It's started to rain, with the approach of night; and as I sit here, listening to the muted patter of raindrops beyond the window, at the same time it has begun to rain inside my body; to fall and run, gently, in come-together streams inside. It is the same feeling that I remember, the way that it felt when she began to tell me where she had come from; when finally I saw it, when finally the thing inside her showed itself to me.*

*Lying together, in her bed in the night. I remember the way her body hardened, became mechanical; how as she began to speak her voice was thick and hollow, only the sound of what she was forcing up, and out, from so deep within. I lay next to her, to how she had become cold and stone, and waited; and when her barely there, toneless voice began to tell me what had actually happened to this little girl I felt the tears well up, felt them and knew that even if I wanted to stop them from coming I could not.*

*Let me set the frame: Isobel as she had come to be, as who she was by the time she walked into my life. The gen-*

65

tler of the two nicknames she had accrued, over time, was the Ice Queen. Less frequently, or at least less openly, it was simply Death. Names given to the person they saw: a person who was silent, who never laughed or smiled. Names given to the voice they heard: caustic, laced with real anger. They named her as they knew her, a way of shielding themselves from knowing more. A way of easing their own discomfort, of erasing the reality of things they preferred to ignore, to pretend out of existence. But because the world had long ago disallowed her from being able to pretend at anything, she saw it all. How the names they gave her masked their own fear; how they saw her as no more than something they didn't want to become.

With no lived experience to tell her that she might be otherwise, she hardened that way; hopeless, bitter, full of hatred. It would rise within her, and she would lash out at the world with violent force; with the intention to hurt, the ability to cut deep.

In those moments I would see what was happening, would listen without saying a word. She'd fall silent, stare back at me with sullen eyes, helpless and hating herself; hating herself for being that way with me, for the fear of making me go away.

I knew that it came from somewhere. From something deep within, down in the dark. That I hadn't yet seen, beyond glimpses. That she hadn't yet shown me. And when her hollow voice spoke from her stone body that night, I felt the tears rise up from deep within my own as I began to cry.

I can tell you that I wept because Isobel told me, for the first time, that she had been raped by her older brother when she was a little girl. That it began when she was impossibly young, that it continued for years. I can tell you that I wept because I knew there would be more, that it was only the beginning of her story, her world of complete darkness. But the reason that my body shook with crying was because the thing that finally turned its face toward me was so deeply, profoundly sad; because I saw how it had climbed inside her heart and how it had deformed her body. I wept because the sadness was so deep and so long, because it needed to be cried for. Because it needed, desperately, to be felt, and I was feeling all of it. I wept, uncontrollably, and my tears became a body of water that ran through both of us in the night. A body of water whose flow washed things away, washed away the accumulations of years and gently, quietly uncovered the shape of something real.

She was astonished. Put her hands on me, her arms around my body, trying to understand the sudden feeling within herself for which she had no name. The darkness she had always lived with was a darkness she lived within; something that always negated everything. An empty place at what she had thought was the center of who she was; the place from which she was speaking to me and where she expected to again find herself, left again alone, with nothing. And then suddenly someone next to her was crying. From a body beyond her, a body she saw as filled with light, came the unmistakeable sound of an empathy that was all and unconditional, a sound that she had never heard before.

Her astonishment came not from the fact that she had found me within the darkness, that I had appeared. It was that I had found _her_; that there was somebody, still very much alive, in there for me to find. I could feel it. Feel how the hardness in which she'd spoken was gone, how she was filled with an inarticulate, searching kind of wonderment as her fingers felt the real tears on my face, as she held me against her. As she felt me not falling apart; how the full weight of her dark and dying pain had fallen across my unguarded body, and yet I cried only for her; that the tears that rose and fell from my eyes were for her and for her only,

67

*came from a care for her that was unbowed, unbroken by her secret.*

*We lay together in the night and felt how the world had changed, was changing; how from within, we were traveling into an undiscovered kind of country.*

My eyes close. I bring the palms of my hands to my forehead, let them carry my head's weight. Something is moving away from me, something I don't know, already too far away for me to see. Faster than I can follow it, memory is receding. I don't know where I am. I know that I should know, but I don't. My eyes open, I look down. Ah yes. I am here to read.

*So this is the story of the deep and intricate sadness within my sweet little girl's heart; how it was all she had ever known, how the sheer weight of it threatened to break her life.*

*She'd been the third and unexpected child, born into a family that was already falling apart. Falling apart, without knowing or seeing how to fall away to an ending. A continuity of pain that broke all of them, and the forms in which they re-grew were mistaken and wrong: nightmare forms, nightmare shapes. Like bodies without hearts and hearts without bodies; a pain that pushed love beyond memory, and never being able to find it they brought back only fear and anger instead. Her father tried to bury himself in alcohol, lived within a confusion and rage that manifested itself in his voice, in his hand and fist. Her parents fought each other with true violence, sought to cut without restraint. Unable to reconcile her dreams and pride with what her life had actually become, her mother chose denial; chose to live within an imaginary, unreal house and to force her family to live within the same bright and terrible walls.*

*I can't know what was inside of Isobel's oldest brother; what really happened inside of his sad young body, what the lessons he learned became.   He was given absolutely no control over his own life, and he took control of someone else's. Having been given pain, he gave pain in return; and she was the person to whom it was given, my sweet little unexpected girl.   She looked to see what the undiscovered world might bring, and her little body was delivered into the darkness.*

*As I write this I find my eyes filling with tears, all over again.   For the child she was never able to be, for how she was never defended; how her only safety came from what she had to find, completely alone, and how even that turned into dust and nothing and fell through her fingers.   How the darkness filled up the mouth and eyes of her little body.   It is a depth of suffering that's difficult to bring to words, to try and write down.   Because I don't want to dramatize it, don't want to mis-convey what's real.   The point is to give you an unmistakeable, clear vision into what happens within a broken heart: that unable to find any kind of reason why the world might hate her so much, what emerged was the belief that it was something she must deserve; that she was somehow fundamentally, incorrectably wrong.*

*Isobel carried what her brother did to her alone within herself, through the course of its mangled and creeping violence and within the long, dark silence it left behind.   What hate does is real, the way it fills up and creates a world around itself.   For her it made happiness into an unknowable commodity; made it seem that delight and joy were things that other people felt only because they were pretending to themselves, or because they just didn't yet know what the world truly was.   The Ice Queen.   Death.   The only possible product of a lived experience that had irrevocably shattered her ability to ever pretend.*

*She was still living in that house when the secret finally spilled over. She was a teenager, her oldest brother had long since moved out, away. Her other brother found something she'd written. Worked up the will, somehow, to tell their parents. There was no strength in that house of lies, no ability to bear or deal with any kind of honest weight, much less a revelation of that magnitude. Isobel was confronted by her parents in all the strength of their terror, met with loathing: it must have been your fault, she was told, her secret brought before her and named as an ugly and horrible thing that she had made. If there had been anything in her life that gave off any kind of light it was gone now; swallowed up, forgotten. Her mother's denial was swift and terrible, falling over the house like a deeper shadow, casting ropes and chains to bind up the brokenness towards some far-off, imagined shape.*

*What Isobel remembers is sitting alone, later. Within that dead silence, sometime late in the night, in a dumb echo of emotion. Sitting alone on the couch, and her father came into the room, drunk in body and soul; sat next to her, less a man than an ocean of sadness and shame, and couldn't say a single word.*

*Hate is what she survived on, from that point forward. The desire to take herself beyond her family's reach, to leave them completely without her and alone. That was how she came to me; the way that she was, when I found her.*

*Recalling these things, and writing them down, is a new kind of strangeness for me. You might see me, sitting in the lamplight and the sound of my pen moving across the paper; you might see, or you might not, how doing this takes all and everything of who I am. To try and re-make the pain that lived in her body, to call out that feeling into the breathable air; to feel that I am doing so with considered care, doing so for some reason…if it's coming out of me, it is only because it's what I think I have to be doing; that in my life, in this world, it is the thing that I have to do.*

Enough. There is more, more words, more pages filled with words, but that's enough. The words are like blue fires burning without heat, indigo and sapphire flames spread across the landscape of darkness that is my mind and memories.

I can't grasp them. The words are too strong, too strange, too terrible. They are within me and I know they are within me but they float, untethered across my night sky. I close my eyes. Instinctively feel myself pushing out, feel the space expand around me. When I open them again it is no longer just the desk and the lamp; a brown recliner sits in one corner, a bed in another. Posters on the walls, shelves lined with books, cd's. But it's all vague, dim. These are ghosts. This is not a place, but the ghost of a place.

As though within some kind of spell I move slowly through the room, searching for clues, answers. A tiny toy racecar. A small ceramic mask, decorated in delicate, swirling patterns of blue and silver and gold. A framed photograph of two young men, pulling funny and distorted clown faces. Find myself standing, staring down at the pages again, the words and images tumbling through my mind, drifting through my body.

Did all this...happen to me? Did I...did I write these things down, some lifetime ago? I can't say no. I can't say yes, either.

Layers upon layers. The blue flames are starting to fade, to die out. I can't linger here any longer. There's a door now, a closed door in the wall, I don't know if it's always been there or if it's just appeared, but it doesn't matter; I feel too stunned, too bewildered to care anymore. I walk across the room and reach out, pause for a moment with my hand resting on the doorknob. I look back, having felt for a moment some stir of movement, some whisper of a voice. My eyes come to rest on the desk, the pad of paper in the pool of lamplight. On the floor next to the desk there is a canvas bag, the kind with a single strap that comes down across the chest and shoulder. I walk back to the desk, pick up the bag and put the pad of paper inside it; sling the bag over my head, feel the slim weight come to rest across my upper body.

Time to go. I turn back to the door, open it and step through, feeling the room fade back into darkness behind me.

# yellow line

He puts the bags in the back seat, closes the car door. Walks back into the house, into the bedroom. Isobel is sitting on the bed, shoulders slumped forward, face drawn and sullen.

"Everything's in the car, time to go. You ready?" She doesn't say anything, just looks up at him with eyes that are bitter, almost angry.

Nearly a month has passed since the night he returned from Iowa. So much has happened, so far in one month they've already come. He knows her secret now, what happened to her inside her family. She knows that it doesn't frighten him. And she knows now, really knows for the first time in her life that she is still alive, still there inside that mountain of pain.

The Thing behind her eyes is clearly visible to him now, the Thing that feeds on her body, that nests in her heart. It hates him. It hates him because he knows what It is, because he knows It shouldn't be there. It hates him because It knows he is not afraid of It. It puts masks on her face, pushes words out of her mouth.

73

Attacks him in ways that are sharp, sophisticated. It turns this way and that, trying to smother him with sadness, to cut him with hate. It takes control of her and spits at him, but he is not fooled and It knows he is not fooled. It writhes, rushes at him in fury, in black waves. He holds her; he reaches into the writhing blackness and finds her, holds her with true hands, speaks true words into her that burn the Thing behind her eyes, that break Its hold on her and cause It to retreat. It sees that he knows and that he is not afraid, that It has no power over him. It is terrified. It lurks, watching and waiting, wholly bent on destroying him.

He sees the clear danger, and yet cannot explain to himself his own lack of fear. Cannot explain the movements he makes that he knows are all true movements, the words that he speaks to her that he knows are all true words. He can explain neither the power he feels within his body nor the fact that he knows exactly, always, how to wield it.

It has been nearly two weeks since she moved in with him. Her living situation deteriorated quickly, drastically. A fight with Tess and the other roommate in the apartment, and something that had been festering broke open, spilled out a corrosive poison. Isobel had to get out, suddenly.

He looked, and saw that the choice to make was a clear one. Even so, he hesitated a moment. Could hear, distinctly, the voice of the careful, rational world saying, unequivocally: What are you doing? Are you crazy? Do you not see the incredible danger? Are you blind and ignorant, or just a reckless, utter fool?

He heard, and he hesitated. He looked again and saw that the careful, rational world neither saw what he saw, nor knew what he knew. And as such he saw also that when he made this decision he would make it alone, unsupported. That when he made it he would be leaving support and safety behind; moving forward alone into a strange, unknown and dangerous country.

He chose, stepped forward. Isobel looked at him.

Really?

Yes.

Are you sure?

Yes.

She looked. Looked at the world she was walking into, at the new things growing and taking shape around her. The new world that she and he were living in, were creating together. Tentatively she touched the hope, with her fingers traced the intricate, tangible reality of trust, of belief. She looked up at him as he watched her, quietly. Okay, she said, and stepped forward into his arms, deeper within him.

Now, two weeks later, she sits on the bed; her face is pale, her eyes are dark clouds. She looks at him and then away, her mouth twisting. He sighs, sits down next to her.

"Look, we don't have to go," he says. "But this trip was your idea, not mine. And there's no reason not to go. I'll be there with you, the whole time. Nothing bad is going to happen. And in fact, believe it or not, we're actually going to have a good time."

"You don't know," she says, looking down. "You don't know what they're like."

"No, I don't know," he says. "And it's time for me to find out. You say that it's bad, that every time it's bad. I believe you, of course I believe you. But you've never been there with me before, have you." They both know it's true, and that it makes this a test. That going to see her parents, that going back and going into that house

75

again is a test: a test of the two of them and what they are creating, a test of all the things that are so new and precious to Isobel, a test of everything. She is afraid.

He reaches out and takes her hand. She tries to pull away but he clasps tightly with sudden force and pressure.

"I want to go. I want to go there with you, to be there with you. There is no reason not to go. You can go anywhere you want to go now, anywhere you need to go now, because you will be there with me."

The words carry the power, they sever the binding ropes and chains. She looks up at him as the clouds disperse, as the color and light return to her eyes and face. She squeezes his hand and takes a deep breath and says, Okay.


They drive south, over the small mountains that hem in the oceanside town and down into the long, flat valley. They listen to music as the car hums down the highway, cutting a line between the farm fields that recede into the distance to the east and the low hills that line the western horizon.

The feeling is deeply pleasurable within him. The juxtaposition of stillness and fast motion, the rhythm of music in tune with the views of surrounding, open country. And her: looking to his right and seeing her sitting next to him. Seeing the shy smile that steals across her features because she's happy, because she can't believe that she's so happy.

Small anxieties surge through her system and he whistles at them, nonchalantly waves them away.

What if this happens?, she says. What if that happens?, she says.

What if it does?, he says. What if the next time it rains, instead of raining water it rains little bits of poopoo?

Eww! Why would you say that? What's wrong with you?

Well, you never know. We'll see what you have to say when you're hiding under my extra-wide, heavy-duty umbrella and asking to use my extra gas-mask.

You're a very dumb person she says, giggling.

Minutes later he's watching the car hungrily swallow up the road ahead and he hears her make some happy little sound and then she's pressed against him.

"Why do you have to drive the car? Why can't you just stop so we can be together?" It is a child's voice, a child's words of sudden overwhelming, joyful desire. In this reverie she wraps herself around his arm, jerking it downwards.

"Hey, watch it!" he says with mild alarm as the car shimmies, swerves slightly. She sits back immediately as he guides them back into the lane. He looks at her and her eyes are wide, she sits still and chastened, looking back at him. It is not the first time something like this has happened in the car, either.

He shakes his head with an exaggerated grimace. "All right," he says, "your new nickname is Yellow Line, because that's where you always send me." She lets out a squeal and looks away, squirms in her seat. He sees her and in that moment his vision is overlaid with the memory of the quiet, taciturn girl who sat on his kitchen counter a couple short months ago, and the unnamed feeling moves deeply within him.

Night has fallen by the time they arrive in the great city. The sea of electric light spreads to all horizons, they zoom along with the cars and trucks along the sweeping curves of freeway. Isobel is high, riding the joy of transit, the speed of traveling through space and time. The song coming through the car stereo is soaring and she is soaring with it, untethered and free.

"Look at it all," she breathes. "It's so huge and strange and beautiful." Their hands reach out, find each other in the darkness; fingers interlace and press for moments until he returns his hand to the wheel. It's my job, he thinks quietly, to carry us safely; always mine, to carry us safely.

They're staying with Samson, her other brother. He is tall, his shape is bear-like, Teddy bear-like, more accurately. He is a gay man who has sought and found an anonymous niche within the vast city, created himself in a quiet corner. The affection between brother and sister is clear, if guarded; like soldiers who survived, glad in reunion but careful to stay well away from old wounds, old memories.

They go out to dinner. Road-weary he lets Samson and Isobel talk, lets himself rest. Quietly information-gathers as he listens, as he watches.

In bed she curls against him. She says nothing but he can feel her fear, feel her reaching for the security within him before she falls asleep.

They have breakfast with Samson and then leave, piddling around town for a bit, killing time before the early afternoon meeting. Ostensibly Isobel is responding to her mother's ceaseless, importunate requests for her daughter to come visit; ostensibly, as well, there are a smattering of belongings in boxes stored within the house that Isobel wants to retrieve.

These are the ostensibles, the plausible excuse. The reality is the test. The test to see if what she has found with him will die in this house the way every other thing that she has ever wanted has died in this house.

It's time, he tells her. Reluctantly she puts the magazine back on the rack, follows him slowly out of the store.

As they drive he feels the shadows come into her, feels them tightening their grip. He doesn't say anything, doesn't reach for her hand to squeeze with reassurance. They are not shadows he can dispel; he doesn't try, knows this place is very real to her. Knows it is something she has to feel, something she has to remember.

"There it is," she says tonelessly, pointing.

The house is aged, unremarkable. As they walk across the street and step onto the concrete walkway leading to the front door, the door opens. A woman stands there with an awkward smile, a man stands with his hands in his pockets and not quite facing the door in the darkened interior of the house several feet behind her.

"You're here!" says the woman in a voice that strains to not sound strained. She embraces Isobel and it is like watching someone embrace a wooden board. In the house behind them the man shifts his hands in his pockets, looks down at the floor.

Standing just behind Isobel, he takes the moment in. *So here are your monsters; yes, I see who they are.*

The woman turns to him with eyes that struggle to hide both defiance and desperation. He takes her outstretched hand in both of his and smiles. "It's good to meet you," he says as he looks into her face. *Yes, I know who you are.*

The house feels old, feels as though it has been lived in for years and years and still never become a home. He shakes her father's hand, sees that he is barely noticed, that most of this man is very far away somewhere.

Isobel sits down on the couch, sits like a piece of iron, and her mother sits next to her, a couple feet apart and turned slightly, awkwardly, in the piece of iron's direction. Hands in his pockets still her father remains standing.

Her mother's words fall around Isobel like dying birds, to questions she delivers answers stripped to the bare, hard necessity of relaying information. He watches as her mother turns her conversational attempts toward him now, the defiance giving way to the desperation, a plea given as the dark sea begins to rise, as the shadows proliferate through the room.

But they don't touch him.

He speaks them away. He speaks his light into the room as he answers her questions, as he tells her who he is, what he does in his life, where he comes from. The words are just simple words, but the sound of his voice is a sound that has no fear and it commands the shadows, causes them to retreat. Some kind of sharp, insensate curiosity emerges in the woman's eyes as she looks at him, feels her desperation receding. From a million miles away Isobel's father realizes that he is hearing something, almost unconsciously turns and looks at the people in the room, almost animal-like her father's eyes come to focus on him as he continues speaking.

From deep within her walls Isobel hears, looks, remembers; sees him, that he is here with her. The walls stay firm, but a tiny door opens somewhere.

It is enough. The conversation doesn't flow, but it doesn't need to. He pulls it into shape around them, pushes it forward, carrying three confused passengers; all unclear as to where this boat has come from, but all grateful for its security, for the sense of unexpected relief. The firm reality of it pierces their confusion, and they begin to respond in kind. Food, says Isobel's mother, returning from the kitchen with small plates of carnitas and peppers, and he eats with sincere, obvious pleasure. Long-disused machinery within her father comes to life with a jerky start, he leaves the room and returns with tequila. No it's not quite the right thing, but it doesn't matter; it's a simple adjustment for him to respond, to receive in the odd spirit with which it's given. He can feel them concentrating on him as he eats, as he drinks, as he talks. Feels them concentrating on this unknown force that has willed this room into being alive; on a light that has flickered into life within a far-off, distant memory.

A couple hours later they're leaving. Isobel has gathered the things she wanted, she holds them in a small box in her arms. He shakes her father's hand; the man is still too far away to really look back at him, but he can feel him in the distance trying nonetheless. Her mother hugs Isobel again, and Isobel lets a tiny piece of her mother in through that tiny door.

Her mother's eyes barely hide enormous questions as she takes his hand.

"You'll take care of my daughter?" she says, and he sees the change work across her face as she realizes it is not a question.

"Of course I will," he says as he looks back at her. "Of course I will."

Isobel is looking out the window as they drive away. After a few minutes she reaches out and finds his hand.

That night, safe and alone with him in bed, her walls come down and the tears come out. She shakes, sobs wrack her body as the sadness rises in a great, overpowering swell. He holds her in his arms, letting the tears flow into the containment of his body.

"They're so sad," she whispers. "They're just... they're just so sad!" Her voice breaks as another sob tears loose, her body twisting in the sadness, beneath its aching weight.

He doesn't say anything as he holds her close. These are not the contortions, not the manipulations of the dark Thing. This is the pain as she sees the truth of her monsters. This is something she needs.

"Of course they are," he says after awhile, softly. "How could they not be? Yes, they are very sad." Minutes pass as she presses tight against him. The sobs subside. The flow of tears becomes a trickle. His hands begin to move, fingertips across the lines of her face. Fingertips softly, nimbly across the skin of her back, drawing intricate shapes, figures of wordless meaning. Fingertips like painless needles, tattooing patterns of life, of ancient, powerful symbols into her flesh that sink down into who she is, that sink down into her body. He feels himself somehow both creating and bowing down in the same moment. Her body is gentle now, quiet now, as across her skin he traces this wonder.

They spend the next day in the city with Samson. They eat delicious food, find fun shops, turn to each other holding odd, curious items for inspection. The sun is warm, the day is filled with light. Isobel twists in her seat belt as he drives, talking to Samson in the back seat, laughing. They wander through the large, cool spaces of an art museum, stand before riots of color and twisted metal, before natural forces pulled by creative will into messages, into deep mysteries.

At night, in the bed, there is no crying. The darkness gives birth to desire. The kisses are long poems, tongues twist together like silver flames, bodies like dark orchids in the jungle's hidden secret deep. His hands make the shape of her body, his arms close around her with the strength of iron and she cries out, softly, whispers a plea to not stop, to never stop creating this beauty. Even still they hold back; even though they are so close to it this is not the time, this is not the place. The fire burns with a soft glow, they are walking into everything with eyes open; the moment will come, it will rise when it rises. And they both know: as they lie together in the tender darkness, they feel it and know it is a thing that is very close now.

In the morning they have breakfast with Samson, say nice goodbyes. As they drive, as they are driving through and away from the city she is quiet. He glances at her, sees that she is thinking.

"I'm glad we came down here," he says. "I had a really good time."

"Yeah," she says. "Me too." He looks over at her again and she's looking back at him as she realizes, as it dawns across her face.

He smiles. "I told you we would, didn't I," he says, reaching out and taking her hand.

"I didn't believe it could...I didn't know..." Her eyes are wide as she stares back at him; as it rises within her, as she stares at emerging, long-forgotten dreams.

"I had a really good time here with you," she says as she takes his hand in both of hers and squeezes, tightly, her voice filled with meaning. "I had a really good time," she says again, listening to the sound of it as she sits back in her seat.

Yes, he thinks as they drive away from the city. As he feels his hand in hers, her fingers tracing the lines of his palm, the contours of his skin and bones. Yes, he thinks as he feels them moving further into this strange, undiscovered country.  We will keep going.

# home

I'm walking again.

Walking in this place, aimless wandering. Lost. I don't know what to do.

The walls and darkness recede, I am walking through a great, nameless vague city. Everything is dim, the images are blurred and remote. Cars drive by, people fill the sidewalks, but there is no sound. No one sees me, no one feels me, the motion around me is thickened and slow. Not here, nothing here. A gray mist begins to fill the air, becomes an opaque white fog. I cannot see the ground, beyond the fog can see nothing further around me; the only living quality is the sound of my footsteps, a muted echo from somewhere far away.

The white fog comes inside, fills the caverns of my memory with its quiet safety and peace. How did I get here, I wonder dimly to myself. Words pass like slow, single ships across a far horizon: Where…did I…come from? There must be a place where it all begins. I push off from the unseen ground beneath me, I rise up and the fog breaks, disperses into great white clouds in a vast blue sky. Far below me is a long, sunlit plain, broken into patches by fields of green corn and golden wheat, ribbons of trees that follow the paths of creeks and streams. In the distance the plains rush up to a line of great mountains, ranges of peaks piled on top of one another for as far as I can see. They pull me; a deep, strong current of memory in that place where the plains rush up to meet the mountains pulls me. As I come nearer I can see the cities and small towns, up and down along that line; massed against the bulwark of the great mountains, spreading out amidst the valleys which lie at their feet.

This is the beginning. I need to know what happened here. What happened before I came to this place, this shadow world. This is where the trail begins.

I drift downwards, the current of memory growing stronger, running deeper and faster as I see the small town beneath me, the details emerging as I come closer and closer. The neighborhood with its modest homes on large plots of land, the streets without sidewalks, strips of black asphalt that bleed into the grass, that pool into cul-de-sacs; and the house, the single-story, simple brick house with its trees and shrubbery, expanses of green lawn, the wooden playset beneath the shade of the enormous cottonwood, next to the sprawling vegetable garden and the floodgates of memory fly open, the waters of memory burst upon me in a torrent, a tremendous rush.

Tomato worm, says grandpa as he plucks the fat green caterpillar from the vine. Dark green guts explode from its body as he grinds it with a stick into the dirt. Two small children, a boy and a girl with heads of hair blond as corn-silk. They run through sprinklers, lie down with wet bodies on sun-warmed concrete. In the tall grass beyond the garden they lift up boards and watch the gray roly-polies and red centipedes scurry for holes, they seize the garter snake as it tries to quickly slither away. They pass through hallways of cool bedsheets hung on the line, they eat popsicles, they sit with mother and grandmother on the patio, shelling mounds of peas as the sky dims, as it gathers the soft, blue evening light.

In a world covered in snow they wander. Little feet snug in boots, little bodies snug in puffy coats through a still, white world heaped in piles of snow they tramp with delight, they fall and lie in the quiet with red cheeks, seeing the white puffs of breath in the cold, cold air.

Scraped knees find band-aids, hungry bellies find good food, small bodies find comfort inside strong arms, listen with heads nestled against shoulders to soft, soothing voices. The world is a safe world, the world is a protected joy.

But not only. Not always, not only. In the great river there are darker currents, shadowed, swirling eddies. The world lurks. Beyond the protected joy the sense of a larger, an impossibly larger world. A universe. Where does it all end? How could it end? How could it ever begin? The question is too impossible, a massive weight bears down. The boy cries out in the darkness, they come, they sit at the side of his bed. How, he asks them, afraid to ask, reluctant to say it aloud because he somehow knows it is too big. A great wheel in the darkness, says his father. When I was a small boy I would imagine a great wheel in the darkness. We will always be here honey says his mother as she bends to kiss his forehead, smoothes the hair back from his brow.

Not answers, but enough. The dark questions

recede, the sense of comfort, of safe comfort is enough. What it teaches is to learn. What grows is a hunger to know, a desire to learn.

For a moment I recollect myself, within the flow of the rush of memories. What did he learn?...where did I come from?...I reach out, searching...

The swirls merge, distill again into recognizable lines, shapes, figures. The little boy stands in his room, amidst the wreckage of a set of dresser drawers that he has torn apart in a frenzy, a fit of rage. His father stands in the doorway with a shock that slowly gives way to disappointment, written across his face. He shakes his head, says nothing as he walks away. The boy is filled with a tremendous sense of loss, the sudden knowledge that he has the power to break things, the capacity to destroy. He wishes desperately that he could remove that sadness from his father's eyes, feels the pain of an action that cannot be undone.

He screams at his mother. I hate you he screams as he stalks furiously away. His anger subsides, he forgets, he is playing with his toys. He hears his father approach, feels the rise of curiosity as he looks up, as his father comes down into his small world, comes down on one knee. When you say to your mother: I hate you, it hurts her, his father says in a quiet voice. It makes her feel very bad, he says. The boy is looking into his father's face and eyes and he sees it. He sees what it is to say hate, he sees what hate is. He takes the gift of this seeing into himself. He never thinks of speaking hate to his mother now, he never says hate to his mother ever again.

She kicks him. She is frustrated, tired, overburdened as she works and the boy doesn't know as he pushes on her, begs for nothing, incessantly pleads as she works and it breaks her and with an angry voice she kicks him. Shocked, in silence he walks away. There is no physical hurt, but he is shocked by a new understanding. Minutes later she comes to him, comes down to him. I am so sorry she says, her face and voice filled with pain. It's okay Mommy, he says in her ear as he puts his arms around her neck. Understanding dawns within him as they hold each other. It's okay he says, his cheek pressed against her hair, her face.

Anger and rage. He can hurt things, break things, a power that causes pain. Forgiveness, love. He has the power to heal wounds, to make pain and hurt go away. First lessons learned within the protected world, they become a part of his little body and who he is. But beyond yet lies the dark universe; moments when his joy in everything that surrounds him is so great that it soars beyond him, breaks the containment of his protected world and soars into a vastness that is beyond the reach of his imagination, that he cannot comprehend.

Learn, learn, learn. Everything has a name. His hunger for knowing is unending. The knowledge brings joy, the power to name is the same as the power to shape, to create. He devours the knowledge faster than it can be fed to him. Special, he hears. So smart, they say to his parents. He has a gift, he hears them say. The words sound like magic. He is magic. He feels the power swell in him, pride in the power swells within him.

But he is going too fast, they cannot feed him fast enough. Moved from one school to another to another. Then, finally a right place. A school that can feed his hunger, that piles more and more onto his plate. For a time it is enough. Everything seems to work, his knowledge grows, he feels safe. One year, two years, three years. But in the fourth year shadows begin to emerge, widening cracks, and before the fourth year is over it breaks. In the spring of that year his parents pull him out of the school which can no longer contain him. Searching for answers they bide their time, trying to find what to do next.

The boy sits on a swing. On a gently warm, sun-filled spring morning, in the shade of the giant cottonwood tree the boy sits on a swing. His feet no longer dangle in the air. He pushes his toes into the green grass, moving himself back and forth, slightly, listens to the wooden playset creak as it carries his weight.

He is still, inside. He feels no desire to run, to play. He knows this will all be gone soon. He knows they will be leaving, that his parents have decided they can't stay here.

He cannot say: Stay. He does not want to go, but he knows that he can find no answers. He feels the world of protected joy receding. He sees shadows all around: shadow figures in the branches of the tree, shadow figures running across the lawn, shadow voices and laughter that echo silently and fade.

He looks down at his feet as he pushes his toes into the cool grass. He feels the invisible future all around him, the great, looming world just outside the door. He is not happy. He is also not afraid. He knows that he wants to know. He is quiet inside, waiting.

I stand a short distance away. Watching the boy. I want to go to him, to speak to him; but even if he could hear me, I don't know what I'd say. He stands after a bit, walks slowly toward the house, hands in his pockets, head down. He goes into the house, the door closes behind him. I know that if I were to follow I would not find him in the house, would find no one in the house any longer.

When this world of protected joy disappeared, where did it go? Was it just gone? What did the boy carry with him? I feel the strap of the bag across my shoulder, the slim weight within.

I sit down at the base of the cottonwood tree, back against the solidly corrugated bark of its broad trunk. Lattices of leaf-shadow play across the grass, the breeze brings the sweet spring scent of lilac flowers as I pull the pad of paper out of the bag and begin to read.

*Sometime near the end of that April I was away from her for four days. I left early in the morning, drove across the day it takes to get from Santa Cruz to Portland, heading for the annual end-of-the-school-year celebration at Reed called Renn Fayre; which, is not actually a renaissance fair, in spite of its name, the origins of which are shrouded in the mists of time. It partakes of a similar fair-like atmosphere, but with punk wizards and glam pixies, and motorized couches and a drunks vs. stoners kickball game and a lot of fireworks and a glow opera.*

*But what it is mostly and more than anything is a fire-like and profound expression of community joy, unlike anything I've ever elsewhere come across. The beginning of my first experience with it, when I could feel the energy building but had no real idea what was going to happen, felt like a shattering kind of awesomeness: the enormous firepit full of burning theses, the champagne-soaked celebratory parade…and then the uprising of the hippie peasants besieging the wooden castle, the Mad Max knights essaying across the lowered drawbridge, and finally the dragon, rising from its hiding place within the castle walls…the spectacle alone was enough to blow the fuses of my still very young and inexperienced mind. But what planted itself* deeply within me was not the sheer energy itself but its embodiment within distinct individuals; I'd never before seen people who were so purely happy. The tremendous sense of release from all constraints, of being alive and free; but more than that a sense of joy with a directed purpose, a deeper meaning.

And that was only the beginning, the gateway, as such, to the rest of the weekend-long event. That year, and each year afterwards, I found myself: within that deep and extended magic-time, at some point uncovering a new, different emotional shape within my body; a truth of the motion in my life, of who I was, or was becoming. Now I was coming back, with a new quality in my heart; coming through the dry hills of northern California and the forests of southern Oregon, coming to a gathering of my friends and the love in my life; coming with a patient curiosity, a glad excitement.

Saturday night. The summit night, the deepest part. Seven of us, together. Tyler and I and his younger brother Matthew eat some mushrooms, try to soften them in tea before we end up just chewing, forcing them down, Tiffany and Jack, Eric and Trisha all swallow pills of MDMA; and then, over the rest of the night we are a clan, a family, a seven-part harmony. We run into Erganon, who tricks us with his latex gloves and water babies; I can't get that guy's voice out of my head, says Matthew, over and over again. We stand for what seems forever in a concrete stairwell, a resonance cave, blending our voices in sung tones like ocean waves. Charlie Sheen-Chaplin's face is about to eat you, I said to Tyler, cringing. His face?...or his butt?, said Tyler. Oh yeah, definitely his butt. I thought so...well I accept my fate, said Tyler and nodded stoically.

I was happy, lost in this gathering of my friends, this circle of my love; and so when it came it came unlooked-for, *a pure revelation. It was during the glow opera; seated on the benches of the ampitheatre, outside in the dark night, hundreds of people huddled between the tall pines murmuring and roaring and responding as a body to the surreal performance in the clearing below; a kind of delight that exploded before your eyes and within you, fell tumbling over rocks like water, gathering in small and secret pools; and then, I remembered her. Remembered Isobel, like a forgotten bright star in my pocket, a beautiful kept secret. The world left me, the sights and sounds of the world withdrew and left me alone. A rain of golden sparks fell, drew a slow arc across a field of velvet darkness.*

*The glow opera came to an end, the space of it dis-assembling, fading as people began to move, dispersing into the rest of the night like streams of fire and water; and as we also got up, began to move out, something broke open inside of me; shattered within my body, like a crashing wave that had always up till then been seen only far out upon the water. As though a circuit completed itself, and a potential was achieved. It rippled up, raced outwards, I flew into the sky like an electric arrow; found myself atop a picnic table, giving a performance in concert with the table, a young tree next to the table, and a ridiculous cartoon monster, an inflatable plastic toy with colorful appendages of multiple arms and eyestalks that I had somehow somewhere attached myself to. A mad performance, wild and free. I shouted proclamations, whirled on the tree as it tried to sneak up on me, berated the monster for its faults and failures, broke free from the trap of its hypnotic gaze. I solemnly thanked the table for its solidity, my friend Marcus stepped forward, lifted the table, tilting it, I shrieked as I grasped the edge and felt myself about to slide off into the universe, Marcus laughing as he set the table down again.*

*People gathered, laughed and applauded, watched and*

*didn't watch, stayed for a while in my world and then moved on, within their own; I cared and didn't care, moving from one moment to the next, without plans or attachments, responsive to everything.   I moved within a living joy: unkept, unkeepable, it fell across the night like a starry rain, sang like drunk electric birds; I was a wind-bender, a natural force, a body beautiful and alive.   Plans and blueprints, studied and re-worked over and over again, frustrated glimpses, the hopeless moments and years of searching, of doubt and anger and sadness.   A resounding yes.   An extraordinary sense of triumph, of grace and blessing.   A gift that could only truly become mine as I gave it back into the world around me.*

*Take that, ye devils, and know thy master!   Mine is the victory!, I shouted at the table and the monster and the tree.*

*Congratulations, O Prince Idiot, said Tyler, laughing. You've vanquished these powerful enemies, at long last. Can we go now?…it was something like that, the things I said and he said, words to that effect.   Years ago now, exact words and actions are lost to memory.   I remember the broad gestures, the feeling.   I remember my friends and how we were together that night, the play we created out of the intricacies of our relationships; the sense of deep, abiding devotion to these people who I knew loved me.*

*Later on I felt something different stir, move inside.*

*I need to be alone for a bit, I said.*

*Are you sure?, they asked.*

*Yes.*

*Okay.   Do what you need to do.   We'll come and find you.*

*I left them, walked away, past trees filled with colored lights, pockets of the party spilling from doorways, all fading behind me; went to my car, in a quiet parking lot beneath tall, old trees.   I got inside, shut the door; turned the ignition* *switch on and put Neutral Milk Hotel into the cd player, then crawled into the back seat and covered myself with a blanket, pulled it all the way over my head and lay still. Felt the strange music in the deep forest of my body as I lay there, the starlit dream. The soft chattering sing-song of night creatures within that forest fell off, a sudden hush, and Isobel rose. Not an angel, or a vision; a kind of tender question, a deep and intricate, singular body of feeling. I saw it; how it was not just within me, but instead <u>was</u> me: a still-unfolding path I had chosen to walk, but at the same time, a thing I had become.*

*Time passed. A noise outside, a knock on the window. I stuck my head out from the world beneath the blanket and saw that my friends had come to re-gather me; faces pressed against the window, peering in, laughter, voices calling. As I watched them a song began to play, a song called "Ghost" that sounds like a promise, that rings slowly and suddenly into the air with an immeasurable spirit and fire. I threw off my stillness like a cloak, turned the volume way up, rolled down the window and scrambled out and on top of the car, stood there with my arms raised as my friends' cheers and cries rose to greet me, calling out my name. And it felt as though they were celebrating my true entrance into the world; as though the soul they had seen and believed in was emerging for the very first time.*

*Alright Prince Idiot, now get down from there before you fall and break your face.*

*Roger that. But first, did you notice it's a full moon tonight?*

*Nice try, not fast enough. No, we're not going to open our eyes to look at the "beautiful moon", pull your stupid pants back up and get down from there, they're about to start the bouncy ball drop...*

*Or something like that. I don't remember the exact*

*words.  I just remember the feeling.  The feeling of being whole, and happy.*

I look up from the page.  I feel…I don't know what I feel.  The words and images are so strong, charged with so much emotion; self-discovery, the beauty of relationships and human connection, but—what I feel is this—sense of deep, drifting sadness…I can't…I don't…

I shake my head, the movement feels thick and slow. There's a tingling sensation in the back of my neck.  Am I supposed to connect these dots?  Who wrote this? Did the boy, the same boy who climbed through the branches of this tree, who felt this world dissolve around him?  I scan the pages again, trying to under-stand: "…streams of fire and water…a wind-bender, a natural force…the deep forest of my body, the starlit dream…"

I stare at the words, trying to force them, to will them into saying more.  The closer I get, the more the darkness grows.  What's standing in my way, why can't I remember?…

The tingling in my neck grows, spreads upwards into my head, down into my chest and becomes a burn-ing.  I can't move, can't lift a finger.  Icy beads of sweat form, drip down across my face.  Staring out of eyes I can't shut at the world around me I see the cracks begin to appear, spider-webbed racing through the sky, the grass, the house, through everything.

Without a sound it breaks apart.  Without a sound it shatters, shards falling like snowflakes in the darkness. Without a sound falling so slowly and I feel myself falling too, falling so slowly down into the darkness.

# thai food

Driving south, driving back to her, his mind wanders. Cruising along the black ribbon of highway his mind wanders out into the low green hills, into the masses of cloud on the far horizon. His mind touches the opaque future, tentatively; touches this thing in the future that is suddenly so close, so near. This thing within its amniotic membrane that has been growing between them, that has been waiting between he and Isobel to be born. His mind touches the thing; softly, tentatively. It stirs, turns over, he can feel its movement within that crimson, velvet dark.

The next day he's walking along the beach. The day is leaving slowly, the sun in the haze is a low, pink ball of fire. The ocean purrs. His mind churns, turns over and over again. The sun is an unceasing, smoldering eye, the waves curl with a grace that lies beyond him, the ocean crashes in on itself, daring him to believe.

That night it happens. In the bed and the moment is upon them, but the moment is so large that it blots out everything, fills his mouth and hers so that they cannot speak. They fumble as though in a race against time, like senseless beings they tumble into and suddenly back out again. It happens and nothing happens; a false nature, it drains away.

Unremembered time passes. Perhaps once, perhaps twice, perhaps three times the sun passes in its track across the sky. The ocean meditates, murmurs in the night.

Skin-on-skin, body against body they curl, sway like a boat on gentle waters. The garden grows up around them, the green vines, the heavy, tender violet flowers. Tongues push through lips, gathering a sustenance, a slow power in the wet dark.

Wait, she says.

Let me show you, she says.

She rises, a pale, figured moon.

He feels the weight of her slim body as she comes down, feels time disappear as she brings him inside of herself, as they merge for the very first time.

Something is born. Something made of light and bones and bodies; a wind comes up and a wind comes up suddenly in all the leaves in all the trees and the shadows are an ornate moving gorgeousness across the ground; are shadows, cool and dark and full of wonder.

Never before, he thinks without words; never, he realizes, before now. The power inside of it, the way within the infinite breadth of possible experience it stands alone. A wind comes up and a wind comes up and you notice that the trees sing for the sky, notice that your heart and body are yours, apart and complete and enough.

There is no urge to climax. No desire within them to move beyond this oneness, to seek its ending. Curtains of sleep draw gradually around them as they drift, dreams gather within them as they fall asleep within each other's arms.


It is the afternoon of the following day. He is at home, alone with his thoughts.

Sex. Intercourse, sexual intercourse; now a part of who they are together, of the way they communicate with one another. It feels momentous, enormously momentous, and yet at the same time so smoothly, seamlessly integrated into the whole.

It just gets bigger, keeps growing; and as it does it takes him further away, deeper into this floating, un-tethered realm. Everything is changing. Things within the world that once caused him jealousy, that provoked anxiety or doubt; all these are just simply things now. He sees them as they are, takes them into himself as they are, no longer measuring himself against these values, within these artificial systems of meaning.

He understands, and he is astounded. It emanates from the core and spreads outward, a wordlessly perfect art. He stands shirtless before the bathroom mirror in the muted, calm afternoon light, and sees what he feels: in the reflection of the contours of his chest, the sinuous muscles of his arms; in the reflection before him, he sees that his body is the containment of a radiant power.

He knows that it is not that he has changed. That what Isobel has catalyzed is not a change, but an accep-tance. That what she has wrought in him is an ac-knowledgment of who he is, an embrace of his true inheritance.

But for her, this thing that exists between them is entirely something else. The entirety of her life, as far back as she can remember she has lived in the shadow;

in the grasp of the dark Thing that her brother put within her so long ago. And for the first time now, the first time ever, she has discovered her own heart. Hope, blooming, a flower she beholds with awe, presses close to with exclamations of delight.

It is a juxtaposition of exhilarating joy and of a deep, abiding terror. Joy as she feels the dark Thing's hold receding, weakening. Terror as she feels how strong Its grip yet remains.

He feels Its hatred. How all of It, all of Its rage and fury is bent on his destruction. It seizes her, her eyes grow dim, her body goes rigid as the color drains from her face.

Get away from me says her empty, hollow voice. You shouldn't be with me, no one should be with me. Get away from me, leave me alone.

No. No, I will not go away. What happened to you is not who you are.

You don't understand, she says bitterly. You don't know who I am, what I've done, what I will do to you.

You have no more secrets from me. I know who you are, and there is nothing in you that can frighten me.

Get away from me!

She struggles to rise from the bed, he bends over her, holding her down as she looks wildly around the room, looks anywhere but at his eyes, but into him.

With force he presses his lips against hers, pushes his tongue into her mouth. His arms encircle her body like a vise, with power he squeezes and she gasps, stares at him, and then her hands are on his neck, fingers running through his hair as her body melts, as her heart surges, beating like a drum with the intensity of sudden awakening.

He stands motionless before the reflection in the

bathroom mirror. So far you have come, it says in silence. So much further, yet, have you to go.


The colors of sunset bend across the darkening sky. The lights of civilization are a passing blur as the car swims smoothly along the black stream of freeway.

"What if they don't like me?"

"Then I'll punch them in their noses."

"C'mon, seriously."

"Of course they're going to like you. You're smart, you're funny, you're cute, what's not to like?"

"What if I don't like them?"

"Then I'll punch you in the nose, obviously."

She rolls her eyes, smiles, lapses into silent acceptance.

A trip to see friends, a couple hours drive to the north. He is unworried; Daisy, Timothy and P.J. are as nice as people can be. But it's more than that. When he thinks of Daisy his mind automatically adds: Annie and Daisy, and the syllables conjure up a treasure chest within his memories.

He had found them at a time when he needed to find them. A gift, that restored something to him he hadn't realized he was looking for, hadn't realized he'd lost. The two of them, Annie and Daisy, had been friends since they'd been little children, make-believing together on the playground, and had forged a way of being between themselves that had continued on into their adult lives unbroken. When he found them they welcomed him in, with arms spread wide and open. The triangle-friendship world they made together had lasted for nearly half a year, coming to an end only when Annie and Daisy moved out of the apartment they shared, when the practical necessities of life declared that it was time to move on. In his memory that apartment, that home, existed as a kind of magic, human-sized terrarium; a place in which all they'd ever done was have fun, in which everything was open to re-invention, in which the simplest objects became the simplest joys. It had been the essence of kindred-spirithood, the finding of lost soulmates: sharp, clear delineations about what was good and what was bad, and always agreed-upon with a three-part harmony. He could remember, clearly, the last day; loading the boxes on the truck, lingering together, for a long moment Daisy's head resting on his shoulder. A sadness that was too sweet to be a true sadness, too strong and clear to be anything less than a gift to the long body of memory.

This short trip, to visit Daisy, her brother Timothy, and her boyfriend P.J. in the town where they all lived now, was simple on its surface. A trip to see friends, to have fun, to visit loved ones.

But it was more than that. It was a trip he had chosen carefully, purposefully. An example of the kind of world Isobel needed to discover, to know was real. She needed more than just being with him. To believe in the change happening within her she needed to see it reflected beyond him, to see it in other eyes, hear it in other voices.

A test. Another test, carefully chosen. Both he and she knew it, and it was why she bit her lip and fidgeted in her seat as they sped northward.

They exit the freeway, drive slowly through town, following the directions Daisy's given him. He sees them standing on the sidewalk in front of the restaurant, gives a wave as he pulls into the parking spot.

Daisy's all smiles as he gets out of the car, arms open as she comes forward. "Hey! You're here!" she says, wrapping her arms around him.

"Hi, Daisy-boo," he says, lightly kisses the top of her head. "I brought a friend with me."

"I know!" she says, letting go and turning. "Isobel, is that right?" Isobel nods with a small, hesitant smile. "Well I'm Daisy, and I'm really glad to meet you!" Daisy's clear, sincere enthusiasm ripples outwards, and Isobel's smile deepens, shyly, as she takes Daisy's hand.

Daisy turns, pointing: "This is my brother Timothy and my boyfriend P.J." Each of them nods and gives a little wave in turn, Isobel returns the gesture. Daisy stands with her hands on her hips, smiling at all of them.

"Oh old friend, I'm so glad you're here!" she exclaims again.

"Well…sorry to have to tell you, but it's not actually me. He and Isobel were busy, unfortunately. The two of us are robots they made and sent in their place."

"Oh no! Robots!" Daisy cries, clapping her hands to the side of her head.

"Hm, could be serious business," says P.J., squinting at me. "Are you evil robots?" he asks suspiciously.

"Oh no, no, we're definitely good robots. We've been programmed to only use our superior strength and intelligence for the good of humankind."

"Well that's good, as long as you don't get into a classic sci-fi quandary about what's best for us puny humanoids," says P.J. "Can you at least eat Thai food? Because that's what we're eating tonight."

"Of course! Robots loooove Thai food, after oil it's like our favorite thing."

103

"Oh right," P.J. says, nodding. "I'd forgotten, haven't hung out with robots in awhile."

"Well…I guess robots are okay," says Daisy mournfully. "But I wish you and Isobel were really here."

"Hm…well, do you want me to tell you a secret?" he asks her. She nods eagerly. He leans toward her and stage-whispers behind his hand: "It's actually us. We're not actually robots." A huge smile breaks across Daisy's face, she claps her hands: "Hooray! Not actually robots!"

"Dang, you had me fooled," says P.J. as he shakes his head. "I was starting to wish I'd brought my, y'know, ray gun or whatever, in case you malfunctioned."

"Since you aren't robots, I think we should celebrate," says Daisy, hands on hips again. "By eating Thai food?" suggests P.J., gesturing to the restaurant's door. "Yes!" says Daisy, beaming. P.J. opens the door, props it with his foot as they all walk through; Daisy leads the way and gives P.J. a curtsey with a giggle as she passes inside.

The restaurant is busy, cheerful, smiling waitstaff in white shirts and black pants bustle back and forth. They sit, order Thai iced teas, hem-and-haw over the menu; Daisy gives another "Hooray!" when they decide to share dishes, family-style, so they can try as many different things as possible. Daisy's laughter bubbles like a clear spring found in a dry country; just as he imagined it would, just as he remembered. He and Daisy and P.J. do most of the talking. Timothy listens mostly, laughs frequently; repeats things he particularly enjoys, as though they are small treasures he is storing up somewhere. Isobel sits in the conversation's corner. She gives short, shy answers to questions, looks down at her lap when she laughs, when she finds herself laughing.

Appetizers appear, spring rolls in their cool, translucent wrappings, disappear quickly with mms and ahhs! given through crunchy, delicious mouthfuls. P.J., Daisy, and Timothy excuse themselves for a cigarette before the arrival of entrees, "Because that's the best," says Daisy, "when you come back and find your food waiting on the table!"

As they walk away he turns to Isobel and is caught by the look on her face, the commingling of frustration and hope.

"I don't...don't know how to be, I don't know what to say!" she says.

He can't help but smile, looking back at her.

"Do you see how nice these people are? Just be who you are, the same person you are when it's just you and me. They're curious about you, they already like you. Say whatever you want to say." She takes a deep breath, nods, and her eyes fill with something. He takes her hand and squeezes as a waiter approaches with a food-laden tray.

Daisy and Timothy and P.J. return as the waiter is placing the last dish on the table.

"Yes!" says Daisy, pumping her fist with a grin.

"What up, Thai food," says P.J., rubbing his hands together.

Noodle dishes, Thai curries, bowls of white jasmine rice; everything looks delicious, everything smells delicious. They start passing dishes around the table, piling food onto their plates. Daisy hands the curry across the table to Isobel, but he puts his hand out as though to wave it away, and they both look up at him.

"Isobel shouldn't be eating anything that rich, Daisy. If she's going to be with me, she needs to maintain her figure," he says as he takes the curry and sets it aside.

"Hey! Bad, bad boy!" Daisy says, wagging her finger at him with a severe frown.

"Hey, I didn't sign up to be with a fatty," he says.

"Yeah, no horrible fatties," says P.J. through a mouthful that he's choking on, a moment later, after Daisy's punch to his ribcage.

"It's okay Daisy, I'm used to this," says Isobel, reaching for the bowl of curry. "Stop that!" she exclaims, slapping at his hand as he tries to take it away. "Besides," she says, leaning in toward the table a bit, "my figure's about to change anyway. What he doesn't know yet is that, as of quite recently…I'm eating for two now."

He freezes with a forkful of food halfway to his mouth, mind suddenly racing. He turns to her and at the look on his face she bursts out laughing.

"Gotcha!" she exclaims.

Daisy squeals with laughter, claps her hands. "Oh, good one! That was a really good one, you scared his pants off! Take that, bad boy!" she says, reaching across the table to exchange a high-five with Isobel.

Shock gives way to relief, relief gives way to wonder. The girl sitting next to him, mere minutes ago, the shy, anxious, silent girl…is just gone now.

"Aww, did I scare you?" she says. She pats his cheek, makes a kissy face, turns back to the table and whatever Daisy's saying now. He stares at her, at the changing happening within her before his eyes.

The Ice Queen. Death, they called her.

No, I will not go away. What happened to you is not who you are.

To say it, even to believe it is one thing. To see it happening, though, is to see the true nature of what is at stake, the enormity of the decision he has made…something moves deep within him; something happens, deep inside his body, at the sight of her in this moment, unchained and free.

The rest of the evening is filled with the light; Isobel's light. She talks, she laughs, her happiness flows and everyone can feel it, can see. The conversation at one point is focused between Isobel and P.J. and Timothy. He looks across the table at Daisy, finds her watching him.

She knows. Her eyes sparkle: she's so wonderful, this is so wonderful, her eyes say.

Yes, say his eyes in return, his slight nod.

Yes it is.

## mirrors

How long I kept falling, I don't know. How long I've been lying here for, I don't know either. I have no memory of hitting something, of coming to rest on solid ground; just, at a certain point, realizing that I wasn't falling anymore.

I sit up gingerly, anticipating pain. But there is nothing except an ache in my chest. An ache like a hollow place, an echo. I realize, in a quiet kind of way, that this ache is an old thing; but my darkened, fractured memory has nothing more to tell me about what it is or where it comes from. I look around and find the canvas bag and pad of paper lying next to me. I put the pad in the bag, stand up and sling it over my head, take in my surroundings.

I'm in a large room. The floor is composed of tiles of white stone, but there is no ceiling. Instead, above me is blackness, pierced by tiny points of white light like a starry night sky, but there is no star-like motion, no sparkle or glimmer; as though they are arrested, frozen in time. And on the walls, all over all the walls around me there are mirrors. Hundreds and hundreds of mirrors, in all kinds of shapes and sizes: small round mirrors, mirrors taller than I am, mirrors framed in wrought iron, in golden-gilted, ornately carved wood.

Immediately I feel a strong sense of unease. And as I look, turning round slowly, I realize that none, not a single one of these hundreds of mirrors is holding my reflection.

I hold my hand up in front of my face, reflexively, to see a part of me, to see that I am still there, and as I do I sense a murmur of movement at the corner of my vision, within a small oval mirror in a simple wooden frame. I turn, my heart begins beating faster as I step towards it and the movement sharpens, a blurred image appearing, undulating in waves as I come closer. I stop, less than a couple feet away as the undulations begin to vibrate with a greater intensity, and then suddenly the image freezes, snaps into coherency. I stagger backwards involuntarily, my mouth dry, at the reflection in the mirror of my eyeless face. The reflection doesn't follow, or change, it stays frozen in place: my face with two dark holes where my eyes should be. I touch my own eyes, my trembling fingers touch my own eyes and my breath comes out in a shudder as the fear of touching two dark holes dissipates.

I wrench my gaze away from the frozen image and again I feel, as much as see, off to the side a flutter of movement. What is this, what the hell is happening here...I don't want to, but I can't stop myself, I turn, take slow steps towards the mirror where the movement came from, a mirror taller than I am and nearly again as wide. Again the undulations within it as I approach, the increasing waves...and then I am standing before it, paralyzed.

The figure on the left is me; clothed like some kind of ancient warrior, his face that is my face broken with pain and rage and lost hate, as he thrusts a spear through the heart of the identically-clothed figure on the right, who is also me, whose face that is my face is a picture of bliss, of pure release.

I back away, the sheer force of it pushes me back and away and again the reflection stays frozen in place. Again the glimmer of movement in some new mirror, again the irresistible, hypnotic pull towards it, again the sharpening undulations until the unbidden, incomprehensible reflection snaps into place. Images of me crying or maimed or dying or dead, images of sadness and despair and rage, over and over and over again, I cannot stop myself, until the mass of unknown reflections threatens to bury me beneath its accumulated weight, a mountain of pain; the sweat is pouring down my face now, my breath ragged, gasping.

Can this possibly be me?…my future, my broken past?…this is madness, insanity. My heart is pounding, racing, my mind whirls and churns like a storm-driven, terrible sea; I crumple to my knees, bent double, my hands balled into fists, forehead pressed against the stone floor. Somewhere amidst the dark, swirling chaos inside there is a dim thing; a voice calling softly, urgently, words that are so far away that I can only barely, only maybe hear: …power and pain and choices… shattered…chose…no choice…truth and hope, believe…believe….

I shut my eyes tight and ride my wild breathing, my hammering heart. I cling to the reins with a memory, battling, fighting until there is a rhythm, until it is my rhythm, slower, and slower, and slower…

I blink. My breathing is low, steady. The tile floor is

cool against my forehead as for long moments I let the breath in, and back out again. I move, finally, and it hurts to move, all over, my body feels as though it has been used up, wrung out like a wet rag.

I don't know how much time has passed. But I can sense it, that something has changed.

Slowly, painfully, I sit upright; look and see. All the mirrors with their frozen reflections are still there, but the images are dimmed now; darkened.

All but one. One mirror remains untouched, tall and bright in a silvery frame worked with small, dark-silver flowers at the corners, dark-silver vines that crawl along the edges.

I do not want this. Somehow I know that I would take anything, anything at all but this. But there is nothing else left.

I rise; on unsteady feet step forward. This time it is different: the mirror is filled with mist, a dense fog. As I approach, slowly, I see a figure within, coming closer. When I am nearly a yard away the figure emerges, or the mist recedes, it happens too quickly for me to perceive.

It is me: just as I am, clothed as I am, a bag over the shoulder just like mine, and this time the reflection stays a reflection; it moves as I do, breathes as I do, blinking eyes stare back at me. It is me, within this mirror, but something is…wrong.

I unsling the bag over my head, let it fall to the ground, my reflection doing the same, continuing to follow me.

I stand still for a moment, staring.

I have to know.

I pull my shirt off, let it fall next to the bag. I stare down for a long moment before I will myself to look up and see.

There is a dark shadow like a hollow just off the center of my reflection's chest. I feel it as I see it, the dull ache: a shadow left behind in place of a thing that was once within me. Thick dark lines begin to emerge from the shadowed hollow, black vines with thorns like razors that crawl across the body within the mirror, wrapping around its torso, twining around its legs and arms, twisting, until a last vine coils around its neck. Blood trickles down in places where the thorns have pierced the skin.

The silence is vast. The dull ache sits within my chest like a stone. My body feels empty, cold. I raise my gaze to my reflection's face, find immeasurably sad, lost eyes staring back at me, eyes filled with shadows and ghosts. I stand motionless as the reflection raises a vine-entwined arm, now; pointing, down to the bag at my feet. I sit, kneel, reach into the bag and pull out the pad of paper, my body moving as though at the whim of a puppeteer's strings. I look up at the mirror one last time, see that terrible reflection standing, looking down at me: those lost eyes, that endless sadness. The mirror and its reflection fade slowly into darkness, as I bend my head towards the pages and begin to read.

*As we drove away from Santa Rosa, later that night, Isobel said, in a shy kind of way, I think I made three new friends tonight.*

*I think you did too, I said.*

*Really?*

*Yes. They all really liked you.*

*I really liked them too. Daisy especially, she was so nice to me.*

*Well yeah, that's how Daisy is when she's fond of some-*

*body.*

*Isobel was quiet for awhile, and then she sighed, in a way that was almost like singing. I looked over and could see the smile on her face, her eyes shining in the dark.*

*It was late when we got home, near midnight. We should've been tired, but we weren't; the world felt full with the buoyant energy of being alive. I followed her into the house, as she walked across the living room she stopped and twirled, once, laughing. I followed her on into the bedroom she now shared with me, the room that contained the secret garden of our life together; we went into it, and closed the door.*

*I call it that because it is the clearest way of saying what it had been for us: a garden in which we discovered each other and this world we were creating, a secret garden full of things that were alive and growing; things we had never seen before, but even so we knew, somehow, that they had yet a different, unseen incarnation, something else to still become. And what made it so strange, what made it fairly impossible to articulate, even to each other, was that these things were already so beautiful. It was beyond words to see that they were partially obscured, and to see at the same time that their deepest beauty was unseen, would be invisible until they stood fully revealed.*

*When I say beyond words I'm trying to make a literal description. I'm writing this now, more than five years later, and maybe because it has taken the words that long to find their way to me; that much, all that I have learned and lived through in the time since then, for me to be able to finally bring them together. They are the strongest and most secret words and yet the most simple as well. They are the hardest words to come to know and I have not wanted to use them until I have come to know how to use them; until I know that when I use them they will say what they can say,*

*say all of it.*

*I don't remember most of what happened that night, beyond that buoyant energy that kept us from sleep; we read comics, listened to music, told each other stories, kissed each other, lay still together; those are all best guesses, the specific details are lost to memory. But that makes sense; makes sense because it's not that I forget things but that I do remember the way it felt; the way it felt the whole time; the way it felt perfect. And what I mean when I say perfect is that Isobel and I saw that we were happy together: that it was the same moment still unbroken, regardless of where we were or who we were with; and we stayed awake in the room with that feeling between us that night; we played with each other like children, like children in the sun in spring. Played in green and golden shadows, silhouettes of mountains and trees silent beneath moonlit-silver clouds in the deep night sky; played within and beneath a beauty that edged the darkness, showed in different pockets of light. And what I mean when I say perfect is that all this was ours; that it was something we had produced, and that in this secret garden of wonders what we saw and looked at was each other. In the center of all of it, a shape silent and true.*

*Towards the end of the night, as the light of dawn was gathering beyond the curtained windows; towards the end I saw the end, could see it clear approaching. Quiet, ready to sleep, I did not see it; did not see what I was seeing.*

*I don't remember what she said; it was only part of the conversation we were having, and I didn't see it. I don't remember what she said, only that she was on her back on the bed and that I was propped somehow above her; that I was looking down at her when she said it.*

*And then suddenly there was something in my body bigger than anything that had ever been there before; bigger and far bigger; so big that it was simply everything. With-*

out warning or sign, not there and then just suddenly somehow there; a river that went right through me and that I was: a river of nameless light in the body of air. And then it came to me, rose up in silence; came to me only as it was, and I saw that I had never really spoken its name. It came into the back of me, hidden from her; came behind me and I felt my head bend forward under its weight, felt my eyes close; felt it burning, a silent, shattering truth, and felt absolutely nothing else.

My head bowed down, my eyes closed, my body shaking. Isobel put her hands on me; put her hands against what she could suddenly, unmistakeably feel.

"There is a word inside of me; it is bigger than any word I have ever had, and it is also the only word left; the only word there anymore, and I need to be able to say it to you."

And as I said it I raised my head and looked at her. As my body rose up like a force of nature I held it, as though you could be able to hold the wind or the water; still I held it, trembling, as I looked at her and waited, because I had asked.

And she looked back at me; seeing what she was seeing, not believing that she was seeing it, but clearly seeing it nonetheless, she looked at me with eyes that I had never seen before; with eyes wide and wordless she silently nodded: yes. yes. yes. The tears began to run down my face, the river of light flowing: and it came out of me like the song of angels, not just words but a way of choosing to be alive. Like nothing I had ever said before I looked into her eyes and said, "I love you...I love you, and it's the most beautiful thing I have ever seen."

Because I saw it then; as my heart said "love" I saw it; closed my eyes, or just as possibly didn't close my eyes, and saw it within. It shone like a light, but it was not a light; it was nothing else than what it was, alone and whole unto *itself. It was red, a deep and illimitable redness, bright and true and strong. Uncontainable and yet somehow it contained itself, and it rose in the air above an unseen lake set in the high, stone-walled depths of unknown mountains that rose up just beneath some kind of sky; above the green and silver water it shone. As I looked, as I saw, I came to see that there was another. The color was lighter, a pink rose, but just as single and deep; and it shone just as bright and strong but lighter; with its own individual truth, it was next to the other; those two, together in the air. And the way that each shone, that each was shining, was a kind of song; a kind of song that each was singing to the other; for the other. It was that song that made them each so beautiful; the way that each sang for and to the other; the clear, unbroken sound of the way they sang together.*

*It came to Isobel several seconds, a minute later; just kept coming until she could no longer find her disbelief, until it was simply no longer available. "I love you," she said, with a helpless kind of light and surrender. "I love you, I just do."*

*And that was it. Saying it was the last thing left undone between us, and now we had done it. We had made a new whole together.*


I sit; motionless, still. Within a void, a sphere of nothing.

It seeks for me. Dimly, as if from very far away, I can feel the pressure of it surrounding the void, feel it seeking a way in.

I will not allow it. I will not allow it to enter me again.

I've remembered it, now. Remembered... everything.

You've been watching me, yes? Following me. I

116

spoke to you, I remember, some nonsense about the "landscape of a heart." And something about this place, about promises and secrets, shadows and ghosts.

Well, now I remember. Remember the hole in my body. I will not feel that pain again. Promises and secrets no longer concern me. I remember power.

I push, hard, and I feel the pain beyond the sphere change. Feel it darken, begin to boil. Feel the power surging.

For the betrayal there will be a price. For the pain there will be a reckoning. What was stolen from me will be mine again, and I am coming to take it.

# II

## silver threads

The sky above is leaden, gray. Everything here is gray, a landscape of ash and rock, of broken things. The endless dead forest stands directly ahead, looming, stretching to the far horizons. The wind rattles the branches of cold, black trees, the wind sings of dying, all around me.

I look down at my hands. The light in my fingertips flutters; inconsistent, weak. Imagined from within the void this place was one thing, but being here it is another...no. The pain. I will not feel that pain. I clench my hands into fists and feel the anger stoke the fire. I hear laughter; somewhere out there I hear It laughing at me. The anger within me surges; I push, hard, and the closest tree explodes in fire, blooms with a thousand burning, white-hot flames.

"No," says that quiet voice. The word rings out, a tone struck from a bell. I whirl and find Dawn standing a few short feet away, her eyes hard and clear like two black diamonds.

"What...what are you doing here? How did you

get here?"

"It doesn't matter how. I came to talk with you."

"I don't need to talk to anyone anymore. I'm through talking." She stares at me in silence. I look away, irritated, scowling.

"Go away. There's no reason for you to be here. Leave me alone, go away."

She sighs. "Do you really think there's no reason why I'm here? Do you think this is a place I would choose to come to on my own? Yes, you're right, I shouldn't be here; but that's only because you shouldn't be here either."

"Then go. Leave, like you left before. As I recall you gave up the ability to have anything to say in my life a long, long time ago."

Her eyes narrow. "What do you think you're doing here, exactly?" she says, pointing at the tree and the flames behind me. "Do you think that what you will face, here in this place, is nothing more than some dead tree you can simply burn away? Do you honestly think —"

"Enough! What the—who the fuck do you think you are to come here, to talk to me like this!" The words come tumbling out, hard and fast. "I found something with you and you ignored it, you took the easy way out and pretended like you didn't see, like you'd never seen me! So who the fuck do you think you are to be standing here now trying to tell me what to do? I didn't ask you to be here, I don't want you to be here...so *leave*!" I hurl the words with force, the earth cracks open, jagged rents running through the ground to either side of her. She stands unmoving. The black diamonds of her eyes stare back at me.

"Do you really think that it was easy?" she says, an

edge of bitter anger in her voice. "Do you really think that just because I was the one who chose to say no, that it was easy?" Something comes into her face. Her voice softens. "You heard what I said; I know you were out there, listening. It was just too hard, there was nothing easy about it. Remember? I said it because I meant it, because it was what I felt when you held me that last morning: it feels like I'm being cheated..."

At those last words a lock clicks open. As she stands before me my eyes remember her face, my heart remembers her voice, my hands remember her body. Silver threads coalesce in the air between us, bridging the distance, connecting her body to mine; a network of gossamer filaments that causes the breath to catch in my throat as the anger dies away. Her eyes close, and she sighs in a way that causes the silver strands to quiver with feeling.

"Of course it hurt me to let this go," she says quietly as her eyes open. "Of course it did."

From nowhere a memory rises, fills my body. Words come suddenly, flowing up and out of my mouth.

"I was walking in a field, alone at night. I had not remembered you in years. In the darkness and a rushing wind, and a full, pale moon in the dark sky. Something moved in me, and I sat down and the wind came and the moon came and you came. From nowhere, you came and knelt by my side. I spoke with you, felt you next to me; it seemed as though if I could remember something that was just beyond me then I would be able to reach out; to reach out and feel my fingertips against your face. I didn't try. You stayed with me, until finally the wind and the moon carried you back away." I look at her as I finish saying this, and it is as though I am surfacing, emerging from something as the words leave me, and I hear myself ask: "Who did that happen to? Is it mine? Does that memory belong to me?"

"I…I don't know," she says, hesitating. "It's not—it's not a question I can answer."

I look at her as the memory echoes in my mind; I look at her, and suddenly the clarity, the resolution I felt after that room of mirrors, suddenly all that is slipping away, running like water through my fingers.

"Why you?…why is it you, here now?" I ask. She is silent. "I…I was just talking to you, as though I remembered you, as though the feelings were mine…as though it was years ago, as though I was years ago again…but I…I…"

Memory is receding again, fast. The lights are dimming, the things I know are sinking down, down back into the dark. "What's happening to me?" I ask her, almost pleading. "What is this place, how did I end up here…why can't I hold onto anything? What's happening to me?"

I see the sadness in her eyes. "I can't answer your questions. I wish I could, I really do, but I just can't." She shakes her head, takes a deep breath. "But…but I do know why you've come here. What It is that's here waiting for you." Her voice falls, softly. "And I know that if you try and face It, without knowing who you are, then…then It will destroy you."

A branch breaks off from the burning tree behind me, crashes to the ground. From somewhere in the far distance I hear the laughter again, and it rings in my ears, seems to vibrate in my bones. The cold, cold wind rises, the silver threads between us start to darken, to tremble in the rising wind as through they might snap and break.

Dawn takes a deep breath, and reaches out; runs deft fingers along the strands, reversing the darkness, and they begin to luminesce, to pulse with a faint glow.

"What you have seen is one possible truth, but there are many others. You can't give up, you have to keep going," she says as her fingertips trace the memories. "You have to know more, much more, before you will become able to hold the truth within yourself," she says as the threads begin to resonate, to hum. "You have to become stronger, much stronger, in order to know who you really are." Her hands move swiftly in the air, weaving the threads together into a single rope of silver light. She walks forward, holding it before her, and places it in my hands. Leans in and softly kisses my cheek. "Take this," she says, letting go, stepping back. "It will take you away from here. But where you go next is up to you." I look down, the ball of light in my hands aglow, growing, ringing out. "Don't ever forget that I cared for you," she says, the sphere of light growing, enveloping me, "and don't ever forget that you cared for me," is the last whisper I hear before the sound and the light swallow me whole.

# letters

Five weeks. I'll only be gone for five weeks. I'll be back before you realize I even went anywhere.

He has to say it, but they both know it's not true. She will know that he's gone, will *feel* that he is gone the moment the door closes behind him. She will know it and the ghosts will know it and the Thing inside her will know it too.

He is worried. He's talked with Tyler, asked him to spend time with Isobel while he's away, but he knows that it's a tiny measure in relation to her need; tiny at best, and maybe nothing at all. He and Tyler have drifted too far apart. Since moving here together, nearly a year ago, their lives have gone in very different directions, and the best-friendship they've had for years is frayed, no longer what it once was. Asking Tyler to spend time with her stirs up misgivings within him, but he pushes them down, has nowhere else to turn.

He can't not go. For their twenty-fifth wedding anniversary his parents have decided they want to visit Italy, and to bring he and his sister along. Hope said

Hey, let's stay longer and travel around Europe together after Mom and Dad fly back home; they gave us that "free trip anywhere" christmas present, let's use it now.

He can't not go. He has his own life, with its own responsibilities, wants, needs; he can't discard them all to stay with Isobel, even if he wanted to do that he couldn't, he can't. He knows where he comes from, what the things are that make him who he is. That make him who she loves.

But what has opened up within her is so young, and so fragile. His presence is what nourishes it, what protects it. He is the force that exerts control over the dark Thing within her, what keeps it at bay.

He can't just disappear for five weeks. He has to find a way to also stay.

He buys time. He's going back home, first, they're all meeting there and flying out together. Come, he says to her. I want you to meet my family, to see where I come from. The idea makes her anxious, clearly; but she has placed all of herself and her trust within him. Okay, she says. Okay.

He flies out first. Three days later he takes his mother's car and drives to the airport to pick Isobel up.

He is unprepared. It takes him by surprise, completely: standing there waiting and he sees her as she turns a corner and a wave of feeling crashes, slams into him. Exterior sounds and shapes blur and run together, an indistinct swirl framing this figure who is carrying his love. She takes his hand, she looks into his face and what is inside of him and her eyes fill up with light. I didn't know, he thinks, dazed; it was only three days, I didn't notice the lack; didn't know it would feel so much like joy to come together again…

In the night, they make love that goes on and on;

not just making love but building it, unlocking the secrets within human bodies. Hot, slow, tender. This way she says. That way she says. Oh my god she whispers. God...god. Oh my god. In the day he takes her up into the mountains and the surrounding beauty takes them, fills them up; they run across the high mountain meadow and into the trees until they know they are alone, the hungry gravity of love pulls them down into the grass, to the ground. Fuck me, she pleads as he pushes inside. Hard, fuck me hard she pleads, gasping. The words are a slap across his face; an awakening to the violence this is to her, to the violence this is within her: the force he is bringing into her and its power to break and re-make. He knows that he cannot fall away; that he can't forget, that his eyes must remain open.

Isobel can hardly bear to be with his family, she disappears. He finds her in the basement guest-room, lying on the bed. The tears fall slowly across her pale, colorless face. All the shadows are sad ghosts and he sees them crowding around her, the immense grief of her memories pouring, crushing down.

He sits down on the bed. Her hands come to her face, they cover her eyes. Her body convulses, slightly, as a tiny sob breaks free.

"I shouldn't be here," she whispers. "I'm not...I shouldn't be with you, with your family. I shouldn't be in a place...like this...," and her voice breaks, she curls into a ball as her body convulses again beneath his hand.

"Are you afraid to be here?" he says. "Are you afraid that there is something in you, that will hurt the goodness you see here, the goodness you feel here? That you will hurt me? Sweetheart...you can see this place, you can see what there is here. Do you think I would ever

126

risk it, that I would ever bring anything dangerous here? This is where I come from. I love you, and that means this is a place where you belong."

In the closet in this room there is a large bag filled with his old stuffed animals. He goes to the closet, retrieves the bag. Sits back down on the bed and starts pulling animals out, introducing them to her one by one.

"I've been wanting you to meet some old friends of mine. This is Turtley, my grandma made him for me. He's a bit shy. This is Roscoe, he's a reindeer. He gets scared easily, that's why he's always looking off to the side. This is Tron, he's a tyrannosaurus; he's pretty fierce, but only to people who aren't my friends." He places each of them next to her. The ghosts begin to fade.

"There was this one time, when I was little," he says, continuing to pull animals from the bag, pile them around her. "I had a nightmare and woke up crying, ran out and found my dad. He took me in his lap, and said I should go back to bed but that I should bring a bunch of my stuffed animals into bed with me, especially the big ones. So I did, and it worked; I know it sounds kind of silly, but it did, it made the fear go away. I mean, I always knew that they were just stuffed animals, but I loved them all the same." He pulls out a blue lamb with a pink nose, posed with his head kind of looking back over his shoulder. "This is Lambert. I could never get over how cute he was. I know it's a bit ridiculous, but look how cute he is. It used to drive me a little crazy." She reaches out and takes Lambert; looks at him for a moment and then brings him in, into her arms against her body.

"He's nice," she whispers. The ghosts are gone. He

127

strokes her hair, gently. Turns off the light and goes back upstairs after she falls asleep.

The idea has been forming over the last couple days, and now it clicks into place. That night after leaving her asleep, he writes her the first letter. In the morning he puts it in the mailbox, so that it will arrive and be waiting for her by the time she flies back. Again, that night after she's asleep, he writes the next one. Every day a letter; every day for the next five weeks he will write to her, every day there will be a letter waiting for her when she comes home after work. It will build; when she sees, when she realizes what he is doing it will build inside of her. One page, two, three. Whatever it takes, letters that are long enough for her to hear his voice, for her heart to hear him speaking. It is the most that I can do from across half the world, he thinks; I hope it is enough.

"One last kiss," he says at the airport, taking her in his arms. "Five little weeks," he says when they break apart. "I'll miss you. I'll be back before you know it." She nods, her face set with the determination not to be afraid. She walks down the jetway and he watches her go. Before disappearing around the corner she stops, turns back and waves. Sudden anxiety flares as he sees her from this distance, he wants to run to her, to call her back to him. He stands still, his hand waves goodbye, a moment later she's gone. Gone, gone. He stands at the window, watching her plane back away from the gate.

His limitations. The responsibility of love, the implacable force of reality: the necessary choices pull him apart, push him down. His family knows. His parents don't ask questions but it sits in their eyes. Later that night he and his sister talk.

"Are you sad?" she asks.

"Yes. No. I don't know."

"It's only five weeks."

"I know. It's not that long, I know. It shouldn't matter."

"But?"

"Yeah. It shouldn't matter, I know. But I'm afraid that it does."

"It's…it's pretty serious, isn't it, brother." Her face has care in it, has worry in it. He shrugs, looks down at his hands.

"Yeah. Yeah, it is."

The next day is a new day, though. Too busy: they are packing, driving, boarding the plane. Somewhere far up in the vast deep blue, listening to music through headphones his thoughts drift to Isobel but drift only; too much to look forward to, the imminence of the present adventure claims his attention and the anxiety disperses away.

They spend the next two weeks in cities and trains, in small towns with narrow cobbled streets; sitting poolside at a country villa, green vineyards running across the golden hillsides all around. Exhausting at times, the closeness of foreign travel; all the strangeness that they don't know, the busy and dust and heat. But within it all they find the moments of family solitude, the blessing his parents have brought them all here to celebrate.

Pointing at the statue his dad says, See, look here, it's Romulus and Remus nursing at the wolf's tits. He and his sister, their eyes meet. Um, Dad, I believe the word you're looking for is actually pronounced "teat". His sister collapses into giggles; Honestly, Ted, says his mother. His dad pokes Hope in the ribs, she squirms and whoops, slapping his hand away. Walking along a

129

dirt road in the countryside, they have turned back too late. Night falls, someone stumbles, worry coalesces about finding the way. Look, says someone as they round a bend, and the worry is forgotten before a field full of fireflies, forgotten in the dark sea full of tiny, drifting lights. He hems and haws over whether to buy an intricately-patterned but expensive piece of pottery. His frugal, farm-raised mother surprises him by telling him to buy it, telling him that "it's good to have beautiful things."

They get lost and tired, crabby and annoyed with one another. They tease each other, laugh and play. They stand before gorgeous paintings of gods and angels, talk in low voices as they walk through immense cathedrals full of coolness and stone and golden shafts of sunlight. Taking in this country's ancient, decaying beauty, the life it lives with its particular and careless grace.

And he writes to her. It is as much work as he expected, and a bit more, to find the time each day. He doesn't announce to his family what he's doing, but they notice, ask him.

"Every day? That's a lot of letters, sweetheart," says his mom. "Do you miss her that much?", her voice has just a touch of concern.

"No, it's not like that. It's hard to explain. She... her life has some difficult stuff in it, that's hard for her to deal with sometimes. I'm just...I'm just trying to do what I think is the right thing."

"Hm. Well, I don't think I have to understand everything you do. I know you're a smart boy," she says with a smile and a wink as she reaches across the small table and pats his cheek. She stands and walks out of the hotel room, headed downstairs to meet his dad and sister. At the door she stops and turns back: "We just want you to be happy, you know."

"I know." He gets up and stands at the window for awhile after she leaves, watching dusk gather over the city, the gradients of a Roman twilight. I know, he thinks as he sits down at the table, as he bends to the page and begins to write.

The letters he has written her, up till now, have been simple. Not about love, not about anything in particular; just thoughts, experiences, written in the way that he speaks to her, intended only to carry his voice.

But this…this letter is different. Her birthday is approaching, will happen while he is still away. He knows that it will be hard for her, will be a day particularly crowded with memories. The letter he is writing tonight is a birthday letter, and it is a gift. A gift of power; of seeing, of a light that will turn the dark sad ghosts away.

He begins to write and the words come; one-by-one, flowing out of him and through the pen, spreading across the page. The world is no more than this, than his hand moving across the paper, his body in the pool of lamplight. The words come and fill the page, they work together: building, making, saying until the final word is written and the thing is said, and the gift is made and solid and true.

His breathing is slow, shivers run through his exhausted body, from which he has just extracted so much. He has no more words, and the power of what he has done is almost frightening. He folds the letter and puts it into an envelope, writes "Do not open until birthday" across the back; has to do all this and finish it before he can't, before he can try and change his mind. He fills a glass with water and drinks it down, sits before the window and stares out across the night of the city without thinking for a long while.

Three weeks later he and Hope are lying in bed in a small hotel room in London, watching *Braveheart* on the TV. They are quiet, tired, ready to fly home the next day. He watches William Wallace go through his violent trials and tribulations from a removed distance; it all passes through the filter of his exhaustion, nothing is really reaching him right now.

After his parents left, or after he wrote the letter. He doesn't really know when, exactly, it began. But being away from her, at some point it started to become...difficult. Moving across the European landscape, through Budapest and Vienna, Amsterdam and Prague; there has been no lack for new things to do, for new people to do them with, for ways to satiate his hunger for things new and novel, for experiences unnamed. But at some point a hole appeared within him that he has found no way to fill, an empty thing that has become larger and heavier with each passing day.

It is awkward, uncomfortable. It is also very real. And as he lies in bed next to his sister as she falls asleep, he realizes that he has lost his battle with it. That he is only a body carrying need now; that he will be doing nothing more than watching clocks, than counting the hours between now and his need until the moment when she is within his arms again.

# suburbs

Once again I have no idea where I am. Floating in the trackless void; there should be things, objects, feelings, but there are none of those, the void is within me.

I see that figure in the mirror again. See the endless sadness in his eyes, the shadowed hollow in his breast.

God. Nothing makes any sense. I don't know if I'm moving into light or into darkness. I don't know if I'm moving anywhere at all. These ghosts, these spirits seem to come and go as they please; deliver puzzle pieces that just create more questions, cast light that just creates more shadows. Bring these sudden emotions that overwhelm me and suddenly I'm running like a terrified animal, or burning with an anger that's out of control.

And that Thing. I remember Its laughter. Remember It out there somewhere laughing at me…

Enough. That's enough. I know I am more than this, more than just something afraid of darkness and shadows. I have to believe there is a reason; have to believe that if I walked into this world at some point, then there is also a way back out again. You have to know more. You have to become stronger.

My broken memory is a thing I can't worry about any longer. I have to put my trust in what I feel. I want the truth, more than anything else I want to know the truth. Yes, that Enemy is out there, with Its dark power. But this is also my world, and I have power here too.

From within the void I concentrate, feel things begin to shift, to change around me. Bright lights, big city. Deep in the isolated wild, alone with the animal gods. I flex the power, feeling it, seeing it as images and scenes flow by. So many choices that resonate, but there is a current I'm searching for…there. There it is.

The great mountains, rising up, up; the ranging peaks that melt into the vast rolling plain, rolling away into the haze of the far-off eastern horizon. But something is different this time; it's all muted now, further removed somehow. As though there is something that refuses it, that stops the beauty and majesty at the door.

I pass through the wide roads, fronted with strip malls and parking lots, supermarkets and chain restaurants. The neighborhoods are full of houses that look the same, that look like almost nothing at all. There is one I stand before for awhile, largely indistinguishable from the rest. I can feel that he is here, much of the time. But the sensation is vague, the pull is muddled. This is not what I'm looking for, at least not now.

I close my eyes, searching. I hear a car door, opening and then closing again, and there he is. Standing on the curb, waving briefly as the car drives away, then turning to face the nondescript edifice of brick and mortar. The boy pulls the backpack onto his shoulders. He is late, and so he stands there alone. He takes a deep breath and starts walking towards the door.

Silence. And a bell rings, doors open and bodies

and noise pour forth into the halls. It is a true ca-
cophony: the bodies gesticulate wildly, the voices yell
and shout, locker doors slam back and forth. The news
spreads like wildfire, did you hear about so-and-so and
such-and-such, alliances are made and unmade in the
space of a few breathless words, of fluttering hands and
heartbeats. Just as quickly as it all begins it all ends, in
reluctant streams the bodies pass back into the doorways and the doors shut and the halls fall into silence
again.

The boy sits in his desk in his row. Throughout the
day he moves from room to room, in each sitting in his
desk and his row. The teachers say things about writing
or science or math, with chalk they inscribe figures on
the chalkboards. He knows he is supposed to pay attention and he does but it requires very little; the pace is
slow, plodding along and he wanders off. He wanders
into the sea of new faces and names that surround him,
trying to understand who they are and what they are,
what are the mechanisms by which they relate.

The first ones he chooses are a mistake. He realizes
quickly that they sit alone at the bottom of this world,
unnoticed and apart. He sits at the table in the cafete-
ria and picks at his tray of food, listening with distaste
to the conversation of these mistakenly chosen compan-
ions, looking for his way out.

He begins to generate connections in the rooms,
sitting at the same desk next to the same names and
faces day after day. He is more cautious as he begins to
perceive the hierarchy, he treads carefully now.

The days become weeks become months as the year
rolls by. The walks home in the afternoon are long, a
tallying of progress, of time spent with particular names
attached to particular, pretty faces.

And finally, as the year is drawing to a close, a breakthrough. The cool kids come to him. So-and-so is out, they say, and you're in. Welcome to the posse says Brian Johnson, giving him a high-five. Elation. A sense of victory.

But a victory over what? Over the remaining days the initial flush of success fades. Are these people he's supposed to spend his time with now his friends? What are they supposed to do, what is he supposed to do with them? At recess he roams the playgrounds with them as they talk about nothing, as they do nothing, hands in his pockets in a state of utter confusion.

In the afternoon, after school. He is walking with a small contingent, walking his bicycle alongside. His home lies in the opposite direction. Why am I doing this, he asks himself silently, and the silence returns no answer. Daniel Foster asks to ride his bike; Sure, the boy says. Daniel Foster rides a short distance on the boy's bike, then dismounts and, using his fingernail, lets the air out of the bicycle tires. Stop!, says the boy, bewildered. Why are you doing that? 'Cause I want to, says Daniel Foster, as he laughs and the others laugh and they all walk away.

Tears of frustration and shame sting the boy's eyes as he walks his crippled bike home that day. No, these are not his friends, there is no friendship in this. Frustration with the clarity now that he has accomplished nothing. Shame as he realizes that this is the reward for his pursuit of vanity. The school year ends; a long, slow summer awaits.

Time itself slows down now, in fact. I remember; I don't know if they are my memories, but I remember enough, all the same. Adolescence spent in a dreary suburban purgatory, a long road of almost nothing. The boy bundles up and takes the dog out for winter walks, for walks in the snowbound winter silence. There is beauty in the silhouettes of trees against the cold white sky, beauty that he sees alone, feels alone. There is no one to whom he can say Do you see this beauty, no one to whom he can say, My god, what is this that I feel inside of me that is beauty. The roads and the curbs and the sidewalks and the lawns and the houses are an un-speaking monument to nothing, to a life that is nothing. His parents watch him with wary eyes but he lives deep within, in some kind of hidden, solitary cave. He tries, it is not that he stops trying. But the language of his dreams is not spoken here, never spoken here; and so within his dreams is where he lives alone.

Again I want to say things to him, but I know he couldn't hear me if I tried, and again I don't know what I'd say even if he could. Keep on, keep going, pick your head up?...going to what, to where? I can't promise him anything about where he'll go, or what he'll find, and I know that. He had to go through this, and I have to go through it with him. As much as I might want to avoid this dull suburban desert, it is what lies before me. I have to know more, I have to know as much as possi-ble. There are reasons why I am here; there are things in here that I know I need.

The boy's life is this. He wakes in the dark of the early morning to the buzzing of the alarm clock. He hits the button and stares at the red numbers and rolls over, his mother opens the door and says Get up. At the breakfast table he eats the omelette, or the oatmeal, or the pancakes. Dimly he remembers how the pan-cakes used to be animals, dinosaurs, What do you want me to make you his mother would say; but his mother is too busy and he is too tired, the memory fades.

The desks and the rows. The next several hours are the desks and the rows. One room after the next. Figures, names, dates. The bell rings, the long walk home, alone. In front of the television until dinner time. A struggle to find the will to do his homework. And finally he is in bed, with a book, wandering in some unknown world until his eyelids begin to sag and he turns off the lamp, and the darkness fills the room and he is asleep.

The remaining two years in the middle school pass in this generally monotonous fashion. He tries to do the things that he is told he should do; he tries to understand why he should do them. Strongly-worded references to a vaguely described "future" fail to captivate or convince him. The work given to him is too dull, too boring; his ability to will himself to do it erodes slowly, inexorably away.

The debacle of that first year has left him cautious in his pursuit of relationships. He still engages, he is far too hungry for this to do otherwise. But the friends he makes pass only through a limited sphere of his life. There is still too much that confounds him in the things they want and the choices they make. His instinct, his memory, his hope tells him that this cannot last forever; he watches, biding his time he waits.

And the walks home in the slow afternoon sunlight are filled with the names and the pretty faces. Angela Kline. Selena Duran. The syllables conjure up palaces of dream in his inner landscape, tap wellsprings of feeling that become vast, flowing rivers within his heart and soul. The boy with his backpack, walking past the dullness of the fences and the front yards and the drab houses with his head down, with a sweet ache in his imagination for which he can find no cure, no answer.

The disappearance of the protected joy has left almost no world around him, has left him only the world inside that he walks in alone. Knowing that it will not last forever does not change the fact that this is melancholy, that this is a long blind winter of sadness and discontent. As with the world of protected joy this too will end; and again I wonder, when it does end, where will it go.

Are all shadows the same? No; no, I don't think so. They may come from the same place, may represent the same absence, the lack. But this is not the same, this is not the shadow whose source I'm searching for. That dark creature whispers in another world somewhere; no, some shadows are darker than others.

Is this boy the one who will later write all those words on the pages I found in that room? Is he the figure in the mirror? Will I ever truly find him, will I ever truly find any of them? The questions are birds that fly away, that fly away from me and disappear. The road unrolls in a long ribbon before me, dwindling into the far-off, vague horizon. Stubborn resolve is all it generates now though: all things end, and so this will too, and I will find this ending.

Three years have come and gone. There is no great emotion as the boy finally leaves the middle school behind. Relief, of a sort. Curiosity, of a sort, about what comes next, what lies ahead. Summer rolls by in hot, dry, slow afternoons. Behind the roaring lawn-mower, the air full of the scent of freshly cut grass. He pushes it through the last turns, lets the engine sputter to a silent halt. Finds a glass of lemonade in the kitchen, shade on the back porch as he idly reaches down to scratch behind the ears of the dog. There are tennis lessons in the morning, baseball practice in the

139

early evening. The summer rolls by in a hot, hazy wave.

Are you ready?, his parents ask him. He feels their anxious love reaching out to him, trying to pull out the words, the answers from wherever it is he is hiding inside. Sure, he says, wishing that he could find what they are looking for. Of course, he says, knowing within himself that it is a resolution that stands on nothing at all.

The first day arrives. He shoulders the backpack without knowing why, enters the building without knowing why, and dissolves into the streams of bodies that fill the high school's classrooms, that shout and careen inside its walls.

Everything is bigger, louder. There are strong new forces here, currents that he barely knows as they sweep him along. The classrooms are almost a refuge. He tries to focus, to do what he is supposed to do. In the halls he is overpowered by his anonymity, by the forces he doesn't know. As he walks home in the afternoons he tries to find the pieces, to sort them out. There is more here, he realizes. Something more like freedom, at the same time more like danger. The directives are the same; but within them is hidden an acknowledgment, somehow, that there are forces here beyond their control.

As the days and weeks and months go by his anonymity is slowly displaced by a new word, a new name. Potential, they say. The teachers look at the work he half-does, the portion of the work he is able to will himself to do, and they shake their heads: But you have so much potential, they say to him.

Okay, he says. I will, he says, nodding his head. But he cannot. Try as he might he cannot find what they see in him; cannot find anything in the work they put before him that tells him anything about what they say he is supposed to be. He does enough to get by, but can find no more than that. A gulf opens up around him, a wide space he cannot cross between who he is and who they say he is supposed to be. Potential becomes his unsolvable riddle, his curse, his name.

And all this while the new forces have been gathering in him, collecting in pools throughout his body. They catch fire, conflagrations of desire burn wild across his inner sky. A fantasia of girls and women and sexual goddesses; eyes and lips and curves of bare skin, of secret places, physical actions his young body imagines in fevered dreams. Locked in the bathroom he cleans up the mess he's made, fear of discovery mingling with shame at the mundanity of his solitude, and with the stark reality that this is a thing within him that is an animal that is too powerful to control. Somehow he knows that it is another thing he will not find in this place, another answer that he will never find here. The walks home alone are a long rhythm of things he cannot reach, a litany of slow forevers.

The year ends. Summertime again, a respite from the things he cannot do and cannot be. He sits in the shade on the back porch with a book, reading. The dry heat dulls his senses, the whispering leaves sing softly. In bed at night the fan blows the cool air across his body beneath the sheet, blows his anxieties away from him, lulls him into a cool, dark sleep.

I sit in the darkness of the room for awhile longer. Listening to the sound of the fan, the movements of the boy's sleeping body as he turns within his secrets. Then I rise; above the house, above the town; up, up, into the darkness of the starlit sky.

The pools far below me of electric light pulse gently,

a steady orange glow. Different sizes, different shapes. A scant few miles to the north lies the town where the boy lived before. What makes them so different, one from another, what makes them so much not the same. Still to the west is the vast mountain boundary, still rolling away to the east is the long, undulating plain. The pools of orange light are gathered at the line where the plain and the mountains meet; they nestle here, they draw sustenance here, hoping for a framework, a life-meaning, a place that will tell them how to be.

The eastern horizon begins to glow, dawn bends across the great dome, calling to the sleepers, calling them to their work to find the ends, to find where the ends meet. I walk the streets of this town the boy lives in now and do not understand the life lived here, as the boy does not understand the life lived here. A life of boxes. A box they live in, a box they move in, a box they work in, a box they sit in front of and stare at, day after day after day. The boy can find no reason, but he knows nothing else. Glimpses of other worlds tantalize, places far beyond him which he cannot reach. The god-beauty of the ranging snow-capped peaks is still there, always; without words he calls to them, without words they tell him stories of who he might become, of who he might be.

He listens. He turns away, turns back to the town. If he is here, now, then so be it. He will not stop searching for a way to be free.


They walk in a long, single-file line as they enter, looking out into the sea of surrounding faces and waving and smiling at those they recognize, they know, they love. One-by-one they take their seats on the metal folding chairs that have been brought out onto the floor for this occasion. They gather the long blue gowns beneath themselves as they sit, adjust the blue caps from which hang the golden tassels. When they are all seated the restless tedium of ceremony commences: the speeches designed to commemorate accomplishment, to impart purpose, to grasp meaning. The energy begins to build as the names are called, as one-by-one they rise and walk and receive the handshake and piece of paper as they cross the stage. The last name is called, the last blue-robed body returns to its seat, the energy rises, straining to be released, and as the tassels are moved from the left to the right and the final words are spoken the assembly erupts with a roar of approval, a wave of relief, of joy, of gratitude as the blue-robed bodies toss their caps up into the air, into the hopes and dreams of the future that spreads out, suddenly, wide and open.

It is this which captures the boy. Amidst the tumult, the hugs and back-claps, the smiles and grins and tear-streaked cheeks; amidst this swirl of emotion he looks up and finds himself suddenly, incredibly alone; alone with the impossible vastness of this future that spreads out now before him. Alone in this moment he sees all at once what has not been said, what has not been told by any of the teachers, by any of the books, by anything they have ever set before him. All at once he sees it, the nigh-infinite terms of the true world, the true difficulty of being alive, of existence as a sentient being. He is stunned, astonished. The panorama of the true world on whose doorstep he stands unfurls in all its complexity and strangeness and wonder, a vision that makes its place within him as it takes his breath away.

A hand finds his shoulder, a voice calls his name, calls him back to what he has accomplished, finally, to

143

what he will now leave behind. He moves in this web of relationships, moves from embracing one body, one set of tender feelings to another, and another, and another. The warmth suffuses him, the sweet nature of farewell.

But there is no sadness. The sense of accomplishment is the sense of having survived; many battles won but many battles lost, and it is a thin margin. This vision of the world he is about to enter is in many ways a reckoning with those losses, and the reality is a sobering one.

I know. I watch him as he moves through the crowd; I have seen all of it, have watched him for so long.

Everything freezes. The bodies are motionless, time-locked by the power I wield here. I want...I don't know what I want. I move through the frozen scene, walk amongst the statues. Almost all of them he would call friends, now; but at the same time there is no real connection, no true support. I feel a rising sense of frustration with all of it, almost anger at how I have watched this world and these people try to cut him into pieces, try and box him up; I—wait. What is that? Movement? Yes. Someone is making their way through the statues. Coming towards me. I push from inside and reach out but it has no effect. Christ, not again, this shouldn't be happening...but it is. I brace myself for what's coming as the figure emerges from the crowd not twenty yards off and walks straight toward me.

She stops a few feet away and looks up at me. There is curiosity in her eyes, in her open face. It reaches inside me and touches a memory: I know who you are. She smiles, nods. Looks around, briefly, with that same curious intent, and looks back at me.

"Can we go somewhere else, where we can talk?" she says. "You can do that, can't you? Take us somewhere else? There's no reason for you to be here any longer, I think." Without saying anything I nod, reach out. She takes my hand, her eyes look into mine; curious, unafraid.


The stream flows. The little stream makes little, clear water-noises, songs in quiet water-language as it flows by. We walk on the path that runs alongside, within the cool shadow world beneath the tall pines. Invisible creatures move in the undergrowth, birdsong comes down now and again from somewhere up in the trees as we walk along in silence.

"It's beautiful," she says after awhile. "It's the kind of place he loved the best, I think. You…you look so much like him, like what he might've become. But I know that you aren't him, are you."

"No. No. I don't really know who I am. But I know I'm not him."

"You don't know who you are?"

I stop, and release a sigh. The stream gathers into a small pool here, behind a kind of natural dam. I sit down on a log at the water's edge, she sits down next to me. I pick up a small stone and toss it into the pool; hear the splash, watch the ripples spread outwards across the water's surface, slowly diminish.

"No, I don't," I say. "Sometimes I start to think I do. But then something happens that makes me feel like I don't know anything, all over again."

She picks up a stone and tosses it into the pool, too. Splash.

"Like me?" she asks.

"Yeah, like you. I didn't think you, or anyone else back there, could see me, all on your own like that. I didn't think you could see me, talk to me like this...I think maybe I'm beginning to know, and then something like this happens, and I don't understand."

"Well, I didn't see you, at first. But something happened; like waking up, or coming up from underwater, or something. And I looked up and the first thing I saw was you, standing there. And everyone else was not there, anymore; everyone else was kind of shimmery, all around you."

We sit quietly. A slight breeze lifts, rustles leaves. Insects flit above the water's surface, draw lazy curlicues in the air.

"I can't tell you who you are," she says after awhile. "But I can tell you about him, at least, and maybe that will help you." I reach down and pick up another stone, roll it around in my palm. I look at her and nod, okay; look away into the pool again as she starts speaking.

"I don't remember, anymore, when I started to love him; and I can't say, either, when it might've been that he began to love me. The only thing I'm sure of is that we both knew; without ever saying it, ever needing to say it, we both knew that we loved each other."

"That's what made it different. Special. It didn't have desire in it, or need in it. It wasn't romantic, but it wasn't just a friendship, either; I can't categorize it like that, can't give it that kind of name. It was just these... just these little moments. One day in math class we were working together. I saw his name written at the top of the paper, with the middle initial M. What's the M stand for, I said. And he looks at me coyly and in this super-cute girlish voice says, It stands for Meredith.

And I laughed, because it made me happy; I mean, because it was cute and funny, yes. But what made me happy, is that I knew he said it to make me happy. He knew it would, and he was right…little moments. It was enough to just let chance bring us together; here or there, now and again, to look up and see the face of someone you loved, and who you knew loved you right back." I look over at her, she smiles at me. She looks back out across the pool, thinking. We sit in silence for a bit before she speaks again.

"I can't say that I thought he was happy, not really. I'd watch him when he didn't know I was watching, could see it in his eyes. And there were moments, times when the light within him broke free, and he *was* happy, in a way that made everyone around him happy too… when I saw that, and realized that the rest of the time it was trapped somewhere…I knew how much it must hurt to have something like that trapped inside you; to know what lives inside you, and yet to not know how to let it out."

"But he was never like that with me. Never the sadness I saw in him, never that kind of, force of nature, I guess, that he sometimes became, either. Those were things I saw, from a distance; but he was never like that with me, in the short spaces of time when we were ever alone together…because he knew I could see him, I think; because he knew I loved him without conse-quence, loved him just as he was. And, maybe most of all, because he knew that I would let his love come to me, that I would take it in…with me he was always just this warm, steady glow."

"I told him once, a long time ago now; I wrote it to him in a letter, because I realized that he needed some-one to tell him, that he needed to be told. I told him about—about the light, I didn't know how else to put it…it was after we'd graduated, after he'd gone away. And I thought of him out there in the world, and wanted to write to him, to tell him. This light in you, that is so strong and good, I wrote; I can close my eyes and still see it, still feel it…"

She falls silent again. After awhile looks over at me, with that curiosity and intentness in her eyes, her face.

"I think something has happened to him…something serious. I think that's why you're here, why I'm here; why we're here together right now. And I think you're supposed to help him, somehow."

"How am I supposed to do that?" I say, hearing the frustration in my voice. "He's the one I can't talk to, can't reach at all. All I can do is follow him, watch him. His memories are my memories, but I know that they are also not my memories. I don't know how I ended up here, don't know anything; how can I help him, if I don't even know myself?"

"But you made this place we're in. This beautiful place," she says. She reaches down and plucks a small, violet flower; she holds it out to me, patiently, and after a moment I reach out and take it.

"You made this, all of this," she says. "I asked you to take us somewhere and you made this beautiful, wonderful place. I think…" She hesitates, I look over at her, and she is looking at me. "I think…that what has happened to him has left him lost somewhere. That he can't find his way out. But you, you can still do what he can't anymore, you have the power to make a place like this. I think he needs you to find him; to show him the way back again."

We are looking into each other's eyes. She nods, decisively. "I think…I think I have to go now," she says.

"I'm sorry to leave you alone," she says as she fades. I see her eyes, staring deep into me.

But you have it too, says her voice as she fades away. You have that light in you.


I sit for a long while after she's gone. Sit quite still, without thoughts or thinking. A feeling within me rises and falls, rises and falls in a slow, steady rhythm. After some time I become aware of the bag again, the weight of the strap across my chest and shoulder. I'd forgotten it; honestly, I'm not sure that I hadn't left it behind somewhere, that it hasn't just reappeared now. But that doesn't matter. I'm starting to understand, maybe, what is and isn't important here, what does and doesn't matter.

As I unbuckle the flap and reach inside I know there is more within the bag than there was before. My fingers move amongst various items until they find the plastic lighter and the pack of cigarettes. I light one up, noticing without surprise how familiar it feels. I watch the thin line of white smoke curling into the air. I pull the pad of paper out and rest it on my knees, taking a long drag from the cigarette as I begin to read.


*And then; and then at some point something began to happen to me; something that had never happened to me before. I began to feel...to feel what, I don't know what; something like an ache; like the sound of a mistaken empti-ness. Underneath everything, and as the days went by it only grew; an invisible burden that began to feel heavier and heavier; or maybe it wasn't actually growing, it was just its constancy; the fact that regardless of whatever I was doing it was there. Visiting Annie in Hungary, traveling alone on the train, out walking the night-streets of Vienna and Prague; wherever and whenever I was I could feel it; silent, single and breaking. It was unshakeable, and it took a little bit out of everything; took a constant part of my attention, took always a piece of my capacity to be where I was; a steady and unnegotiable pull. It tired me out; it was more than me, more than the strength I had available; and as the time went by I could feel myself starting to bend beneath its weight. It felt beyond me, unanswerable; or rather, it had only one answer, waiting for me back in California. It came not so much as a surprise, but as a question I'd never expected; a question I'd never seen, hadn't even really imagined. I had no idea what to do with it; no idea but to wait; to wait for her eyes, for her arms; wait to finally feel myself folding into her again. In the end I felt collapsed by waiting; felt like I simply gave in to counting the days and the hours, checking them off in my mind, my awareness fixed on the moment when I'd see her shape walking toward me again.*

The following page is empty. All the following pages are empty. Just so. I nod to myself as I return the pad of paper to the bag: so it is, then.

Evening is drawing up, the light is a rose-edged violet, fading. I walk uphill, away from the stream until I emerge from amongst the trees and find myself in a long, gently sloping meadow. I lie down in the soft grass; as the last of the great light leaves the world I watch the untold multitudes of stars appear in silence across the black velvet sky. I light a cigarette and lie still in the whispering grass, lie still in the dark night beneath the stars, waiting.

# the dark thing

There is the convulsive jerk as the wheels hit the tarmac, the shuddering roar that dies away as the plane's motion is arrested finally, brought to a slow roll. Ding. The voice telling everyone that it's safe to move now is lost in the noise of unbuckling seatbelts, of luggage being retrieved from overhead compartments, of the general impatient energy of passengers ready to leave this airplane.

He is too tired to feel impatient. Too tired of carrying the burden of this empty place within him to feel anything outside of the fact that she is so close now; the proximity increases the pressure, takes everyone and everything he sees that is not her and makes it all into the same dry, drab nothing.

A part of him, somewhere inside, knows this isn't right. But the ache of the hollowness, the sheer exhaustion it has created has overwhelmed all else. I will deal with this, the same way I've dealt with everything, is what he tells himself. But he knows there is a note of question in that voice that hasn't been there before now.

There she is, in the terminal up ahead. But Tyler is there too, along with Kevin and Joseph. They are holding a sign they've made, they're wearing stupid, silly hats or something, burbling with some weird, antic energy that grasps at his presence. It doesn't make sense, doesn't accord with this occasion: a supposed Welcoming Committee that feels very unwelcome. Her smile is awkward, almost embarrassed. The whole scene locks him out: he can't feel what he needs to feel, can't reach out for what he needs to reach.

Instead of being taken home he is taken to some restaurant. There is a continued expression of sentiment that this is for him, that this little party is for him, but it clearly isn't. He has neither the desire to participate nor the will to even pretend; but it doesn't matter, there is something else driving things forward here, something he is too tired and annoyed, now, to try and identify or explain.

He looks at her in a way that tries to say: I need this to be over. The look she returns is sympathy and anxiety and confusion. She turns, at someone's childish and ceaseless claims for her attention. He doesn't understand, but is too tired in soul and body to care. When someone suggests moving to a bar his foot comes down, unequivocally: Take me home.

Okay, they say, okay. But Isobel, you can come out: they cajole, insist, plead. She looks at him, and as much as he doesn't want to ever constrain her, yet something in him clamps down. Even if he wanted to, he knows he could not remove from his eyes the clear expression that he needs her, in a way that he has perhaps never needed her, very much right now. She sees, and something comes into her face, quietly inside her changes. She turns to them: No, she says. Take us home.

They walk into the house, into the room. He sets his bags down and turns to her and she comes to him, and finally; finally. He folds her body into his, folds his arms around her and he *feels* it; feels it flowing into him, filling up the emptiness. It's so visceral, so immediately visceral, this feeling of his body knitting something back together, of a deep, profound release. As though he has been trying to hold a tension from thousands of miles away. As though he was holding something taut from across half the world, to be able to still discern the vibrations, the potential need. But she is here, still whole, and he is holding her, and his entire body is sighing a vast relief.

"Are you glad to be home?" she asks.

"Yes. I missed you. It was a good trip, but I'm glad it's over. I missed your face."

"I missed you too. It was…hard. I'm glad you're here again," she says quietly. He can feel it in her hands, the way they brush his arms and shoulders, gathering memory.

"Your letters…" She moves to the desk, fingers a stack of envelopes. "The first one was here when I got home. And then another the next day. And then another, and another…I started to think about it at work. I'd come home, and a new letter would be waiting. Sometimes I'd read it right away, sometimes I'd wait. Sometimes I'd get into bed and read it before I went to sleep…I read them over and over again. It was like you were almost here with me…I couldn't believe that they kept coming, that it kept happening." She picks one of the envelopes up. "This is the one that came today. I haven't read it yet. I thought…I wanted to read it together; I wanted to hear you, reading it."

Something that he hears in her voice, sees in her

body as she stands there. Something like hope and the fear of hope; as though she is some kind of animal-child that lives within him and his protection.

He takes the envelope from her and opens it, takes out the folded pages. They sit on the bed, she nestles into him as he reads it aloud. It is the last letter he wrote. It is about missing her, about the feeling of missing her. About the deep, strong wish that he could be with her as she reads it. Some kind of quiet electricity gathers between them.

She looks up at him as he finishes. "But...but you are here. Did you know this would happen?"

"No. I didn't remember what it was about. I didn't remember what I'd written until I started reading it."

"But then, your wish, your...your wish came true?" It is a small true thing. I am afraid of wishes and dreams, say her eyes as she looks at him; I am afraid of what I know is happening, they say.

He wraps his arms around her, she pulls in close against him. He can feel her heartbeat. Can feel her fear and all the things she's afraid of. He is so tired. He closes his eyes, holds her tight and close against his body.


"What do you mean 'weird'?"

"...I don't know. Just weird."

"That doesn't tell me anything. What happened?"

"I don't know...we had a few drinks, and he started talking about some stuff...it was just weird, okay?"

"No," he says, anger rising in his voice. "No, it's not okay. I asked him to hang out with you so you wouldn't be all alone for five weeks; because I thought you might have a good time together, that the two of you might get along well. I didn't ask him to get drunk and say a bunch of weird shit to you. What did he say?"

"Nothing, I don't know. Can we just forget about it?"

"I asked him to be a friend. It sounds like instead, he decided to be a jerk. So the next time I see him, I'm going to ask him what the fuck his problem is."

"No, you can't, please. He asked me not to say anything, okay? He asked me not to repeat it to you, okay? So can we just please forget it? It's over, it wasn't a big deal. I'm fine: okay?"

Her discomfort and anxiety push him into an angry silence. Something happened with Tyler, just like he was afraid it might. Angry with his friend for his lack of control; for the inability to *be* a friend, to keep his promises anymore. Angry with himself, for ignoring his own earlier misgivings, for having put Isobel into a possibly harmful, possibly even dangerous situation.

But as he looks into her anxious eyes he knows he cannot be this, cannot be this anger.

The further he brings her out of the darkness, yes: the more into the light she grows. But the darkness remains, with its hunger and its hate. As she grows away from it, so in turn grows her sense of the distance she has traveled; and so, in turn, grows the fear of falling and the danger of being re-claimed.

He sees all this as he looks at her, as he looks away again. Things are changing. He feels the ache of five long weeks again like an old wound. The power she has awoken within him is vast, but he is discovering its limits. He cannot spare himself for feeling regret, anxiety, anger. His strength is what carries both of them, and he can't let it be less than what she needs.

"Okay. I won't say anything. I'm just glad I'm back

now; glad I'm not going away from you again anytime soon." He reaches out and takes her hand.

They are driving as this conversation takes place, headed out on a weekend trip. By the time they arrive and check into the hotel the earlier discord has been forgotten. It is only a couple days since he returned; she has been busy with work, and he has been tired, resting. But as he closes the door to the hotel room she comes to him, kisses him. They are alone and far from everything.

"I'm going to take a shower," she says, smiling shyly as she goes into the bathroom and closes the door. He waits until he hears the water running, and he undresses and goes inside.

"Did somebody come in here?"

"No, nobody's here."

"Ok-a-ay," she sing-songs. He pulls the curtain aside, steps into the tub. She's facing away from him, into the stream of water, and she turns her head, looks over her shoulder, her eyes bright: "Hey, you lied!"

He slides his hands onto her hips, pulls himself against her body.

"You want me to go away?"

"No. I want you to stay." Her lips come onto his, he slides one hand up her wet body to the fullness of her breast, with the other he pulls her back, pressing her firm bottom against him; her back arches, her tongue dives into his mouth, hungry. She turns in his arms and he moves his lips across her neck and down, the taste of her mingling with the wetness, the water that runs in streams down her bare skin. He takes the round nipple into his mouth and she sighs, her body shivers. She pushes him slightly away.

"I missed you," she says softly, pressing her hands

against his chest. Her dark wet hair plastered across her head, her round wet shining eyes: all he can do is stare as her beauty fills him, as it flows like a great river through his body and soul. I missed you she whispers as she leans back against the shower wall, as she reaches down and takes him in her hand; as she takes him deep inside of her.

The sex is deeper, longer, stronger; apart from everything else, its own world, a creature of force and tender beauty. No, she says. No, not like this; never anything like this.

Before, she tells him, with other partners it was just physical. Not mechanical, not unfelt, but physical: desire like an animal, pleasure like an animal. Something she found, she says, that was strong enough to break through her hardness. Something she could feel, an action that endowed her body with feeling.

From within her numb, dark, angry world she peered out, trying to perceive why anyone did anything. Sex, when she found it, seemed like it might be an answer, and she pursued it as such, from this vantage point of intellectual remove.

But I never knew, she says as they lie amongst tangled bedsheets in the pale morning light. I never found this, never knew it could be like this. I had no idea, she says softly; I thought I knew what it was, but now I feel like I didn't know anything at all.

She kisses him; kisses his lips with gentle need, pressure. Her hand grasps his cock as it hardens quickly, she bends over him and takes it into her mouth. The feeling is a wave that flushes up his spine, stars rain with a slow burn through everything. She rises and takes him in her hand, guides him within and as he feels himself sliding into her soft, hot wetness she sighs and the universe hums with the vibration of unity, of home. His hands cradle her face, her angel's face as she stares back at him. I can't believe I found you she whispers, his hands come to her breasts and her eyes close as her head tilts back and as one body they rise up with love.

It is such a power. Such a magnificent and strange power. In some ways he has always known: the feeling that came into his small body the first time he saw a picture of a naked woman, the sense of awe, of perfect wonder that filled him the first time he found a naked breast against his fingertips. Scant hours before the first time he'd had sex, he had understood that he was on a threshold of a categorically different kind in his still-young life; scant hours afterwards he had written a poem about a little boy running away from him for the last time, about a dead man who walked in his bones and died at the end of each day, who "fell softly in light the first and last time she sighed beneath my body."

But this...this is beyond anything he has ever seen, ever felt, ever known. Maybe, possibly it lay at the previous borders of his imagination...but no. He knows in his heart that he has left those borders well behind now. If it were only the depth of the feeling, the visceral beauty, that would be one thing. But it is not; because of who she is, where she comes from.

He cannot help but know that it is the same force that first mangled her. That long ago crept into her small, fragile form in the night and swallowed her, that stopped up her eyes and mouth, that drowned her in sorrow and pain and shadows.

Of course he knows this. Of course he knows that

he is now using that power to drive all those shadows away. That when he enters her, he is *entering her*: that his love is flowing into her, working in her against her wounds in a way that nothing else could ever do.

He cannot help but know this. She cannot help but know it too. They lie still, silent, locked into each other's eyes, staring at this beauty and wonder they are slowly giving birth to. He watches visions pass across her face. Feels how they are so far away from everyone and everything he knows. He wonders what death is, what death really is. He takes her hand in his like a prayer. They lie together inside of what they have created; they watch, they wait, they hope.


Here comes Time, now. Nothing stays the same way always, and here comes Time, knocking at the door.

In a little over a month Isobel's company is moving to the city, miles and miles to the north. Too far away to stay where they are, and she needs this job. So what will they do.

"Look; we already live together."

"…I know."

"And I'm not staying here, that's for sure. The whole reason I moved here was because Tyler invited me to, and that pretty much went nowhere. I would probably already be gone if I hadn't met you."

"I know, I know. But what about going back where all your friends are? Or back…back to your home, with your family? I know…I'm sure that they all miss you."

"Sweetheart…I'm not going to just go back to somewhere I've been before. If there were some kind of real, solid opportunity in one of those places, or anywhere, for that matter, then I would certainly consider it. But there isn't. And anyways; either way, do you really want me to go? Do you really think it would be a good idea for me to go away somewhere?"

He says all this gently; she looks at him and then down at her twisted-together hands in her lap, shakes her head with a barely perceptible, acknowledging No.

She looks and sounds miserable. Her face is filled with all the shadows, those of the past mingling with those of the future, the looming unknown.

It is changing as it grows, this thing between them. He can't contain it all, can't keep track of it all now. He can feel the work, feel what it's costing him, the sense of fatigue settling into his bones. He has not lost the clarity, can still see the right choices, still knows what to do. But the consequences are murkier, shifting out there beyond his vision and its reach.

The Dark Thing. The Dark Thing inside of her. Where is it now. A fact he has come to know like his own breath, his own heartbeat. It no longer comes, attacks. It hides away from him, hidden somewhere. Where is It, and what is It doing there.

It doesn't matter. He knows who he is, what his promises and responsibilities are. He knows what his love is. He looks into her eyes and says these things, again speaks this into her. She is still afraid, but she trusts him.

Two weeks later they co-sign a year lease on a one-bedroom apartment in the city. She looks at him as the future coalesces and it is as though a spell breaks, suddenly the clouds disperse from her face. She looks at him with those bright eyes full of hope, of happiness. The love within him swells, ignoring the fatigue, disregarding the ache. I will never let her be taken back, he thinks. Let the world come, let the hate and pain come at me, none of it matters now. I love and I will not stop loving, no matter what it takes.


Late in the afternoon, nearing evening. The sun's warmth is a thing he feels and doesn't feel. He stares out across the endless water as the sun begins to melt the western sky. The rolling whitecaps, the pelicans skimming along the curl of wave. He sees and doesn't see, feels and doesn't feel. The forms are shadows, the world receding, becoming dreams.

Last night. Late in the night in the room. The nights left are few in number now, they will be leaving so soon.

Late in the night and inside a moment and it is time and he says in a way he's never said before: What did your brother do to you.

She opens her mouth and can't make it work, no sound comes. Physical pain draws angles across her face. It is in her.

He presses his hand against her heart and closes his eyes, pushing forward into the darkness.

And he touches It and like a whip It recoils from the touch. It sinks down, fleeing from him, the Dark Thing. He feels Its retreat and he doesn't follow. He is stunned by Its agony, by the howl of Its agony at being touched that backwashes into him.

He couldn't tell her. When his eyes came open he saw how she was confused and afraid, and he knew he couldn't say: I don't know.

But he doesn't. Doesn't know if he is strong enough for both of them.

But it doesn't matter, it can't matter. Things are moving faster and faster. The feel of It keeps echoing within him.  He is carrying her, he wonders if he's wounded inside somewhere.  It doesn't matter, he can't stop now; he can't see it but there must be some place they have to get to.  He can't stop, can't rest, the questions are a dark woods around them closer now.  He is carrying her, in his arms, he can't stop until they get there.

Everything is in boxes.  The boxes are in a truck.  The room in which they grew together is a closed chapter now.  Tomorrow they move into their new life.

Tonight is an antechamber, a hotel room several stories up, up.  He stands at the window, the colors change as the day bleeds slowly into night.

They make love on the bed, something in him wants more this time.  He pulls himself deep within, an inarticulate sound escapes from between her lips.  He pushes deeper, feeling the sweat on his skin, feeling all the muscles of his body acting in concert, straining towards some indefinability as he pushes deeper and deeper.  Her hands come to his neck and shoulders, grasping, fluttering.  As he comes her eyes close and her mouth opens; her entire body seems to sing out some single, silent tone, to be floating for a moment in the air.

He lets everything go, lets his body down on her, collapsing, breathing deep.  Her arms come around him, fingers gently stroke his back.  He feels her love, her wonder; in the quiet, in this afterwards of stillness.

That was…that was different, wasn't it.

Yes, she says.

What was it, he says.  Pushes himself up so that he can see her face.

It's…it's a different kind of coming, she says.  A

question and a peace move together in her eyes as she looks at him; flow from her fingertips into him as she gently touches his face.

I've felt part of it before, she says. Started to feel it, I guess. But never all of it, never like that. It's not from the same place. It comes from some place deeper inside of me.

She is staring into him, searching. He lets her eyes and fingers roam over him, through him. He can find no words for this feeling. A single thing wells up within him until it is him, until it is all of who he is.

The words appear quietly, without fanfare, unadorned.

I want to marry you.

It is true and it is trapped within him. He sees it forever and knows it is true forever.

He can't say it.

But…how can he not say it?

She knows, he feels it. He buries it away before she can know what she saw, what she felt.

He can't. Bewilderment breaks him apart as some absolute necessity pushes it down, as his heart cries out.

How can he *not say it*?

She kisses the tears from his eyes, with soft lips kisses the tears from his eyes. She whispers love, into him she whispers her love.

And he feels his body quietly begin to break down.


As the days pass he feels it slipping away. She tries to pick him up, he can see the fear in her growing. He knows it's too late. Five weeks was too long.

All he can do is hope that he's carried her far enough.

They're lying in bed. A single lamp on the bedside table, the rest is darkness. The rest of the world is darkness.

They're talking about something in horrible, strained voices. What happened. While he was gone. She is telling him she has to tell him. But she can't, she can't make it come out.

He has to say it.

He is looking up, into that darkness. He knows there is no escape. He can feel the Dark Thing's eyes. He can see the immeasurable force of the blow that is a moment away.

He looks at her. Even though he already knows there is still bitterness in his voice.

"You slept with him. You slept with my friend. You had sex with him."

Her face is a pale, pure terror as she mutely nods.

It is as though something falls upon him and falls inside of him. He feels his body absorb the impact of a thing that is far too massive for it to absorb.

Deep within his heart there is a timeless moment. There is an immensely powerful, purity of righteous anger within his grasp. But he's already made this decision. He turns from this power, this last possible defense. And as he chooses this he closes his eyes. The last moment he has left is some kind of wordless prayer as the Dark Thing strikes its precise and deadly final blow.


In the numbness of the aftermath I see the thing I have chosen. It is so small, so delicate, such a fraction of what it was. It is for her.

When I give it to her what will I have left? Will it

be nothing? Will I be left with nothing?

She waits, there is hopelessness in the way she is staring at me. My god, why. Why is the world this way.

"Come here," I say quietly. "If you love me then come here." A light flickers in her pale face. It is the hardest thing I have ever done or felt or known. "It doesn't change the fact. It doesn't change the fact that I love you." I put the gift in her hands. Her eyes, her face, are a thing I have never seen, a thing I will always remember. She reaches for me, lies against me.

Did we make it. I am too exhausted to know for sure. Too broken down to be afraid. I know I have lost something, that something is over. My god, I hope I took us far enough. I have no idea what happens now.

# III

## strangers

Something has happened. I can feel it, first. Then I see it. The stars have begun to move across the sky. The movement is slow, random, as though they have been cut free of their moorings and set adrift upon the black sea of the night. I lie in the grass looking up for a long time. After awhile I start to see some purpose in the drifting: a line that is more direct, a group that clusters together and breaks apart again. The firmament has been broken and a vast migration has begun.

The light of dawn begins to gather, to re-color the world. I stand, stretch. Two figures emerge from the line of trees below, climbing steadily towards me. I stand still, watching them approach.

"Whew," says the first one, plopping down in the grass. He is a bit shorter than me, with closely cropped dark hair and delicate almond eyes. He looks up at me and shakes his head. "You and your damn mountains," he says.

The second one smiles. "Oh, poor lil buddy," he says, reaching down and patting his friend on the head.

He is tall, broad-shouldered like a lumberjack.

"I'm not your little buddy. Get your damn hands off of me," says the first one, swatting the tall one's hand away.

I sit down and fish a cigarette out of my bag, light it up.

"So you're smoking already. I was wondering about that. It's bad for you, y'know," says the first one.

"Bad for you," echoes the second one. He squats down and plucks a long stalk of grass, places it between his teeth. "Try grass instead."

I look down. I can feel them watching me carefully. I take a drag, look at each of them in turn. "A lot of things are bad for you," I say.

"Yeah, you would say that," says the first one. After a moment he reaches out. "Lemme see that." I pass him the cigarette, he takes a drag and holds it before exhaling. "Filthy habit." He smiles at me, takes another pull and hands it back.

"Dumbaffef. You are bofe dumb, affef," says the tall one through his teeth clenched around his stalk of grass.

"It doesn't matter here though, does it. Nothing I do here, nothing that happens here really matters, does it." I smoke the cigarette and watch them. Waiting.

They look at each other. The tall one shrugs. He takes the grass stalk out of his mouth, stands and stretches, sits back down with his legs crossed, indian-style. He looks at the grass stalk as he twiddles it between his thumb and forefinger.

"That's not true, obviously," he says, looking up at me. "I can imagine that things have been confusing and difficult for you, up to this point. But you wouldn't have gotten this far if you really thought it didn't matter."

"Okay. I'll re-phrase, then. Let's say it does matter, okay. But for who? Does it matter for me at all? Or does it only matter for him? And you know what I'm talking about, don't you."

He looks back at me for awhile before nodding, slowly. "Yes. I do. But that doesn't mean I can answer that question for you."

"What I want to know is whether or not you know who we are," says the first one.

I look at him, at both of them. Calm, serious faces. Care and purpose in the questions in their eyes. In their familiar, long-familiar faces.

"Yes. Yes, I know you. You are Jamie,"—the first one nods—"and you are Leandro,"—the second one nods, also—"and you were his friends. But you are also not really Jamie and Leandro, are you."

"No," says Jamie. "No, not really. But close enough."

"Close enough for what?"

"Close enough to help you."

"To help me?"

"To help you do what you're supposed to do."

"And what am I supposed to do?"

Jamie looks over at Leandro. Leandro shrugs those big lumberjack shoulders. "It's a long story," he says.

"And I haven't had breakfast yet," says Jamie.

"Why should I trust you?"

"Well. Why would you not?"

We sit there for awhile in silence. Finally Jamie lets out a sigh. "Look. You can stop trusting us whenever you want. But do it for awhile and see where it takes you. We're not going anywhere, we'll sit here as long as you want; trust or no trust, for the foreseeable future you're stuck with us."

He's right. I know he's right; that this is part of what's changed, of whatever it is that's happened. And as I look at them, sitting there waiting, I realize that I am tired of being alone, anyway.

"Okay. Okay. Like you said, I'll try it and see where it goes. Where do you want to go now?"

Jamie smiles and nods. "Pancakes!" says Leandro, hopping to his feet. "Delicious pancakes, please."

It only takes me a moment to realize it, to see the right memory. I don't know if it's coincidence or if I'm just learning more about the flow. Either way I point back downhill, behind them, to the town now strung along the mountain valley below. "I think we'll find what you want down there. I think you've been here before."

"Yes. Nicely done," says Jamie, nodding slowly with comprehension. "This is the spot, this is definitely the right spot."

"It is," says Leandro with measured solemnity. "It is also the time for pan-cock-ayes."

"Alright, yes, let's get your stupid pancakes already. Ready for this?" Jamie asks, looking at me.

I look at him, at Leandro. I realize that they are here, that I know who they are.

"Yes," I say. We stand and begin to make our way down the mountainside.

# pancakes


"Brrraaaap."

"Geez louise man, don't burp like that.  You're so gross."

"You're grosser.  You ate like, forty pancakes at least. You know what it's like watching you eat?  Scary, bro."

I lean back in the booth, sip my coffee as I listen to them go back and forth.  The table is covered with mostly empty plates and glasses, the scattered debris of a well-eaten meal.  It's been nice just to sit, to eat, to listen, to feel…normal?  Maybe.  I'm not sure if I know what it means to be normal.  I look out the window, see cars going by on the road.  The parking lots, the store-fronts, trees, the odd pedestrian.  It's comforting to just sit here and watch it all for awhile.

"What's goin' on, Mr. Quiet.  See anything good out there?" asks Jamie.

"Oh, nothing in particular," I say, turning back to the table.  "Just normal stuff, I guess."

"Normal stuff, huh?  I never thought normal stuff was really your thing."

"No? What is my thing, then?"

"…Good point. I guess I was never quite sure about that, either."

"But you're not talking about me, right? You're talking about him."

Jamie is silent for a bit. "Yeah, I guess so…but to be honest, I'm not entirely clear on the difference between the two of you, either. Yeah, I sort of get it?…but not completely. I think it might be helpful for me and Leandro to hear what you think, or what you remember."

I'm struck by the question, something about it catches me off guard. I look down at the coffee cup, turn it around slowly in my hands. Something turns around inside of me, but I can't quite catch it; it slips through my fingers, sinks back down. I look back out the window, seeing but not seeing at the same time.

"What I remember?…That's the problem, I guess. I'm not sure what that word…means anymore," I say slowly. "I don't know how to explain the way it feels… to "remember" memories that aren't mine. To not just remember them, but to *feel* them too."

"How do you know they're not your memories?" asks Leandro. "I'm not saying you're wrong, just saying that sounds pretty strange, right?"

"Yeah. But that's the way it feels. Like…like a whole bunch of stuff happened to me, but I was asleep the whole time, or something?…and now it's coming back, in these random bits and pieces, here and there out of nowhere."

"Okay," says Leandro. "Well, setting that aside for the moment, what do you actually remember? For you, as you are now, what's the first thing you remember? When did this begin?"

172

When did this begin? What do I remember? I'm still staring out the window as he asks these questions. The tops of the trees across the road are swaying back and forth, all the leaves are glittering green gems in the sunlight, but I can't hear the wind that must be moving them; I feel like I'm looking out into water, into a world where everything is under water. What I remember swims up slowly, rises.

"Well…what I remember is darkness. Waking up into darkness. And laying there for a long time. I couldn't move. But I didn't want to move, either, anyways; it's hard to explain, but I didn't have the desire to move. Not like I was depressed, or sad, but just like I didn't remember that I might want to move. And I would kind of hear things, and kind of wonder what they were, like if they had something to do with me… but not enough to make me want to do anything else besides just keep lying there. And then I started to, like, feel my body again. Slowly. And I would lift my arm, or move my fingers. And then after awhile it started to not be just darkness anymore, and I realized I could stand and walk and move again. But what I realized, pretty quickly, was that something was wrong. That I had woken up somewhere else, somewhere I wasn't supposed to be; some kind of shadow world, is the best way I could describe it. And that I had to get out, that was the first clear thought I had, finally: I have to get out of here. That there was a way out, and I had to find it, because the shadow world was closing itself around me…and that if it did, I would fall asleep again…and this time I wouldn't wake up."

I turn back to the table. Look down at the coffee cup between my hands, shake my head and take a drink, look back up at Leandro across the table. "It sounds…it sounds crazy, doesn't it," I say. "I sound like a crazy person. But that's it, honestly, that's what I remember."

Leandro frowns slightly, shakes his head. "No, it doesn't sound crazy. It sounds accurate. But more importantly, it's what you remember, and as such it's what makes you who you are. If you invalidate that as crazy, then you lose the ability to make any rational decisions at all."

"Besides," says Jamie, sitting in the booth next to me, "we *are* here, in the 'shadow world', as you called it; we know it, you know it. And if you didn't, I don't think Leandro and I would be here. But I also gotta say that I'm—impressed, or surprised?—not sure how to put it, exactly. But listening to you say all that just now was pretty interesting; and given the things that Leandro and I know, yeah, it sounded pretty damn accurate to me too."

"What do you mean?" I ask.

"Mm, yeah…well so, you call this a shadow world. And I think that's like, half right. Or, what I mean is that it *was* right. I think what you're talking about is what being crazy is; what I mean is that 'being crazy' could also be called 'living in a shadow world'. But I don't think you're in it anymore, actually. Or rather, yes you are, but like you said, your first clear thought was: "I have to get out of here". And somehow since then you've gotten to this point, where you're here with us now…and you're still in it, but it's not just a shadow world anymore."

"Well…what is it, then?"

Jamie purses his lips. Looks up across the table at Leandro; Leandro shrugs, a don't-ask-me expression on his face.

"Yeah," says Jamie. "Sorry mon frere, but I don't

think that's a question we should try to answer. That's not what we're here for."

Another question forms itself, appears in my mind. I don't want to ask it, but it sits there, hovering, and I know it's not going to go away.

"So…so let's say you're right, about the 'shadow world' being the same thing as 'being crazy'…does that mean that I…I mean…" My voice falters, I can't make the last words come out. Jamie is silent for a bit. He looks at me, his eyes narrowing with focus.

"Like I said, I'm not entirely clear on the difference, between you and him," he says. "So I don't know, I mean I can't say what happened to you. But I know that the two of you are connected, obviously, and I do know what happened to him."

I look back at him for a long moment before I say it.

"Why did he…become crazy?" I ask quietly.

Jamie is silent. The waitress comes by and re-fills our coffee mugs, asks if we need anything else, wanders away again. For a little bit the only sounds are paper sugar packets being torn open, metal spoons stirring sugar and cream into ceramic mugs.

"Because…because of a crazy bitch," says Jamie finally, an edge of anger in his voice.

Leandro shakes his head emphatically. "No, man. That's not true."

"It is so true! She pulled him apart, she tore him into pieces!"

"No. No way, man. He could've said no, he always could've said no."

"So you're saying he just went crazy all by himself, then."

"I didn't say that. I'm saying he made choices."

"Why would someone choose to go crazy?" I ask.

"Fucking exactly! That's fucking exactly what I'm saying!" cries Jamie.

Leandro frowns, drinks his coffee. "Okay. I think that's enough with the 'crazy' talk. That word is way too simple, and points in a variety of directions that are neither informative nor helpful, at this point. The whole story is a lot more complicated than that, which is why that dumbass"—he nods toward Jamie—"wants to try and reduce it to a 'crazy bitch'. Because it actually involves a lot of experiences and perspectives that are very difficult to sort out, and being able to just lay it all down to one thing like that would make it a whole lot easier. But if it were really that simple then the three of us wouldn't be here like this, now would we? So enough with the 'crazy bitch' bullshit, please."

Jamie rolls his eyes, sighs. "Fine. Fine, fine, it's true, blah blah blah. I thought maybe we could wrap this up quickly and all go home, but whatever, have it your way."

I look out the window at all that normal stuff again. It seems very far away. "Why is it so complicated?" I ask.

Jamie sighs. "Oh, god, where to begin. The beginning, I guess…you ready for this?" I turn back to the table, look at him, look at Leandro. I nod, once.

Jamie takes a deep breath. "Alright. I'm going to tell what I know, which, keep in mind, isn't everything; we"—gesturing to Leandro—"only know what he ever told us, which, granted, is a lot, but it's still a safe bet that it falls fairly short of all there was to tell. I'm pretty sure Leandro and I wouldn't be here if this information wasn't going to be helpful to you, but still, it's information that's necessarily incomplete. So, that's my disclaimer. Okay?"

"I understand," I say.

Jamie looks at me, nods. Drinks his coffee. When he begins speaking his voice is measured, detached; a historian laying out the known fragments of a history on the table before us.

"Okay. This story begins, as so many stories do, when a boy meets a girl. Santa Cruz, California, February 2001. Our protagonist is twenty-three years old. He and Isobel, who's also twenty-three, meet, and it's my best guess that the connection is fairly immediate—bang, they're into it from the get-go. Turns out, though, that her personal history is basically hellish and deeply traumatizing, the primary focus and root of this being an older brother who sexually abused her for a period of years starting when she was, oh, something like three, four years old?…Pretty dark, nasty stuff. Unsurprisingly she suffers from bouts of deep depression, has tried to kill herself at least once before they'd ever met. Outwardly her presentation is most commonly deeply cynical, bitter and angry. Nicknames she's been given in her life include the Ice Queen and Death."

"Side note: one of the things, to me, that's always been noticeably odd about the whole thing, is that this girl and this boy ever met, much less were mutually attracted. Whereas she represented darkness to people around her, he represented light. Not to say that there weren't things that they held in common; but in looking at it from that one particular, and fairly important aspect, they were about as diametrically opposed as two individuals could be. Maybe I'm being overly speculative here, I don't know. But it's something that's always struck me."

"But anyhow, they did meet, and they were

177

attracted, and pretty quickly they begin to fall, pretty deeply, into love. Profoundly in love: of a kind and quality to which neither of them have recourse in the prior experiences of their young lives thus far; intensely, exquisitely beautiful, etc., etc. But what really captures, no, what *commands* their attention is neither the intensity nor the beauty of this feeling, of this thing between the two of them, but rather its transformative power: on both of them, yes, but most specifically and especially in regards to Isobel. It is too astonishing, as a kind of revelation, to be something they can really articulate to each other, can truly put into words; but there is a mutual awareness between them that an intensive healing process has begun within her, a process that is reaching all the way down into the core of her fundamental being."

"I need to kind of go out on a speculative limb here again; and Leandro, stop me if you think I'm going too far. But I would say that this healing mechanism is so clear, so strong and of such magnitude, that their relationship consciously takes on the nature of an experimental project. An experiment, on the one hand, to track the nature and possible effective power of love; and on the other, and most significantly, a project designed to heal Isobel: to liberate her from her demons, and restore to her the fullness of the depth of her lost heart and soul."

Jamie falls silent. Leandro is looking down at the table, brow furrowed in contemplation. He looks up at Jamie and nods his head: three times, slow and deliberately. He leans back, crosses his hands behind his head and gazes up at the ceiling. "Yes," he says, and is silent again.

Jamie looks at me, asking if I want him to keep

going. My hand reaches out and closes around the coffee mug and stays there, I don't lift it off the table. Finally I nod, look back out the window. I hear him take a drink and set his cup back down before he begins to speak again.

"Well. At this point things begin to move a little faster. Before April is out she has moved in with him, less than three months after they first met. Given the unique parameters of their relationship it makes sense, the proximity only increases the power. But there is a problem on the horizon, an imminent separation of over a month as he goes abroad on a trip with his family. Anxious for what could happen to her, within her, during his absence, he tries to cushion her, to lessen her isolation. He contracts his friend Tyler (with whom he moved, initially, to Santa Cruz) to spend time with her; and he concocts a plan. Every day while he's away, he writes her a letter, in the hopes that it will provide her with enough of his presence, of his love, to sustain her until he returns."

"But his efforts fall short. He has miscalculated badly. The letters work toward his intended goal, yeah…but the friend brings her only more demons. Somehow, Tyler and Isobel manage to do the worst thing they could possibly do, which is to fuck each other. A double betrayal by his friend and his lover, while he is busy writing her letters from the other side of the world."

The meditative tone of Jamie's voice is gone; he spits these last words out with a frustrated anger. Mechanically my head swivels, turns in his direction. His jaw is clenched, his eyes narrowed. I turn back to the window. It's all I can do, to sit here and stare out the window.

I hear the waitress again, the Would you like, the

179

Yes please, the sound of coffee pouring, spoons stirring. It's a little while before Jamie begins to speak again. His voice is quieter, his tone resigned.

"Okay. Okay. So when...when he returns, he has no idea what's happened, obviously; and she, for whatever number of reasons, doesn't tell him. In many ways they pick up right where they'd left off five weeks earlier, but for him it's more difficult; it strains him, taxes him in a way that it hadn't before. I don't know, I never really got any details from him about this, but I think as things progressed they got...I don't know, stranger, wilder. And obviously the secret she was keeping now had to be mixed in there, affecting things somehow. Like I said, though, I don't really know."

"At any rate, what happens is that at the end of the summer they move, for practical, real-world reasons; for her job, they move two hours north to San Francisco. He was still financially independent at that point, I think; could've gone anywhere, done anything, really. But I don't think there were—I don't think he had a sense of any other real choices. So they moved, signed a one-year lease. And two weeks or so after they'd moved in, she...she finally told him."

Jamie sighs; heavily, resignedly. He's silent for a bit. I turn to look at him; he's looking down at his coffee cup, held between both his hands, resting on the table. He sighs again, shakes his head.

"I was in that apartment once," he says. "Couldn't have been more than a month after that. He didn't say anything about what was going on. I was in my own weird head-space at the time, so I probably wasn't exactly super-perceptive. But it was still obviously not a very happy place. It was kind of a crappy spot, too. The apartment itself was fine, but it was kind of far from everything and right next to the freeway; literally, you looked out his window and there were some weeds and an old wooden fence and on the other side of the fence was a massive, non-stop freeway."

"Wasn't it worse than that? It was two freeways, wasn't it? Basically at the intersection of two gigantic freeways," says Leandro.

"Jesus. Yeah it was, you're right," says Jamie.

"Yeah, I was there once too, way later. Probably February?...March? For like, less than twenty-four hours, real short time. The three of us, me and him and Isobel, had this crazy night, just in the apartment, where we downed a whole bottle of Crown Royal Special Reserve that we didn't even open until, like, midnight. It was fun; I mean, I would say that it was a really 'fun' night, but it was also crazy. It was slow, almost kind of awkward at first, which was weird, 'cause it was never like that with me and him. And then later he was like, flying all over the place. I was in town with Abigail and Richie, and he came out with us for a few hours the next day. He was there, but it was like he wasn't there at the same time. Abigail and Richie asked about what was up with him, later after he left, and I was like: 'I don't know. We drank a bunch, it was crazy.'"

"So he didn't say anything then to you about it, either, obviously," says Jamie.

"Nooooo. Nope, not a word."

Jamie lets out a low, soft whistle. "Goddamn," he says, shaking his head.

"Hey. How are you doing?" asks Leandro.

I don't answer at first. Memories are swimming up, memories that I know aren't really mine...or are they? I can't tell anymore. It's all broken, splintered. Crowds of ghosts murmuring their sad, endless arguments, things

181

further down in the darkness that I can feel crying out in voiceless voices. The feelings I have are real enough, and they are strong and far-ranging.

"I don't know," I say finally, looking at each of them. "There's more, isn't there?"

"Yeah," says Jamie, nodding.

"A lot more," says Leandro.

"I thought so." I think for a moment, trying to drown everything else out. I look at each of them again in turn, and the way that they are watching me, waiting for me, brings a sudden wash of relief. I am not alone; for now, at least, I am not alone.

"I need to hear it," I say. "I don't know if I want to, but I know I need to. But I need some time. Can we do something else; anything else, anything at all, at least for a little while?"

Jamie exhales, dramatically, and puts his hand on my shoulder. "God, yes. Thank god you said that, yes."

Leandro grins, reaches across the table and pats Jamie on the head. "Aw, did Lil Buddy get tired out?"

"Fuck you and your 'Lil Buddy'!" cries Jamie, swatting Leandro's hand away.

Leandro laughs, turns away from the table, looks around briefly until he spies the waitress, signals for the check. He turns back and leans forward, elbows on the table with his fingertips steepled together before him and a mock-solemn expression on his face.

"Gentlemen. I would like to propose a plan of action. The town we're in, as I think we all know, happens to have, oh, maybe the best hot springs pool in the known universe."

"Good choice of venue, buddy," says Jamie, punching me in the shoulder.

I smile, shrug. "I do what I can," I say.

182

Jamie's eyes twinkle, mischievously. "Was that a little joke? Did you just make a little joke?"

"Yes," says Leandro. "He made joke. Little. Life of the party."

"Alright! Life of the party!" Jamie grins at me, and I can't help laughing a bit.

"We're on the right track," says Leandro, nodding with that solemn, businesslike expression on his face. "My plan is this: one, find a sweet motel, chill out and rest in the sweet motel room for awhile; two, puff some ganja; three, go to the hot springs."

Jamie reaches across the table, palm outwards, requesting and receiving a high-five. "Yes! That is the plan, that is exactly the right plan! Ye-ess!"

I look back and forth between the two of them. Jamie is pumping his fist in exultation, Leandro is looking at me, eyebrows raised slightly in question. I see them. I remember them. The clear silhouettes of these two figures within me.

"Yeah," I say. "It sounds like a good plan."

"A good plan? Dude, it sounds like a fuckin' sweet plan! Chill out, get high, check out some senoritas poolside..." Jamie's standing now, doing some kind of shimmy dance-thing next to the table.

"What is that?" says Leandro, brow knit in puzzlement. "What are you doing right now? Are you ill? Do you have some kind of injury?"

"Dancing, bro. When a man's got moves, he's gotta use 'em." He puts on a pair of sunglasses, swings his arms to the left, index fingers pointing away from the table. "I'm outta here. Pay my tab, bitches," he says as he saunters away.

"Idiot," pronounces Leandro. "Ee-dee-ot." He takes a few bills out of his wallet, puts them on the table and stands up. "Let's go. We better catch up with him before he gets hit by a car or something," he says cheerfully.

**smoke**

I wake from a dreamless sleep to the sound of gentle snoring. I blink a few times, trying to remember where I am; raise up onto my elbow and see Leandro in the next bed, sprawled out on his back, mouth slightly open. Momentarily he snorts, rubs his nose with the back of his hand and turns over. With a sighing rumble the snoring subsides into regular, deep breathing.

"Jesus, what a monster," says a voice behind me. I turn over and see Jamie, sitting in a chair with a newspaper in his hands, looking at Leandro with a mixture of irritation and wonder. "I don't know how you slept through it, I had to get out of here. It's basically like having a bear in here, a talking bear that's going to wake up shortly and say When are we going to have pancakes, or When are we going to have fifty cheeseburgers. Jesus. Jeee-sus Christ. Oh, ha ha, real funny huh?" he says as I start laughing. "Well, you can be the one to sleep in the same bed with a bear next time, tell me how you like it."

I roll up to a sitting position, rub my eyes; in the

middle of a yawn I picture Jamie in bed with an actual bear, going through extreme contortions of fear and annoyance and the yawn breaks into giggles as I roll back onto the bed.

"Oh yeah, laaa-augh it up; that's right, go ahead and have a good laugh at my expense, shithead," he says, making me laugh harder.

"What's so funny," says Leandro's muffled, sleepy voice.

"Jamie slept with a bear," I manage to say between giggles.

"…Yeah…Jamie likes animal-sex," says the sleepy voice again.

"No, I don't, actually, like animal sex.  I also don't like sleeping next to a foghorn, either."

Leandro rolls onto his back, bunches the pillow behind his head; yawns, smacks his lips, smiles lazily at Jamie. "Was it a she-bear?  That's why you're mad, huh, 'cause it wasn't a she-bear.  Told you not to make that mistake again."

Jamie raises one hand in Leandro's direction, middle finger extending skyward.  He sits back, crosses his legs, disappearing behind the newspaper again. "You can go suck a fat one, dickweed," comes his voice from behind the paper.

I stand, stretch, and the stretching pulls out another giggle or two. Jamie folds down the corner of the paper, shakes his head at me with a mock frown.

"You could've slept in the bed with me," I suggest, crossing over to the window and sliding open the curtains.  Mountains, parking lot.  Long shadows, the afternoon is giving way to evening.

"Yeah, I could've, if you hadn't passed out in the middle of the bed.  You lay down and mumbled some-

186

thing about resting for a sec and then you were gone; out like a light, amigo."

"What's all this?" asks Leandro. He's standing at the table next to Jamie's chair, examining the contents of a couple grocery bags.

"Bread, cheese, salami, fruit; I went shopping. Someone's gotta get some shit done while you two jackasses sleep the day away."

Leandro pops a couple grapes into his mouth. "Mm. Good grape. Here, catch," tosses one at me. "What time is it?" he says, wandering around the room with a small grape-handful.

"Time for you to load a bowl," says Jamie.

"Me? I didn't bring no weed. I thought you did."

"Shut up and load it."

"Seriously, I thought you had it."

"…You are such a jackass…"

Leandro grins, pops the last grape into his mouth. Sits down on the bed and begins rummaging through his carry-all.

He pulls out a tiny wooden box and what looks like a very small pillow, about the size of a large grapefruit; it's a deep burgundy red in color, patterned with pale blue crescent moons and yellow stars, and two golden tasseled cords knotted together at one end. It turns out to be a padded bag of sorts; Leandro undoes the knotted cords which cinch the bag shut, reaches in and pulls out a glass pipe. The glass is an opaque green, threaded with lines of brown and blue that run down the long stem and lose themselves in swirls around the bowl at the pipe's end. He sits down at the table with the pipe and the wooden box, slides the lid of the box open and empties its contents onto the table: two densely clumped, green nuggets of marijuana buds, covered in fine golden-brown hairs.

He picks one up and hands it to me: "Take a whiff."

I hold it under my nose and inhale deeply; it's rich, complex, the scent of secrets of the earth, the secrets of green and living things. I inhale again and Leandro nods appreciatively: "It's real good shit, isn't it. I've always loved that smell," he says.

I pass it back to him, he takes and begins to break it apart, pinching off tiny pieces and putting them into the bowl of the pipe. When the bowl is about halfway-full, he reaches into the pipe bag and pulls out a plastic cigarette lighter, the butt end of which he uses to tamp the contents of the bowl down and pack the tiny pieces more closely together. The process has the air of a casual ritual; his movements are sure, methodical.

When he's done he puts the two nuggets back in the wooden box, slides the lid shut and sits back in his chair. "Thy bowl is loaded, monsieurs," he says.

Jamie folds up the newspaper, drops it to the floor; claps his hands, rubs his palms together. "Alright boys, time to get hii-iiigh," he sing-songs.

"Indeed," says Leandro. "Are you down for this?" he asks, looking at me.

I nod, slowly but decisively. "Yes. I…remember, sort of. Remember enough, I think. But besides that, I"—I hesitate, realizing it as I say it—"I trust you. Both of you. I don't know why, necessarily—but I know I do."

They smile quietly back at me, and there's a moment in the silence where I know that we all know the same thing.

Leandro picks up the pipe and lighter and passes them to me. "First greens for you, sir. I'm nothing if not a well-mannered pot-smoker."

I take the lighter in one hand and the pipe in the other, one finger instinctively finding and covering, at the bowl's end, the small hole which regulates the air intake. I notice this; notice without surprise the lack of awkwardness, the smooth readiness of mechanisms hidden within me. I bring the pipe to my lips, flick the lighter, bend the flame to the contents of the bowl and inhale deeply; feel the smoke rush within, into my invisibilities as I release the flame and lower the lighter, watch the embers in the bowl turn the green to a glowing orange that fades into black. I lower the pipe, watch the cloud of white smoke as it leaves my body and disperses in the air.

"Well done, sir," says Jamie, nodding appreciatively as I pass him the pipe and lighter. He takes his hit smoothly, holds it, exhales, nodding again as he passes the items over to Leandro. Leandro puffs, puffs, milky-white tendrils curl up from the corners of his mouth and out from his nostrils. I take the pipe, watch the flame bend as I pull it into the bowl with my breath: breathe, bend, breathe and bend again. The sigh and crackle as the embers move through the green mass, leave behind skeletal black, gray ashes.

Around, and around it goes. Slowly. Puff, pass. Puff puff, pass. Leandro re-loads the bowl. Breathe in, hold, breathe out. Pass. Again, and over again. Leandro blows smoke rings: one, two. Three.

How do you do that, Jamie is saying.

Do what?

The smoke ring thing-a-ding.

I use my ring-a-dinger.

Does that mean your wang?

What? My wang!? No, not with my wang.

Just thought it was maybe wiener-related.

189

Because the ring-ding thing?

Yeah. That one. What?

Um…you're high.

Yeah. So are you.

True. I am high too. Also. Too.

Shit. We just got fucked-up, didn't we.

Um. Yes. I believe that is a fucked. I mean a fact, shit. Oh, man. Shit man I'm high.

Jamie is shaking his head now, muttering something. Leandro is giggling; sits up straight, trying to contain himself, can't. There is some lightness in my body, lifting something up. Something heavy? Something I should worry about, or know about, or think about…I look back and forth between the mutterer and the giggler. I wonder if I could giggle and mutter at the same time. There must be a midpoint, a balance point, it must be a matter of balancing…

What are you doing?, says someone. I look down and see my feet in a line, heel-to-toe-to-heel-to-toe, realize that my arms are spread out wide like Jesus. Like Jesus?

Um…I think I'm balancing like Jesus.

Okay, right, cool…how are you doing that?

Are you saying Jesus wasn't balanced?

Isn't that the point of Jesus?

That he was unbalanced?

Yes.

So he should've seen a psychiatrist. Or actually, maybe a psychiachrist.

Wait. What?

Ooh, that would be a cool super-hero. Psychiachrist, no one would want to fuck with Psychiachrist.

What are you doing now? Leandro, look at him.

I'm Psychiachristing bad guys.

It doesn't look like that, says Leandro, squinting. It looks like...like you really need to go to the bathroom...but you don't remember how.

Oh god. Can that happen? That would be terrible.

I'll find out, says Jamie, promptly getting up and disappearing into the bathroom.

Leandro solemnly extends his arm in my direction. I reach out, he drops a cluster of grapes into my up-turned palm. With the same otherwise serious expression on his face, his lips peel back to reveal a grape held delicately between his front teeth. He bites down, chews, swallows. Takes another, tosses it into the air and catches it in his mouth. I follow suit, rolling the grape around inside my mouth for awhile before biting down. A mild sensory explosion ensues: the crunchy-soft, the sweet juice.

Damn. Grapes are awesome.

Leandro nods, tilts his head back and piles several in all at once. Aweshome, he says through his mouthful.

Jamie returns, shaking his head in wonder.

Oh man. Whole 'nother world in there.

Leandro giggles again. How much did we smoke?, he says.

No idea. A lot, I think.

Weren't we supposed to do something?

Jamie frowns. The light bulb appears in the air over his head, his eyes widen, the frown becomes a knowing smile.

"The pool, dude. It's pool-time."

## water

Oh my god. God is in my mind because god must be near at hand, because I feel like I am in some kind of heaven right now.

A gorgeous world. A warm, watery green, endlessly gorgeous world. Like water-creatures we glide, feet skimming across the smooth stone. Other water-creatures appear slowly, arise in the mists and disappear again. Balls of soft light glow in the outer darkness, sentinel lamps that guard this dark emerald realm. Like a night-breeze through night-leaves, we move in silence through these magic waters.

Try as I might I can think of no place else; try as it might my mind can conjure up no conception of a world in which I might be more at peace than I am, right now, in this one.

I have no idea how long we've been here. I have no idea why I might ever want to leave.

The pool's end becomes apparent in the vaporous near-dark. Slowly we emerge from the water, wet bodies shivering in the encompassing chilly embrace of the cold night air. Slowly up the broad steps, across the short stretch of white stone...and down, step by liquid step into turquoise watery heat that banishes the chill instantaneously, we sink into it and submit to the command to sigh out an exhalation, a basic and pure release.

"God," says Jamie quietly. "This is amazing. Partly because it's actually as good as I remember it was before...god. Amazing."

"Part of it is just the sheer magnitude, y'know?" says Leandro. "The main pool's almost as long as a football field, which is huge. And this one is, what—half as big, a third as big? The whole place altogether is just kind of enormous. And then there's the design, all this old stone and the old lamps, and the way you can regulate your body temperature by going back and forth between the two pools...oh, man."

"Like I said," laughs Jamie, "it's amazing."

"Are we still high?"

"I don't know man. Maybe. Probably. I can't tell anymore."

Leandro glances around surreptitiously. "Hey. Do you think everyone here is high?"

"Yeah man. Definitely. Like those little kids over there? Obviously really high."

"Okay, duh, not the kids. But everyone else?"

"Yes. Definitely. I'm sure their parents took some huge bong hits before they left the house, dumbass."

Leandro narrows his eyes. He starts humming the theme song from Jaws and moving slowly toward Jamie through the water.

"Stay away from me. You ask a stupid question, get a stupid answer." Leandro sinks down until the water is just below his eyes, his hands come up, curved into claws. "Stay the fuck away from me, I'm warning you...

goddamnit dude, you're supposed to be chill in here!…"
Jamie has assumed a kind of karate stance. Bubbles
begin to emerge from the water in front of Leandro's
face and he rises up, laughing.

This is a dream, I think to myself, as I listen to the
mutterer and the giggler go back and forth. The heat of
the water is a balm, a soothing of my body that pene-
trates to the core and ripples back outwards in soft, slow
waves. Release. Relaxation follows, in the wake of the
action of release. Let it go, I think; and as I think it I
know it is a thought that foreshadows. It comes, it goes.
Let it go. The mineral vapors rise like ghostly vines
from the water's surface, from an opalescent blue soil
this garden of mist-vines, ghost-flowers.

Dinosaur bones down there in the darkness of earth;
other relics of ancient power, older than time and vast
beyond my reckoning. My candle-flame life, my
candle-flame body. But I know that it is a thing that I
contain, a something from within my body from which
springs this dreaming…

"…other pool. Hey, dingus. Back to the other
pool." I blink, look up. Jamie is a few yards away, waving me forward, beyond him Leandro's figure emerging
from the water as he climbs the broad steps of stone.

"Where does the water come from?" I ask, half a
minute later as we're slowly gliding down the length of
the main pool again.

Leandro shrugs, his broad shoulders rising momentarily above the water's surface. "Dunno. Ask a geolo-
gist."

"No, wait, I read about this somewhere, something
about the water's sulphuric content," says Jamie. "Hot,
smelly…ah, that's right, I remember now. It comes
from Leandro's vagina."

As I start laughing I manage to swallow some water, so I'm laughing and choking simultaneously. I hear the Jaws song again followed by the sound of splashing and Jamie crying out, which makes it more difficult to collect myself since I can't stop laughing long enough to cough the water up.

Shortly, following the extraction of a promise that there will be "no more goddamn dunking!", peace is restored and we're gliding along again. We reach the deep end of the pool, a stretch of another thirty yards or so in which the bottom drops away precipitously and it is no longer possible to simply walk along. Leandro says he's going to swim the rest of the way, splashes forward into the darkness.

Jamie watches him for a moment, then turns back. "C'mon, let's go. He'll catch up."

"Is it always like this?" I ask. "With the two of you, and…and him?"

Jamie glances at me. "What, you mean with the stream of general bullshit? Sure, more or less. But it's different, too. I'd say that we—Leandro and I—are a little more conscious now of trying to inject, oh, I guess you could say lightness?, into things. I think that's part of what we're here for, to like, relieve the burden, sort of. We're sidekicks, basically; this is about you and your, y'know, journey, or quest, or whatever you want to call it."

Somewhere off to my left I hear laughter; the pattering of little feet on wet stone, the splash of a little body going into the water. I think of the small boy I watched, who I followed through his world, and I know that in some other time and place he was once here, too.

"So…so why did the two of you come here, then? Was it for me, or was it for him?"

"Hm...well, like I said before, that separation isn't something I fully understand. The things you said about it were interesting, but still, I dunno...but besides that, I mean, I'm always down for a good adventure, man."

As he says this he lets out a quiet chuckle.

"I used to have this bumper sticker, back in the day when I still had my sweet Ford Bronco II, may she rest in peace; man that was a sweet ride...but anyways, I had this bumper sticker on it: Not All Who Wander Are Lost. He loved to give me shit about that bumper sticker. We'd be having what I thought was a serious conversation, and he'd like, sigh or something, and then go: 'Well, you know better than most, for sure. Not all who wander are lost', and then he'd laugh his ass off. Ha ha, very funny dickhead..."

Jamie is smiling as he tells this story, his eyes gazing off into memory as we slip slowly through the night and the waters. I watch the expression on his face change as he watches the memory, as he follows its thoughts, feels its feelings.

"It's funny...so, that was a cheesy bumper sticker, duh. I know that, I got it in high school, everyone does dumb things like that in high school. And I liked that he gave me shit for it, honestly. That was one of the things that I liked best about him, that made him such a good friend: that he always held you to higher standards, never let you get away with anything, that kind of thing. But it's funny, 'cause he was always wandering, and he was *never* lost; that was the best part, 'cause he would go wherever, and do whatever, and you got to go along for the ride. But then he went, or wandered, I don't know, too far or something...I mean, he came back, or at least someone who was still my friend came

back. But he came back with this obsession, with this…
it sounds silly, I know it sounds silly. But it was like
some part of him…like some part of him had gotten
permanently lost somewhere. Mm. Maybe it doesn't
sound so weird now, though, after all…"

Leandro has come up alongside us at some point
while Jamie has been talking. Jamie's words echo in my
body as we glide on in silence.


Crunch, crunch. Softly. The air is the cold clean
mountain air. The only sound is the dead dry pine
needles beneath our feet. Leandro stops, the beam of
his flashlight knifes through the darkness for a few
seconds before he clicks it off again. "This way. I think
not much further."

The spreading branches are a dark thicket overhead,
blotting out the night sky. Crunch, crunch. Softly. The
beam of light clicks on, clicks off. "There. Just up
ahead." The trees give way, the carpet of dry needles
becomes grass and then smooth stone. We are standing
on a wide ledge of granite, looking back down at the
lights of the town in the valley far below. There are two
small, smoky jewels of green and turquoise. "See the
pools?" says Leandro, pointing.

We build a small fire inside a ring of stones. Jamie
pulls food from his backpack, we tear off hunks of bread
and fold them around wedges of salami and cheese. I
lie back, light a cigarette. I watch them drift, searching
for whatever it is they are searching, the unmoored stars
moving across the sea of the night sky.

"See what I'm saying? Do you see them moving?" I
ask.

"That is…huh. That's really weird. I've never…it's

197

like shooting stars, only they're going really slow and they don't go out," says Jamie. "Weird, man."

"When did you say it started? Just before we showed up, right?" asks Leandro.

"Yeah. And do you see how some of them are moving together, and then there are other groups that are breaking apart?"

"And some of them are just...drifting. Or—yeah, that's two that are definitely moving together. And there's one following them, I think...wow. This is really weird-looking. You weren't kidding, man," says Jamie wonderingly.

"So," says Leandro, "you say you felt something, like something shifted or something; and then you looked up, and saw that all the stars were...moving, I guess?"

"Yeah," I say. We're all silent for a bit, watching.

"I think they're migrating," I say quietly after awhile.

"Migrating?"

"Yeah. I mean, moving from one place to another. Like, they had to re-organize themselves for some reason, and they're figuring it out now. Trying to figure out what...what the new thing is. The new pattern, or something."

"Huh. Well, they are definitely moving, that's for sure. And it is definitely not like anything I've ever seen before," says Jamie.

"Yeah. That's why I wanted to come up here and show you. I mean, we could've seen some of it from in town, but up here away from everything, it's..."

"...Really obvious," finishes Leandro.

We watch in silence for awhile longer as the fire dies down. We rise, smother the last cinders and walk back down the mountain.

"So. What Jamie said, back at the pool. About him coming back, but it seemed like part of him had gotten permanently lost somewhere. And what I'm wondering now is: is that who I am? Am I that missing part of him?"

We're back in the motel room. Pools of lamplight. I'm sitting on one bed, legs crossed indian-style. Jamie lies on the other bed, propped up by a collection of pillows. Leandro is sitting in one of the two chairs next to the table, opposite the beds. They say nothing, waiting. I look down at my hands in my lap, thinking about what I'm trying to say.

"I...I don't know. Maybe that's right. It would answer a lot of questions, in a way. But something about it seems too easy. I'll be honest: I don't like the idea that I'm just a lost part of someone else. But I also honestly don't really think that's what I am, either. Maybe...maybe I was, maybe that's where I began, or what I came from. I don't know if that's true or not; but it doesn't matter, really, because I am more than that now."

A feeling and a memory come into me as I say this. *You have to know more. You have to become stronger.* And I realize that it is a memory that is wholly mine; mine alone, and no one else's.

"So, look: wherever we are, this world we're in, there is no one like me. I have this power to make things, to create things. But not just anything. Everything I make comes from memory; from this pool of memories that I can't identify, but that exists inside of me. But when I bring those memories to life, that's what they do: they come alive. And then...and then what they are, it…it changes."

I look up, at each of them; silent, watching me, waiting.

"That's who you are, isn't it: no, not Jamie and Leandro, but memories of Jamie and Leandro; collections of memory, bodies of memory. Or at least that's where you came from. But memories don't say new things, they don't make new things; they don't do things they've never done before. You are something else now."

"Then where do you think we are?" Leandro asks quietly.

"I don't know. For awhile I thought we were…I don't know, inside of him somewhere. And maybe we are, in a way. Maybe that's where it started. But it's more than that now."

I look down at my hands; close them into fists, slowly open them again. Thoughts move through my mind. Feelings move through my body.

Jamie sits up. He nods, looking intently at me. "Like I said before man: we're here for you. To help you, as far and as much as we can. But it's yours. This is your journey. It's all you."


Sometime later I am lying in the darkness. I can hear their even breathing as they sleep, Leandro in the other bed, Jamie lying next to me. I lie still, feeling the soft pulse of the life within my body. It is a long time before sleep steals within and gently takes me away.

# dreams

*The brother and the sister took the stuffed animals from their respective rooms. They walked back and forth, carrying armloads of stuffed animals and situating them on and around the couch, carefully, so that each and every one had a clear view of the tv set. The brother and sister sat down with bowls of cereal amidst the soft, furry gathering and together they all watched cartoons.*

*Later on they were a little taller and they fought. That's mine, they said. Get out of my room, they spat at each other. I hate you and I hate you too. They preyed on each other's weaknesses, tried to break each other down. Victories were empty, tasted like acid. They fought anyway, always.*

*Later on they were taller and more in command of their own bodies. The sister came home late at night. The brother was sitting on the couch, he heard her stumble and moan. He went into the kitchen with her and tried to keep everything quiet. When their mother came downstairs she looked and said Are you drunk? No, said the sister. Disgusted, promising retribution, the mother marched back to bed. The brother cleaned up. In the morning he was sitting on the*

201

*couch, watching tv. The sister came down and without a word curled up next to him. Unhappy with his own life, he found a place inside to give her what she needed all the same.*

*Later they had grown into their own lives in separate places. They visited each other. The brother was brushing his teeth in the sister's bathroom and she opened the door and said to her friend See, he brushes his teeth like a crazy person. They made paper masks and walked down the street, arms and legs akimbo. For a time they lived together. The brother would come downstairs and put Stevie Wonder's* Talking Book *on the stereo, and the sister would come downstairs and that was how they would start their day together.*

*Later on the brother was broken. He got into the car and left behind a life that had broken into pieces. As he left the city it was night, and he could feel the ghosts he would carry from that life rising up in the dark night and coming to him, coming into his body as he left the broken pieces behind. He drove for a long time and many things outside the window flashed by. He slept in a bed in a motel and got up the next morning and got into the car and kept driving. Late that night he stopped, finally. He got out of the car and went into the sister's house. She was sitting on the couch and he went and lay down with his head on her lap. I'm here, she said. I know, he said. They stayed still that way for a long time.*

\*\*\*

*The boy knows. He knows he is leaving the girl. He knows that he has to, that it has to happen soon. It breaks him apart to know this, but he knows it all the same.*

*He worries, he is afraid. He knows that he is the net*

*that has been catching her as she falls, over and over again. That he has become nothing more than a net because of this; that if he does not leave, he will soon disappear beneath her weight. But he is afraid, deathly afraid that she will keep falling. That without him there to catch her she will fall and break into pieces again; and he knows that if this happens, it will destroy him.*

*Wedged, immobile, between that rock and that hard place; frozen in that position, forced by desperation to look at everything, he begins to see a way.*

*There is another boy, a lost, younger boy who hears music. This lost boy who hears music has wandered into their life, into the life of the boy and girl. The boy who hears music is lost, he is searching. He has a young, unshaped heart.*

*And the boy sees the way. He cannot say it to himself, cannot even let himself think it. But there is no time, there are no other choices. And the young boy who hears music is lost, is searching; he needs something, too.*

*So the boy says: Come in. To the young, lost boy he says: Come into our life, come into our world. The girl knows that the boy is going to leave. And the boy knows that she is terrified; that in her terror she is desperate, will do anything.*

*And so he says to the young, lost boy: Come in. The young lost boy is hungry for meaning, hungry for what he finds in the boy and girl's world. He devours everything they feed him; and as their world enters into his body, he enters into their world. He feeds on what they have grown in their garden, his lungs begin to fill with their air. His heart begins to change, the music the lost young boy hears begins to take shape.*

*The boy sees it. He begins to step backward. The young lost boy is beginning to speak their world's language; his*

203

*voice begins to emerge in their language, to say things. The young boy speaks and the girl speaks, and as they do the boy steps backward. The footing is clear, he continues stepping backward and knows that he will soon be gone.*

*He thinks: When I leave, I think she will not break now. He thinks: That is good. This way, when I leave, only one of us will end up broken. (This is the last of his strength, given to this thought. And then he is gone.)*

# pieces and places

I take a drink, set the coffee cup back down on the table and take a deep breath. "Okay. Let's get started."

The scene is a repeat from yesterday: booth next to the window, empty cups and plates on the table. Breakfast has been a laconic and methodical affair, a thing to be done before getting down to business. I look from one to the other, sitting across the table from me. Jamie is working on his teeth with a toothpick, shrugs and looks at Leandro. Leandro nods, looks down at the coffee cup held between his hands.

"Well, let's pick up where we left off. But to be honest," he says, "neither of us can really tell you much about what happened in that first year, the year they spent in that apartment in San Francisco. He kind of dropped off the map, in terms of communicating with people, while he lived there. And afterwards he never really talked about it, at least not in detail. My sense is that he didn't know how; that it was so difficult and just, kind of fundamentally traumatic, that he just didn't know where to really begin. I don't mean to say that we don't know anything about it, but I don't think we know enough to do it justice; and besides that, I also kind of get the sense that it's not really our story to tell. Does that make sense?" he asks, looking at me.

"Yeah," I say, nodding slowly. "It does. I don't necessarily understand why, but yeah, it does. And anyways it would be kind of pointless to try if you don't really know what happened."

"Right," he says. "Obviously it's important, and I'd imagine that you're going to have to deal with it eventually, but—"

"It's just not time yet,' I say, finishing his sentence.

"Exactly. It's a can't-cross-bridges till you come to them kind of thing." He pauses as the waitress comes by with more coffee, takes a drink and then continues.

"But, having said all that, there is one thing I can tell you, which is that somewhere in there he got lost. What Jamie said last night at the pool, yeah I definitely agree with that. No, like you said, I don't know how that relates to you exactly, either. But the idea makes a lot of sense to me, in terms of what happened to him and what he was like; the choices he made, afterwards. And I think he realized it, finally; realized that he was lost, and that he just…had to leave. So, anyways—"

"—Wait, wait, hold on a sec. Dude what's up?" Jamie asks.

As Jamie speaks, I realize my eyes are closed. I don't answer; I'm focused on what's rising up, what I'm remembering.

*Broken…pieces…ghosts. He knows he is leaving the girl. I'm here. I know.*

"I had…had these dreams, last night," I say slowly. "Two dreams, both about the same thing, but from different…places, or different ideas, I'm not sure how to

206

put it. About…leaving. Two dreams about leaving. With two different people. The first dream, a girl named Hope. And the second, a boy named… Matthew."

I open my eyes. Leandro and Jamie are looking at each other, I can't quite read what's passing between them. "What?" I ask. "What is it? What's going on, do you know who those people are?"

Leandro nods slowly. "Yes. We do. Um…well, the first dream, about Hope. That makes sense. Hope is his sister. And that was the first place he went, when he left. Back to Portland, the last place he'd lived before he moved to Santa Cruz. She'd moved there, most of his friends were still there. Instinct, basically, at least that's how I read it. A person is lost, so that's all they have recourse to. Instinct drove him back to the last place he could remember being in and knowing who he was—"

"But also, he was never *really* there, that time," says Jamie, breaking in. "He lived with Hope for awhile, he lived with Jack for awhile; but he never had his own place, his own space, like his feet never really touched the ground. Like, either he couldn't be alone, or he had to stay extra-close to people; maybe both, maybe they're the same thing. Maybe…maybe he knew he'd lost the ability to form normal attachments and fulfill normal responsibilities, like signing leases and paying rents and bills. But also, he put a lot of strain on those relation-ships, just floating there for five months like that."

"Maybe he had to," says Leandro. "Like he had to test them, see how much weight they could bear; y'-know, like he had to gather a more specific, clearer sense of what kind of resources he had."

"That makes sense," I hear myself say, softly. They fall silent. Outside I can see green trees, blue sky.

207

His...or mine? My friends? My sister? These memories I see and feel and do not remember. That walk into me of their own accord and stand there, staring.

I turn back to the table. "It makes sense. Figure out where you are. Determine the constitution of the battleground. Discover what kind of weapons you have, and know how strong they are. He was following a plan. Maybe he didn't know it, yet, but he was following a plan all the same."

It resonates. The idea resonates between us, I can feel it; see it in their eyes as we sit in silence.

"So then," I say slowly. "The second dream. Who is...Matthew?"

Something else builds up, this time, as soon as the question is out of my mouth. A different kind of resonance. Something deeper, more complicated. Jamie looks down, shakes his head after a moment. Leandro makes a face, sighs. "Well," he says, "that's a part of where things start to get...difficult. Matthew is...in this context, two people. I mean, he's one person, but he has two separate meanings. One of them, is that he's Tyler's younger brother. And the other, is what he became. Which is, um...Isobel's boyfriend."

Everything inside of me tightens, twists like a rope. The world blurs as the feeling wells up from within, gathers behind my eyes.

Without a word, I get up from the table and head for the door. Neither Jamie nor Leandro says anything or tries to stop me. Outside I walk to the rear of the restaurant. I fish the pack of cigarettes out of my pocket, try to light one up but my hand is shaking too badly, I can't do it. I lean back against the brick wall and after a second sink, slowly down against the wall to the ground. I'm holding my head in my hands and looking down, I see the dark spots form on the concrete as the tears fall down.

*A lost boy who hears music…a young, unshaped heart. The young boy speaks and the girl speaks…this way, only one of us will end up broken.*

The dream is a memory and the memory is a dream. The thicket of emotional cross-currents within it is intense and bewildering, almost more than I can bear.

How he…saw it. How he knew it. How he opened the door; how he watched the two of them coming together, even as they themselves did not know they were coming together. How later it tore him apart. The agony of being forced to continually affirm the one thing in the world he wanted to destroy. The dark hatred he fought alone to keep locked away…

The brother. Of the friend who betrayed him and broke his heart. Of all the people in the world…Jesus, *motherfucker…*

I shake my head, wipe the tears away. Lean my head back against the wall and close my eyes. Breathe. In, out. Slowly. In, and back out again. I open my eyes, bring the cigarette to my lips and light it, pull deeply; hold, let the smoke drift back out through my mouth and nose. These memories, feelings are not mine. They are maps, tools. I pull again, deeply, exhale the smoke slowly in a long, thin stream. Slowly, deliberately I put the maps and tools away, in files and drawers and toolboxes. I watch the cigarette burn down, slowly; stand, take a last drag and drop it to the pavement, grind it out beneath my shoe.


Back in the restaurant I sit down. I take a drink of lukewarm coffee, look out the window, thinking. I turn back to the table, Leandro and Jamie are watching me. I shake my head, take a deep breath. "That shit…" I say slowly, "…is crazy." Jamie grimaces, shakes his head. Leandro nods once, deliberately. "Yes," he says. "It is."

We sit in silence for awhile. "It makes a fucked-up kind of sense," I say finally. "It gave him a way out; it put up walls that were strong enough to withstand, later, when he wanted so bad to get back in. But…I mean, Jesus fucking Christ…" I look back out the window. All the normal shit out there. My god, I can barely stand it. "I think…I think I'm beginning to understand," I say.

"Yeah," says Leandro, quietly. "He left Portland after about five months; went to Costa Rica, out of the blue pretty much. The idea was to work as a volunteer on someone's pet project; this woman he knew, some friend's mother, who'd bought a piece of former ranch-land up in the mountains and was trying to re-forest it. He sent these mass emails, that at first were about normal stuff: 'this is what it's like here, this is the work I'm doing,' etc., like travelogues. But then they just turned crazy: about intense dreams he was having, poems he wrote, like this one poem he wrote to Jesus; and he was sending these to, like, everyone he knew. Brutally honest, and really hard to read, 'cause he was thousands of miles away and alone and there was nothing you could do. I know he found out, just before he left Portland, that Isobel and Matthew had basically become a couple; and I know that despite that, she flew down to Costa Rica, alone, and was with him for like ten days or something at the very end of his four months there. And I know that during those ten days some heavy shit went down; I don't know what, exactly, but I know it must've been…I mean, fucking crazy."

I'm looking at Leandro as he says this, and he's looking back at me, and we both see it. It coalesces and clarifies immediately, moving from thought to decision in the same moment. I look at Jamie, his eyes are narrowed and he's nodding, he sees it too. I look inside myself and find what I need, waiting.

"Yes," I say. "Pack your metaphysical bags, boys. Are you ready?" Leandro smiles, nods. "Sweetness," says Jamie. "The adventure continues. Hell yeah I'm ready."

"Okay," I say. "Here we go." I close my eyes. I take a deep breath, and bring my focus to bear; feel myself drawing the power, feel it as the world around us changes.

## so far away

"Jesus," says Jamie wearily, behind me. "Can someone please explain to me why we're walking up a goddamn mountain again? I thought we were going to the beach this time."

Leandro laughs, stops and turns. "C'mon, adventure boy, thought this is what you were all about."

Jamie trudges up next to us, wipes the sweat from his brow. "Eat me, goontard," he says, flipping Leandro the bird. He looks at me, shakes his head. "You could've let us just skip this part, you know. We could already be there, just enjoying the view."

"Nope," I say. "You heard me explain this already. This is part of it, the sense of travel and distance; the fact that it's a place that's literally at the end of the road. To understand that we have to go through it too."

Jamie looks around, grunts. "This isn't a road, this is a mudslide. Re...tarded."

"It is pretty damn primitive, I'll give you that," says Leandro. "I remember him talking about it, in one of those emails. How they had to put these massive chains on the tires of the truck, weigh the bed of it down with sandbags and whatnot; and sometimes, when the rain was heavy, they'd get stuck and just have to back down. It is pretty out here, though," he says, looking around.

"Is it?" says Jamie. "A bunch of green shit, a bunch of brown shit, and a bunch of gray shit," he says, looking up at the overcast sky.

Leandro laughs again. "Looks like adventure boy bit off more than he can chew," he says.

"Suck it," says Jamie. "At least it's not hot, too."

"No, we're too high up," I say. "And I don't think the cloud cover up here ever really goes away, either, at least not for long. C'mon, let's go, it's not much further I think," I say as I start walking up the road again.

Leandro is right about how remote it is. We left the last town behind a few hours ago, and calling it a town is overstating the case. A few buildings, strung along the road, almost hidden by the trees and undergrowth; and calling them "buildings", or calling this a "road" is almost overstating the case, too. It's wide enough, but steep and muddy; pitted with boulders, criss-crossed by deep gullies where the water has washed the dirt away. Jamie is right too, I think as we trudge along. Yes, it's pretty, but there is a kind of monotony to it all, as well.

After awhile the trees and undergrowth begin to thin out a bit, become sparser and patchier. A view opens to the left, down the steep hillside to the bottom of the valley far below, and across to the mountainside opposite. Finally, we round a bend, and the end comes into view. The deep ravine of the valley rises into a shallow, small bowl, at the bottom of which, in a cleared and flattened space, is our destination. We walk the last few hundred yards and stand there, taking it in.

"Not much to look at, is it," says Jamie after a bit.

213

"When he said 'cabin' in those emails, I was picturing something more…well, picturesque."

It's about as utilitarian as houses can be. A concrete box, essentially, walls painted blue, with a tin roof. Solidly constructed, but a concrete box with a tin roof nonetheless. One-story, perhaps twenty feet wide by thirty feet long. A broad covered porch, most of which is taken up by a long, heavy wooden table, two benches at either side. Off to one side are a number of raised platforms, filled with baby trees, a nursery of sorts. The ground around the house is cleared for a wide area, just dirt and gravel. Some power tools on the porch, a couple stacks of lumber to one side. A wooden outhouse behind the house, and just beyond the cleared space, in the grass a falling-down, decrepit wooden shed structure next to a similarly broken down fenced-in area, the remnants of whatever "ranching" operation existed here before, I'm guessing. And that's it; no other signs of habitation anywhere around.

"Yeah, what he said," says Leandro. "Not much to look at. But the setting is pretty impressive. It is beautiful up here." The mountainside rises again behind the house, up to a ridge perhaps a half-mile off, and to the left and the right, as well. Much of the land has been cleared of trees, just pale yellow grasses now and green shrubbery, but higher up the trees begin again, stand here and there in clusters. The house faces down the valley, and the view is a long one. In the far distance discernible clouds beneath the gray of sky, from the valley itself tendrils of mist rise above the trees, floating.

"It is, I won't try and disagree," says Jamie. "Beautiful in and of itself, but also the sense of real isolation… it like, adds something, just to feel so far away from, well, pretty much everything, I guess. If that was the point, I'd say he achieved it."

"Yeah, that was the point," I say. "I don't think he… realized it, fully, until he got here. But it didn't take long for that to make itself clear."

"Those emails," says Leandro, shaking his head. "Remember?" he says to Jamie, who nods, a more serious, even somber expression coming into his eyes and face. "I mean, I said they were crazy," says Leandro, "and they were. But more than just crazy. It felt like…I mean, it felt like he was breaking apart. I half-wondered, honestly, if we were ever going to see him again…"

I'm looking at the house. As plain as it is, there's something about it, some kind of thing in the air around it. Something…something inside of it. Something in there. I look at Leandro and Jamie, I can see they feel it too. Without another word I walk to the front door and open it; stand there for a moment in the doorway before I step inside, Leandro and Jamie following behind me.

The room we enter is dim, cool. Concrete walls and floor, light coming in through the open doorway and clear plastic panels in cut-out portions of the tin roof. It's a workroom, filled with shelves and tools and toolboxes, a small table and a couple of chairs. There are two doors, one in the wall opposite, one in the wall to the right, both standing open, flat against the wall. I walk across the room to the doorway in the opposite wall, step into the room beyond. A double bed, a dresser, otherwise empty. I step back into the workroom; Leandro and Jamie are standing there, watching me, I shake my head. I walk through the other doorway, into what turns out to be the kitchen. The light is brighter in here, a window sits above the sink. All the basic necessities, but again, rudimentary versions of such. There is a cast-iron stove in one corner, a stack of fire-wood next to it on the floor. A couple countertops, shelves with cups and plates, pots and pans. On one of the countertops a two-burner gas range, hose running from it to the propane tank underneath.

"No electricity, obviously," says Leandro. "Running water, at least, from a spring up above in the hills some-where, I think, if I remember right. But yeah, I'd say this all qualifies as remote." The three of us stand there for a moment. I look at both of them, see it in their eyes. I turn. The door in the back wall of the kitchen is shut, closed. I take two steps, reach out and open it, and step inside.

There are three pieces of furniture in the room. A bed, a table next to it, a chair at the table. On the table are a few books, a couple of candles, two pens and a pad of lined, yellow paper. One of the books is Thoreau's *Walden,* another is Thomas Pynchon's *Gravity's Rainbow.* A book about extreme solitude, a book about pure chaos. I put my hand on the table's rough, unfin-ished surface, feel a stirring of...pride?...gratitude? "He made this, I think," I say quietly. Leandro and Jamie say nothing. What is it? What happened in here? What did Leandro say about those emails?...something about...dreams...

I sit down on the bed, a heavy wooden frame of thick planks and logs, a thin mattress covered by a blan-ket, a single pillow. I lay down, stretch out, my head on the pillow and I close my eyes.


Nothing happens. I open my eyes. The room is darkened, as though half the light has been taken away,

216

sucked out. Leandro and Jamie are standing next to the bed, looking down at me but they're blurred, grainy, as though half of them has been taken away too. I start to say something to them but my mouth won't open. I try and rise from the bed but I can't, can't move at all; I'm paralyzed, stuck inside a body that has become a stone.

And then I feel it, become aware of It. And as I do I am filled with a blind terror beyond all thought.

I can see It, out of the corner of my eye. On the floor, against the wall. A concentrated, shapeless darkness in the corner of the room. It is holding me here with Its power. It is here for the only reason that It exists. To turn me into Itself and destroy me.

The terror envelops me, is my entire world. I have to get out. Now. Something inside of me gathers itself; with a complete purity of focus it gathers all of the power inside my body and pushes it into a single concentrated point, straining forward with tremendous force. I feel it as it shatters around me, the breath rushing into my body with a shuddering gasp.

I open my eyes.

Leandro and Jamie are still standing looking down at me. Paralyzed, my body frozen. The room still dark, but less so. And the Thing, still in the corner, but less than It was. The terror again. Have to get out. The gathering of force, pushing, with all of who I am trained on a single, focused point, a cry erupting, roaring from my mouth...


I hear a small, strangled and inarticulate sound escape from between my lips as my eyes open. My body is trembling, drenched with sweat. Leandro and Jamie are looking down at me, both of them standing stock

217

still; Jamie's mouth half open, his eyes wide, Leandro half-bending towards me, his hands half-raised in the air as though he's about to do something but doesn't know what, his face stricken with confusion. I roll up to a sitting position, slowly, elbows on my knees, head held in my hands. Breathe. Just...breathe.

"What...dude. What...what in the fuck just happened," says Jamie. I don't say anything. After a moment he sits down on the bed next to me. "Dude," he says. His voice is quiet, intense. "Where...where the fuck did you go just now?"

"What do you mean," I say, and it's strange to hear the sound of my own voice again, to know that I can speak again. A shudder of relief passes through my body, a wave from head to toe. I raise my head, look at him. "What do you mean," I say again. "I didn't go anywhere, I was here the whole time." He looks back at me, his face as serious as I've ever seen it. Looks up at Leandro, for a long moment, before he turns his gaze to me again; slowly, barely shakes his head. "No dude. You were gone," he says, his voice quiet, even. "You were on the bed, you closed your eyes, and then the next moment you were just gone. We shouted for you, ran into the other rooms, ran outside, shouted for you, nothing. We came back in here and had been in here for a few seconds, maybe, trying to figure out what the fuck to do, and then...and then you were just there again. Lying there with your eyes closed, and then you made that...that crazy, fucking gurgling sound, like something was crawling out of you, and your eyes opened again."

He says all this evenly, in calmly measured tones. I look back at him for a moment longer, then I get up and walk out of the room, out of the house. I come to a stop several yards beyond the porch, hear Leandro and Jamie come out of the house behind me. I take in a deep lungful of the cool air, let it back out slowly as I stare out across the valley stretching into the distance below.

I feel them come up, stand beside me. "I thought… I thought I was shouting. Screaming. And it was just…just that tiny little sound," I say quietly. Jamie's hand comes to rest on my shoulder, a gentle pressure. "What happened?" he asks.

I shake my head. "I don't know if I can explain it all," I say, looking out at the valley. The deep vivid green, the slate gray sky; it all seems both more beautiful and much further away now. "I dreamed a dream that he dreamed, once. Or more than once, I'm not sure. When he was here, in that room. But it was… more than just a dream. Now, this time, and then as well, I think. I was in the room, lying in the bed, everything the same, you were both standing there even. But everything was darker, blurred. And I was paralyzed. Frozen, couldn't move. And there was…there was this Thing, in the room with me. This dark *Thing*, I don't know how else to describe it. And it had come there… it had come there to destroy me."

I sit down on the ground, slowly. Jamie and Leandro move, sit also, facing me. No one says anything for awhile.

"I told you, man," says Leandro finally. "Those emails he sent were more than just crazy. They were like, crying out, almost."

"That Thing…it was real," I say slowly. "And I'm remembering, I'm not sure, but I've seen it before I think. Met it once before, and forgot, for some reason. In some other place, that is also in this world. But…

219

deeper inside of it, or something. All the Thing wanted was to swallow me up. But it couldn't. Or rather, it could have, but I wouldn't let it. It took…it took everything I had inside, every last part of me. But I wouldn't let it…and so it couldn't."

"Jesus christ," says Jamie in a low tone. "That is…I don't know what to say man," he says, his eyes filled with real concern. Leandro's brow is furrowed, his face carries the same expression of worry. But as I look back at them, I am suddenly filled with an overwhelming sense of gratitude; that they are here, that they are with me. My eyes fill with tears, both of them see it and reach out, place their hands on me in the same moment. "I'm so…I'm so sorry," I say, my voice breaking. "That you have to—have to go through this with me."

"No way, dude. Don't say that, don't ever fucking say that," says Jamie, his voice filled with force and meaning. "We're not the ones in danger here, you know that, you said it, that Thing wasn't looking for us. We are here for you. *For you.* Whatever it takes, all the way till the end. You hear me? Don't ever question that, and don't ever apologize to us again." His grip on me tightens, Leandro's does so simultaneously, the tears come rolling forth, run in streams down my face.

"What did I ever do to deserve this kind of…I can't, I don't know how to—to thank you. So much, thank you so much…" I can barely get the words out, my voice trembling, breaking apart.

"No," says Jamie. "Thank you. For trying so goddamn fucking hard. You asked me before, why are we here? We're here because we believe in you. Always have, and always will."

I bow my head, close my eyes. Feel them next to me, what they mean to me.

"You can…you can do this," says Leandro. I look up at him, see that serious, calm face, nodding slowly at me. "You've come so far, already. The end is not far off now, I know you can feel it. More hard shit between here and there?…yeah, probably. For sure, would be my guess. But you can do this. I think you know that. But sometimes it helps to hear someone else tell you."

I smile, or rather feel the smile break through my tears. I look down; take a deep, shuddering breath, sigh it back out. Wipe my face with the back of my hand, look up at them. Leandro's eyes carry that look of calm, clear intent, Jamie is smiling back at me. "C'mon, you big crybaby. We're not done yet. You ready or what?" He stands, spreads his arms out wide. "Adventure awaits!"

Leandro laughs. "Return of Adventure Boy! Adventure Boy, Part Two: Lil Buddy Returns!"

"Adventure Boy Beats Leandro's Ass, more like it."

"You and what small army, good sir?"

"I would pay good money to see any of those," I say, laughing. I wipe away the last of the tears; stand, reach for the sky, shake it all out. I can do this. As frightening, as difficult as what happened in there was, I survived, I'm still standing. I can do this.

"Now that's more like it," says Jamie approvingly. "You ready, what's next? Time's a-wasting."

"I am," I say, and feel it as I say it. "Let's…let's get some food, first. I think I know a place. And then…" I pause, thinking. "And then…I think there's one more stop here, that we have to go to. And then, whatever comes next."

The shadow creature, that dark Thing. I won't forget It, this time. I don't know what It is, I don't know where It came from. But I know what It wants. I know

I will meet It again. And when that time comes, I have to be ready.

# fuck it

*Shit.  Shit, shit, shit.  My fucking broken shoulder is killing me.  It seems like it's made a decision to no longer do, oh, forty percent of what a shoulder's supposed to do.  It says no!, no it screams no; NO!*

*Meanwhile I am fucking poor as shit.  Show me the goddamn fucking money, goddamnit.  Every day I have ten different new ideas that sound great, and then whack!, 'no money' slaps those ideas in the face.*

*Oh, yeah.  Wait, it gets better.  I'm thirty-four years old and I have no career.  The entirety of my future rests on a book I'm writing.  No, no, I don't have anything resembling a publishing contract, ha ha, that's a good one.  No, no, no. What I have is a fairly experimental manuscript that is a story about my own fucking life; and, and, that is being written as a big fucking exercise in self-therapy.*

*So, to sum up: my body is breaking down.  I'm broke. And my working hours are being given to a solipsism with the feeble glimmer of hope that it will matter enough to other people that they will pay me money to hear about it. Read about it.  What-fucking-ever.  And oh, yeah, I think* about all these things…constantly. Demons and ghosts, demons and ghosts all around me. I drink to get away from them, I get high to get away from them, I smoke cigarettes like a banshee. Drugs, friends, women, all these are ways to distract, to try and find some fucking peace for a day, an hour, a single goddamn minute.

The worst part is that I have a wonderful family. Lots of excellent friends. A nice home in a nice neighborhood, a comfortable bed and a pantry and refrigerator filled with food. Yup, exactly: no real room to whine or complain about anything.

That's what I feel like, mostly. That I have no room. Lately I have this new image in my head, of these screws turning into my back. I don't know what's turning them, some nameless invisible force-thing, but it doesn't matter that I don't know, they're going to keep turning anyway, there's nothing I can do to stop it.

Fuck you, life. I could quit, you know. But fuck you, then you win. Fuck you for making me this way. All I want is to be normal, like all these people with jobs and money and cars and families; just to plug in and do the work that someone puts in front of me and get paid and not think and be normal and satisfied and happy.

But no, no, you made me so that I don't actually want any of those things. So that being 'normal' is this dream I keep having that I don't want, any part of, in any way whatsoever. No, instead I have this fucking gift, and with that a stubborn, mule-headed temperament, such that any-thing less than hugely ambitious goals and monumental achievements, anything less than that is completely, entirely unacceptable. Oh, and, I have to do this within an un-breakable, unbendable framework of ethics, morals and responsibilities. Codes and rules, fucking my own, complete-ly internal, otherwise ungoverned, codes and rules, and still

*I can't even pretend to transgress them, much less actually do so.*

*But you know what? Fuck you, life. Fuck you, destiny. Fucking bring it on. I obviously have no choices, so just go ahead and fuck yourselves. I'm obviously not going to accept being some gifted dilettante and all-around fucking loser, I'm obviously not going to quit searching and trying and working and fucking striving, I'm not going to quit until the last stupid breath leaves my stupid fucking body.*

*So fuck you, and fuck you, and fuck you too. Bring it on, bring all the shit, empty your fucking arsenal. Because I don't know how to give up. So fuck you and fuck it, whatever it takes. Bring it the fuck on.*

## blurred line

Oh god. I feel it rising up from the pool and I can't stop it. It breaks the surface and floods my body, fills my mouth and eyes.

"She'd booked a room. A small place on the coast. The beach. Not just any room, the 'Honeymoon Suite'. The last three days. Already it had been so hard to control myself, to contain myself, and then we're getting ready to go there and she's showing me photos on the website, saying Doesn't it look nice, it's the Honeymoon Suite...we're in the ocean, in the water, kissing; she's pushing me away, telling me how she and Matthew want so much for me to 'find somebody', and the words are nothing to me, less than nothing to me; she's in my arms in the water, saying these words that go into the fire that is in my whole body now and the words burn up and away. There's a bathtub in the room and she gets into the bath and her naked body is the only thing in the world anymore that I can feel or see. I can't not go to her as she rises, dripping wet, can't not take her to the bed and she can't try to push me away. I press my face between her thighs and drink the taste of her in a fever until the orgasm takes her body and then she is gone, she is in a corner huddled, sobbing. What it makes me feel I don't know how to say what it makes me feel, except that I find I have fallen to my knees before God and I am asking God aloud if I am this horrible thing that I feel, is this what I truly am God this horrible empty thing that I feel. And then she is next to me saying No, no, and what I hear is God answering: No. But I know it is still a thing that I have done. The next day we are leaving and she is so tender with me, she looks in my eyes and looks in my eyes and sighs with longing and I am lost in it, I have been so alone. But I am also not lost in it, I do not forget the way I felt on my knees before God, I do not forget anything and I see what is coming. As the plane flies she grows colder and colder, the closer we get to San Francisco she grows colder and colder. Matthew picks us up and drives us. We sit in her room and Matthew looks at us and I see that she cannot speak a word and I find the strength inside somewhere because I have to, and I look at him and say Matthew; and I tell him everything. Later I lie in the dark wondering and feel God with me, without calling it God. In the morning it is Matthew and I having coffee somewhere and God is in my heart and I say things to him that I have never said to anyone before and that I will never say to anyone ever again. And then I leave, and then I leave them and I am alone with it, with everything, and I know that I am very far from the end."

It dies away then, lets go of my body and I feel myself floating for a moment, before like a curtain the darkness swiftly descends.

Voices. Voices in the dark.

Jesus…what the fuck was that?

I don't know. I think he's coming around.

A face swims slowly into focus. An upside-down, worried face. Leandro's upside-down, worried face. Lying down, on my back. Leandro's hands, cradling my head, I'm looking up into his worried face.

"You okay man? What in the fuck happened just now?" Jamie, anxious, looking down over Leandro's shoulder. Where am I. What happened…

I remember. I sit up, try to stand up; come to one knee, realize I'm too unsteady to push myself up, sit back down again. My shoulder hurts, I'm not sure why. I close my eyes, press against my temples with my fingertips. Fucking christ…

"Did you…did you hear all that?" I ask. They're both silent, after a moment or two I look up. "I didn't… there was no disappearing this time, right? I was here the whole time?"

"…Yeah," says Jamie, after a few seconds. "No disappearing. And yeah we….heard." A pained expression in his eyes, in his voice. "We…we showed up here and about two seconds later you—I mean, it was like you were in like, a trance or something. And you said all— all that, and then—"

"—passed out," I finish. Silence. After awhile Jamie opens his mouth like he's about to try and say something, but the look on his face tells me he doesn't know what, I hold my hand up, shake my head. "No. Not here. We're…we're done here." I come to one knee again and stop, Leandro moves to help me but I wave him off; take a deep breath, rise slowly to my feet. I look around, briefly. The big room, the four-poster, canopied bed, the large bathtub. The Honeymoon Suite. What in the world...it's incomprehensible. As though together they chose to walk straight into the heart of oblivion.

"No. We're done here. I need...I need a drink," I say. Jamie and Leandro nod without saying anything, Okay. I take one last look around, shake my head. Jesus. I take a deep breath, find what I want inside, and close my eyes.



We order three beers at the bar, take them and walk out the back door, onto the fenced-in patio. We find a table near the back, sit down. The patio is mostly empty, only a couple other occupied tables. Green vines and chains of small, multicolored globe lights hang from the wooden trellis overhead. It's a gently warm, early summer evening, approaching twilight. I take a long pull from the cold bottle, set it back down; take out a cigarette, light it up.

"...Yeah, okay," says Jamie. "Lemme see one of those." I push the pack and lighter across the table to him. He flicks the lighter, takes a drag, exhales. "Sometimes it's just that time," he says, and sighs. We sit for awhile in silence, drinking slowly.

"Where are we, by the way?" asks Leandro after awhile.

"Does it matter?"

"...No. No, I guess it doesn't."

I take another drink, another drag. "Sorry," I say. "Didn't mean to be short like that." Leandro shrugs. "No big deal, you're right, it doesn't matter," he says. "Anyways, I don't really know," I say. "I just...pictured a place I wanted to be, I guess, and found this." He nods slowly, pursing his lips. "Yeah. Well that makes sense."

I think about that for a bit, roll it around in my mind. "Yeah. That's what I wanted. Just to be in a place that made sense, for a bit at least."

"Fuckin' cheers to that, dude," says Jamie quietly, raising his bottle. Clink, clinkety-clink. We drink, and sit again in silence.

"Something's happening," I say finally. "Something's changed, somehow. I dreamed his dream, at the cabin. And then...I mean, that was his voice. Coming out of me. That has to be what that was, what other explanation could there be? Nothing else—no one else—could know that stuff, could've said those things."

"Well," says Leandro, a thoughtful expression on his face, "I don't know if you realize this, but *you've* changed. Agreed, yes?" he says to Jamie, who nods his assent: "Definitely," he says.

"Who you were," Leandro continues, "when we met up with you...I mean, up to that point, I feel like things had, by and large, just been happening *to* you. You were, I think it's fair to say, angry and confused, more than anything else. You'd gained a sense of your power, or significance, maybe, but still had no idea how to, like, wield it; y'know, like the current of things was just carrying you along. But now...I mean, you're taking charge. All this crazy shit is coming at you, hitting you hard, and you're just like, taking these punches and rolling with them, y'know?"

"Agreed," says Jamie. "I'm on board with all of that, one-hundred percent. It's been impressive to see, to watch it happening, honestly."

The words sink in, and I know them. I know that they're true. I stub the cigarette out in the ashtray, take another drink. Jamie stands up. "Lizard-draining time.

230

Three more brews?" he asks, Leandro and I both nod, Jamie ambles away. Leandro picks up his beer, starts peeling the away the label.

"It's just…just so tortured," I say. He looks up at me, eyebrows raised; nods without saying anything, continues his methodical label-peeling. "And so insane," I continue. "Literally; decisions and actions that seem in complete ignorance of reality. I mean, going alone to visit him down there in the first place, that's crazy enough. But the Honeymoon Suite?…she books a room for them called the Honeymoon Suite?… and he goes along with it? It's…I don't know what to say about it. What the fuck did they think was going to happen, besides complete and total disaster?" I shake my head, take another cigarette out, light it up. Take a drag, breathe the smoke back out; watch it drift in the air, drizzle in a thin line from the cigarette's tip. "I mean, look. Given that he was your friend, I'm assuming he was a pretty smart person, yes?"

"Thank you for the implied compliment, in regards to my intelligence," says Leandro, as he pulls away the last part of the label and looks up at me. "Yes, in answer to your question. Very smart. As smart as anyone I've ever known."

"And…"—I hesitate, something catches in me; I realize it's…hard for me, to say her name aloud—"… Isobel. She must've been a pretty intelligent person, as well." He nods again. "So why…how…I mean…," I trail off, can't find the words.

Leandro stretches, grunts as he reaches for the sky. His arms come down, fold behind his head; he leans back in his chair, head supported by his folded arms, cocked at a slight angle.

"The first time," he begins slowly, "that he ever

231

talked about it—at all, to anybody—was two full years after he'd left San Francisco. He was living in Colorado again, had moved back there after Costa Rica, and was living with his parents; had been there for almost a year. We were hanging out one night, and I had to deliver this big bag of weed, like a couple ounces at least—the seller and the buyer were both friends of mine, not worth explaining how I ended up being the transit point—but anyways, I had to deliver this like, enormous bag of weed, and he went with me." He pauses, uncrosses his arms, scratches his head briefly; re-crosses them, head resting in the crook, before continuing. "So anyways we get there, and they're friends of mine, and of course they're like, 'Do you want to smoke?' And he looks at me, with this funny look in his eye, and is like, '…yes?' Because he wasn't a pot-smoker at the time, I mean at all, so he was asking me; and it took me by surprise, but I mean I love smoking weed, so of course I was like yeah, sure of course. So we smoke, and he gets really high like right away; someone puts Finding Nemo on the tv, and he's like all up close to the tv, going 'Is this real?…is that a fish tank?', just really high, and funny, in a good way, I mean like he's fine, it's funny to watch him."

At this point Jamie returns with the beers, distributes them and sits down. Leandro unfolds one arm, picks up the bottle and takes a drink, sets it back down and folds the arm behind his head again.

"So anyways, after awhile we leave, and instead of going back to my place we just walk around. It's a beautiful summer night, really nice out, we're just talking about whatever, having a good time. We end up at this playground, in this park, and he sits down in one of the swings." He stops talking; uncrosses his arms from behind his head, takes another drink; leans forward now, resting his arms on the table.  "And I ask him something—just a random question, no idea what it was—and he's silent for a couple seconds, and then in this super-sad voice says something about Isobel.  And then suddenly he's crying, and all this stuff about her just comes pouring out.  Not wild, not like sobbing; just this like sad, quiet, unstoppable flow.  For a long time; like, two hours maybe. And I'm just quiet, just listening, pretty much the whole time.  We leave, finally, walk back to the car and drive home, and it's exhausted itself, he's basically silent by now.  And we hug goodbye in the car, and he looks at me and realizes, and is like: 'My god.  It's been two years, and that's the first time I said anything about any of that to anybody.'  And the look on his face was…I mean, shocked.  Because he saw, immediately, how crazy that was.  That he'd been carrying all that around for so long, just inside himself."

"I never heard that story before," says Jamie after a moment.  "I mean, not like it surprises me.  But still…" he says, shaking his head slowly as he drinks.

"The point," continues Leandro, "is that yeah, he was smart.  That he was able to see, clearly, how crazy it all was.  Tortured, insane, yes.  But y'know, that's why there's a dichotomy between the head and the heart, the mind and the soul.  Seeing it and knowing it is one thing…but actually feeling it is also still something you have to do, have to go through."

"Hmm…" says Jamie, in a way that causes both Leandro and I to look at him.  He's looking off to the side, thinking; arm on the chair's armrest, beer dangling from his hand, clearly focused on some new thought.  He turns back to the table, takes a drink; looks like he's about to say something, thinks better of it, looks off to the side again for awhile, the wheels clearly turning, before he turns back to the table again.

"So," he says; hesitates, takes another drink, sets the bottle down, leans forward, folding his arms on the tabletop. "So, look. Leandro and I are as much in the dark as you are, overall. Yeah, there's a lot we can tell you, for sure. But still, for us...I mean, every now and then he'd come out with some crazy new story that we'd never heard before, and it always gave me this feeling of being, like, iceberg-tippish, like who but the two of them, he and Isobel, know what really happened, what really went on in there. Like, the 'Honeymoon Suite'... ugh," he says, grimacing. "I'd never heard that shit before, had you?" he asks, looking at Leandro, who shakes his head. "Exactly. And that shit was...unpleasant, to say the least. It sounded awful. Terrible. But also, terrible in the biggest sense of that word. Like all that at the end, about telling Matthew everything, and the feeling of the presence of God, of God being in you...I mean, how do you encompass that? How do you have that kind of experience and then, like, try and live a normal life, act like a normal fucking human being?...well, I think the answer is that you don't. What I mean to say is that you can't, that it's not a thing that's actually possible."

He falls into silence, considering what he's about to say next. Reaches for the pack of cigarettes, takes one out; lights it, leans back in his chair again. Takes a long drag, exhales slowly as he gathers the thought into shape, I can see it working across his face. Leandro and I sit quietly, waiting.

"So, let's take what we've got so far. You," he says, gesturing at me with the cigarette, "wake up into this shadow world. No idea how you ended up here, memory gone; or at least, broken into pieces that don't make any sense. You realize you have to get out, that you're not supposed to be here; so you start working at it, taking the broken pieces of memory inside you and figuring out what they are, where they come from. You learn, you grow and change, become stronger; but still, even as you put these memories together, you *feel* them, but they still don't seem like…I mean, you don't *remember* them. Even though they're inside you, you feel like…like they're not actually *yours*." He looks up at me as he says this. I nod; slowly, silently. He holds my gaze for a moment, then reaches for the bottle of beer and takes another drink, another long pull from the cigarette before continuing.

"Here's what I think," he says, reaching forward and stubbing the cigarette out in the ashtray. "I think, that what you said before is correct. That you were that lost part of him. That the place you woke up in, was inside of him somewhere. But that everything has changed now. That you have become something else, and that this world is no longer just a place inside of him. And that because of that, what's going on, now, is that what's happening here, isn't just happening here. That it's affecting the world that he lives in, too. Like you said, that was his voice coming out of you, what else could that have been?…what I think," he says, his voice slowing down, becoming more deliberate now, "is that the— line, between the two worlds, is getting—blurred. That…that they're starting to…come together."

He's looking at his hands, as he says this, held in the air in front of him; palms down, fingers pointing towards each other. As he finishes, his hands move towards each other, slowly, until they are touching, fingers sliding together, interlocking. The motion stops; he looks for a long moment at his hands, together now, before dropping them to the tabletop. His eyes follow his hands, rest there for a couple seconds. He takes a deep breath, exhales with his mouth in an "o", reaches for the bottle and takes a drink, finally.

For a long time no one says anything. I am…I don't know what I am. The implications tumble through me, turn round and round; refuse to settle into coherence. As though the thoughts are turning in a great circle, around and around a stillness, but I can't manage to arrest them, can't manage to move through them; and I know that I know, but until I see it I can't name it, until I name it I can't be it…

"…I think I know," says Leandro. His voice startles me; no, his *existence* startles me. I blink several times as I realize it, press my fingers against my eyes. What is happening to me…

"…think I know when it happened," he's saying. "When you…woke up." He's looking at me with a queer expression in his eyes, as though he knows what's happening in me right now, as though he sees. He doesn't say anything, just looks at me until I nod, briefly, automatically.

"The accident," he says, looks over at Jamie. "Makes sense, doesn't it?"

"Yeah," says Jamie, clarity rising in his face and voice. "Yeah, that makes a lot of sense, actually."

"Do you remember?" asks Leandro, looking back at me. Something swims around inside, images reflected through prisms, behind shadows. Like a creature from the depths, emerging from dark waters…

That woman. Oh my god. Night. Drunk, swerving, careening into the house. Blind panic, he backs out, three houses down the street pulls into the driveway,

236

into the garage. Sits in the dark of the house like an animal, breathing hard. Time passes, no sirens, nothing. Silence…escape. Escaped, oh god, a cascading waterfall of enormous relief, haha oh god, hahaha holy shit, oh jesus…type-type, haha oh my god, whoopsie holy geez, type-type shit oh man ha drunk wow…darkness. Light, eyes open. Head hurts, hell what…oh my god. Oh no. God. Oh my god. Oh no, fuck no, ohmyfuckinggod…

I'm staring at Leandro. I feel like I'm about to fall apart, to break into pieces. But he holds me there. He doesn't blink, doesn't look away. The depth of the calmness in his eyes holds me, keeps me from floating away.

"Shortly after I woke up that morning, I found two emails in my inbox." His voice is the same as his eyes: a lifeline, a grounding force. "I started to read the first one, then looked at the list of ten or fifteen people he'd sent it to, and thought: oh, jesus. It was completely insane. Rambling, incoherent, I can't tell you anything that it actually said; it didn't matter, it was just plain crazy. Then I read the second one, to the same list of people, and it was like the second half of a whole. A deep, profound apology for being so crazy. Intensely emotional, yes; but so obviously…true. Just, full of light, and clarity. I remember going about the rest of my morning, after, waiting for him to call, which he did after another hour or so. But what I remember is the thought, because it was the first time I'd had it, really: 'I think my friend is going to be okay.'"

Silence. And the words begin to come. Not fast, not piling up. Patiently, one-by-one, they rise as I let them out.

"When he woke up and remembered, he panicked. Went into the garage, saw his mother's car and was gripped by fear, possessed by it. His parents were out of town for the weekend and within the dark fear and swirling panic he tried to plot his escape. And suddenly he stopped. Everything inside of him stopped, and then disappeared. And the light came on, and he saw. Saw that he could not hide this, could not run from this. That it was a Thing within him, a dark spirit that had come to live within him; that if he ran from it, he would be running into its embrace, and that it would destroy him. He sat down to deliver his apology, the fullness of his contrition and regret; and as he wrote he saw the names of the people he wrote to, and they rose into the room as he sat there, filling it with love, and he saw what he had built and lived within, his life; saw the depth and richness and truth of the love and realized that he did not want to die. He walked down the street, saw the badly dented car in the driveway, the clear damage to the house and felt the pain and the weight. He knocked on the front door, afraid as he heard footsteps. The door opened, a woman stood there, and as the tears rose in his eyes he pointed and said: I did this. I did this, and I am so sorry. She looked back at him and said: You did this? You got away with this, and yet here you are standing on my doorstep telling me you did this? Come inside, she said. Come and sit with me. She made tea and they sat at her table and she told him about her son who had died a year ago. With tears in her eyes she told him of her eighteen year-old son, the drunken driver in an accident that had taken his friend's life. How lost in the depths of his own guilt and grief, he had afterwards taken his own life. She told him this story, with tears in the eyes that looked at him as she told it, and he did not look away. He heard the silent voice of God within him and felt the heavy burden, the true weight of the heart. And when he left he felt the pain, heavy upon him, and the long hard road ahead. And he knew that everything had changed."

The last of the words comes and goes. I sit in the quiet left behind. Reach for the beer and take a long, slow drink, until the last of it falls from the bottle, into my mouth and down my throat. I look at Jamie and Leandro, each of them in turn. The gifts of life. "Yes," I say quietly. "As they say, a wake-up call. From what grace it came is a mystery, I don't know. But it came, and I heard it, and I woke up. I…remember."

Years. Not days, not weeks, not months. I was asleep, lost inside that darkness…for years. How…how did he survive, without me?…he almost didn't. At the brink a great force arose, a true reckoning, and it woke me. I awoke, and he felt my waking; and though he could not see me, he saw the darkness that had covered me, the darkness within him that had swallowed me up. And still, for years yet I lay there, unseeing, unknowing; while he battled against the dark Enemy within him, fought and strove to find what he had lost. And yet still, when finally the darkness receded, and I could see, could stand and move again; still even then I remembered nothing, still I was lost in this shadow world. Could see only that I could stay here no longer; that it was closing itself around me, and I had to find my way out. But everything that I have walked through, since then…this world has changed, and I am not who I was. I look up, and though I cannot see them I can feel them, moving across the night sky; the migrating stars, constellating and re-constellating, searching for the patterned order of what they are…

"Do you see it?" I ask softly, bringing my gaze back down, meeting their eyes, both of them in turn, as I ask the question: "Do you know who I am?"

239

Both of them sit for awhile, looking back at me. Composed, as always. Calm, as always. Here with me, as they always are, and always have been.

"Yes," says Jamie. "Or at the least, we've had strong suspicions. But you have to understand, that despite all of that—the being lost, the clear pain, the constant searching—despite all of that, when push came to shove, he was there. Always. In any moment, that either of us have ever had, when we needed him, he was there. I have yet to find a time when I turned to him, an occasion of need, that he was not able to rise to meet; completely."

"And it wasn't just that," says Leandro. "It was also that he was still a...joy-creator," and his hands come up as he says this, his voice expands around the words. "When my daughter was born, he was...I mean, unhappy, in and with his life. Fed up, had lost the trail, was ready to leave. But he stayed, for a whole year, to participate in and support that experience. And the bond, that developed between the two of them, the way that they loved each other..." his voice trails off, he shrugs after a moment; looks out at me from under his eyebrows, with a kind of seriousness in his eyes I've never seen before.

"What I'm saying," he says quietly, "is that it was complicated. But yes, we still...saw it. It's that Thing, isn't it. That Thing, that was with you in the dream."

I nod, slowly. "Yes," I say. "Yes, it is. Whatever this world is, whatever it's become, it is the Dark Thing's world, as much as it is mine. And I have to face It. But I still don't fully understand how I came to be lost here, and until I do...I'm running out of time. I can't explain how I know that, but I do. The worlds are merging, and I can't stop it. I have to find the last pieces and put them into place, because I am running out of time."

I see them inside, clearly now. The memories that are not mine, the path he walked while I lay in darkness. The path that I have followed, have re-traced up to this point. But what lies ahead is still disordered, floating; the resonance of what I want is there, I feel it, but I can't extract it from the swirling mass of time, of experience and emotion...

"Tell me. Not the details, I don't need those anymore. Only where he went, what he did, afterwards. I will know it when you name it." My voice has a clarity, an authority that hasn't been there before. I see it reflected in their eyes, and note at the same time that not even that, that reflection, is something I need anymore.

Jamie takes a deep breath. "Okay. Okay, yes. I got this, I think, but jump in if I forget something," he says, Leandro nods. "Colorado. He sells everything he owns, sets off with a car full of what's left. New Orleans, that was the first place...I remember talking with him on the phone at the end of his time there, as he was driving away; trying to decide which job offer I should take, just after law school...sorry, details you don't need...Chicago, was next...then Mexico...then I think Ut—no, wait, he was in Colorado again, briefly, just before that— yeah, okay...then, Utah, the small town in Utah...and he didn't tell anyone where he was going, didn't tell till afterwards where he'd been, that's right I forgot about that part, I had that crazy dream where I was driving around at night, trying to find him...then Portland again, for awhile...and then the big one, then Japan, for —"

"Stop." It rises up before me, the great, nameless vague city...I remember. No longer vague, no longer nameless. Of course. The purity of the isolation. The

241

opposite side of the world. Of course. I see it and I feel it and I reach for it, pull from deep within and push out. The world around us shimmers, shifts, grows. The sounds change, the smells change, the air is humid, dense. Buildings and buildings and buildings, rising into the sky, raised lines that snake amongst the buildings, trains along the lines that speed back and forth. And people, everywhere; people all around us, smoking, talking, walking, hundreds and thousands of people, millions of them, an untold multitude of human bodies moving, interrelating through space and time…

I turn to Leandro and Jamie, both standing, looking everywhere at once; eyes wide, mouths agape.

"Here we are, my friends," I say. "Welcome to Tokyo."

# choices

*"Fuck it," he said. "Fuck you and fuck you and fuck you too," he said. "Bring it the fuck on," he said.*

*Let me tell you a story.*

*Once upon a time there was a boy. At the same time, there was also a girl.*

*Which, is the beginning of many stories. Of many of the best-loved, most oft-repeated stories.*

*The boy was on the threshold of something. He was in an airport, which is an appropriate place to be, when you are on the threshold of something. The threshold was a choice: a simple yes, or a simple no. Two whole possibilities, nothing else outside, or in-between. Of all the choices we ever have to make in this world, it is easiest and simplest when it boils down to those two possibilities, and this was the threshold the boy was on. Two small, simple words: Yes…or…No.*

*The boy stood on the threshold and could not choose. He got on the plane, the plane flew in the air, it landed. He got off the plane and walked into the airport. He saw the girl, walking towards him, and she did not see him. He stood* still and she walked by him, and he saw in her eyes that she had chosen.

He stood, quite still, on the threshold and did not make a choice.

They got into a car and drove. They sat in a restaurant and ate. They got back into the car and drove to the place where the girl lived.

She got out of the car, and she looked at him. He looked back at her and stood on the threshold and said words to her that were nothing.

She looked back at him, and then shut the door of the car and walked away.

He drove away. Or rather, what I mean to say, is that he tried to drive away, but found that he could not.

He drove and his body started to tremble. The world began to slow down, down. His body was shaking now. The tears began to run from his eyes, veritable rivers, the world stopped and broke in two. Now he was sitting in the car on the side of the road, because his body had stopped and was no longer his, and as such could no longer do the things that a body is normally able to do. The world lay broken, and all the things in the world poured out of the two broken pieces and into his body, a thundering cascade that poured into and through his body, and his body was only now a thing through which all the things that had spilled out of the broken world ran as a great river, a tumultuous, swirling, unceasing flow.

But he was only a boy, only a human being, and so he did not know this; did not know that the world had broken in two and that everything it contained was now flowing through him, did not know what was happening to him. He had seen God once, but even so he was still only a boy, only a human being, and did not know what was happening to him.

He could only see one thing. That he had tried to drive away from the girl, and he could not. That his body was no longer his, and he could go no further away from her. He stood on the threshold and said: Yes. And stepped forward, and the door disappeared behind him, as these kinds of doors do when these kinds of decisions are made.

The world came back together, then, as though it had never broken apart. But it was not the same world that it had been before.

In this new world many amazing things happened; things both wonderful and terrible. The boy battled with ghosts and demons, the armies of an Enemy, a shadow creature he knew only as the Dark Thing. Years passed. The boy began to plot his last attempt, his final assault on the Dark Thing's stronghold. He looked into his memory to find the devices and tools, the weapons with which he would need to arm himself. In order to take them out of his memory and make them real, he began to write them down.

When he came across the memory of the threshold, he was struck by it, and he stopped. He stopped, and sat very still, and looked at the memory for a very long time.

**time**

The world rushes by. Slows, regains stillness, coherence as it comes to a stop. The doors open, bodies pass out and other bodies pass in, replace them. The doors close, the world begins to move again, slowly and then faster till again it is rushing by. The world beyond the windows is a gray blur, mostly. Now and then the near buildings recede, the view opens to more buildings beyond, a sea of gray buildings underneath a cloudy sky. Shiny towers of glass and steel clustered here and there, near and in the hazy distance. Gray apartment blocks decorated with fluttering patches and squares of color, the laundry on balconies hung out to dry.

Islands of green. Sometime islands of green, nestled amidst the gray sea.

The dark-haired bodies on the train sit in orderly silence. Some have headphones in their ears, some have books open on their laps. As many as not press buttons on cell phones, thumbs silently tippity-tippity tap, tippity-tippity tap-tap-tap. Reading, peering down at the screen; smile, or frown perhaps. Tippity-tippity tap-

tap-tap. Some stand, one hand grasping the strap over-head, body swaying in rhythm with the train's move-ment; rocking, gently to and fro. Some sleep, heads nodding onto chests, drooping sideways onto shoulders.

I slide my hand into my pocket, retrieve the phone. Look at it briefly, considering. I type:

**Where are you. I need to see you**.

I press Send, slip the phone back into my pocket.

The train slows, stops; the doors open, the streams of bodies, the doors close, the train slowly gathers speed again. Station after station after station, the rhythm repeats itself, the still dark-haired bodies and the blurred world beyond the windows rushing by. The streams of bodies begin to dwindle, to thin out, the number of empty seats gradually increasing with each stop. I cross and re-cross my legs, fold patient hands in my lap, as the world passes and time passes all around me.

Ding. End of the line.

I exit the train, exit the station, turn right. The air is cleaner here, cooler here as it flows inland, carrying the fading breath of the sea.

I hear it before I see it, a murmuring voice, a dim roar. Then I am standing on the low sea-wall, looking out, the blue-gray of waves rolling, curling whitecaps, the water racing up the smooth sand until the momen-tum dies, the sheet of water sliding back, rushing into itself, all beneath palaces of darkening clouds piled high into the further sky.

I sit down, on top of the wall; cross-legged, hands in my lap. Sit staring out across the water: into the rhythm of waves, the lost depths of evening sky.

I remember her eyes.

The dimming blue light of the surrounding world,

day fading into night. Standing on the sand, suddenly no longer walking. The way her lips moved, mouth came so slightly apart as the wind blew dark strands of hair across her face. Staring back, into the depths of the feeling as it rose into her eyes.

The phone trembles in my pocket. I pull it out, press the button.

The message is a single word:

**Why**.

I stare at the screen until it goes dark. Put the phone back into my pocket, sit for awhile longer, thinking. I stand up, brush the sand off my pants, step off the wall and walk back the way I came, the roar dying into the murmur behind me.


I turn the key in the lock, pull the door open. Step inside, set the bag of groceries on the floor as I bend down to unlace and remove my shoes; pick up the bag, push the door closed behind me with my foot as I stand up.

"Well?" says Jamie as I walk into the room. He and Leandro are sitting at the table, beers in hand; I shake my head as I walk past them, set the bag of groceries on the kitchen counter. "Nope," I say as I pull items out of the bag, set them down. I cross the kitchen to the small refrigerator, open it, take the rest of the bag's contents out one-by-one and place them inside. I take a can of beer out before I shut the door, turn and lean back against the refrigerator as I crack it open, take a long drink.

"Nice and cold. Thanks for getting," I say as I push forward off the refrigerator, walk the couple steps to the table and sit down.

"Yeah man," says Jamie. "We weren't sure which kind to buy, but figured they were all probably pretty much the same."

"They pretty much are," I say, taking another drink. "They all pretty much taste like beer."

"So no luck, huh?" says Leandro.

I shake my head again. "Not surprised though," I say after a bit. "Understandable. It's going to take some...coaxing, is probably a good word. What about you guys, how was your day?"

They look at each other, shrug. "Um...trains, clean, getting lost, more trains, more getting lost, more clean, eighty billion people everywhere..." says Jamie, his voice trailing off as he shakes his head.

"Sounds about right," I say, laughing.

"The clean thing is crazy," says Leandro, wonder in his voice. "It's like no one knows how to litter, like it doesn't exist here. Even cigarettes; all those people outside the train stations, smoking at the designated spots, all of them throwing their butts in the ashcans. It's awesome, and also slightly creepy?...dunno, man. Pretty interesting place."

"Yeah," I say. "There are rules here, and people follow them; the phrase 'to a fault' definitely comes to mind. I mean, clearly part of it comes from an over-desire to not offend, overcompensating for remote possibilities of offending that barely, if at all, exist. But it's also just about respect; perceiving animating spirits in not just people, but things and objects. Which, is correct if you think about it: an ashcan, for example, is a shaped thing, a thing that has a purpose, a utility and value. It's not just surrendering of ego, it's also a surrendering of your time; to give your time, in the form of your respect, back to the world around you. It was...

one of the things he came to appreciate the most, I think, about his time here." I take a long drink, set the can back down, stand up. "We're all hungry, yes? Gonna make some food," I say, crossing to the fridge, opening it and taking things out. I fill a pot with water, put it on to boil. Take out a cutting board, a knife, start slicing up leeks and napa cabbage.

"So this is where he lived, huh? It's not, like, super-tiny," says Jamie after awhile.

"Yeah," I say. I tear open a packet of powdered broth, pour it into the pot, along with some soy sauce. "Not the only place he lived, but the last, the longest, and the best. Fairly central, cool part of town. Had a Japanese roommate, really great guy. Everything he could need or want, and then some, pretty much." I put the sliced leeks and cabbage into the boiling water, along with several clumps of thin, white enoki mushrooms; cut open two packets of thick, fresh udon noodles and put them in the pot as well, turn the heat down. After a few minutes I turn the heat off, ladle everything into three bowls, sprinkle bonito flakes on top of each bowl; carry the bowls to the table, set them down, along with three sets of chopsticks. I sit down, pick up my beer and raise it in toast, Leandro and Jamie follow suit: "Bon appetit, my friends," I say as our cans meet in the center of the table. "It's not exactly traditional, but it should still get the job done."

Jamie picks up his chopsticks, takes a clump of enoki and puts it in his mouth; chews, swallows, nods. "It's good man," he says appreciatively. The only sound for awhile is noodles being slurped, sucked down.

"Y'know," says Leandro after awhile, "you don't have to…hang out with us, or whatever. I mean, you said time was running out. We'll be fine, you should do whatever you have to do, y'know."

I pick up the beer, tilt my head back as I swallow the last of it down. I get up, take another can from the fridge, pop it open and sit down again. "I don't have much time left, it's true," I say as I pick up the chopsticks. "But that doesn't mean I can hurry, either. There's a process to everything: making food, sitting with people to enjoy it. The time I don't have anymore is the time to make mistakes. But I still have to do things the right way." I stop, udon noodles dangling from the end of my chopsticks, poised above the bowl. "It's not that I'm not worried, or afraid," I say quietly, without looking up. "It's that I can't afford, any longer, to be worried or afraid." After a moment I bend to the bowl, bring the noodles to my mouth, slurp them down. We finish the meal in silence.

Later I'm standing on the balcony smoking, alone. The cloudy sky is a dark crimson above, the lights of the city below, stretching into the distance. It's different, this time. Yes, much of the body of this memory is still dislocated, something within me that is not mine.

But not all of it.

I stub the cigarette out in the ashtray, step back into the room, slide the door shut behind me. I change into pajama pants and a clean t-shirt, walk across the kitchen to the bathroom; brush my teeth, wash my face off with cold water. I pat my face dry, hang the towel on the rack, and stand for a long moment; looking into the mirror, into the deep eyes of memory.

I walk back into the bedroom, pick up the phone. I type:

**Because you saw me. Because I remember**.

I press Send, put the phone down. I turn off the light, slide my body between the blanket and the thin futon mattress on the floor.

I turn over on my side, the way I did once before. She is almost there next to me, but is not there. Her lips do not part, slightly. I do not hear her soft voice, almost a whisper, saying Come closer...

I close my eyes, waiting for sleep to take me away.


The thin line of smoke, curling lazily into the air. Clink of cups on saucers, some kind of quiet, moody jazz music from the stereo, conversations in low tones. I take a last drag, lean forward slowly and grind the cigarette out in the ashtray, exhaling through my nose as I do so. I stand, drink the last of my coffee, set the cup down. Pull a couple bills out of my wallet and leave them on the table, walk outside. I turn right as I exit, take another right into the first street I come to, walking away from the main road. The shops and storefronts dwindle, become less frequent. After awhile I turn left, into one of the narrower streets opening off to either side.

The neighborhood is quiet, the narrow road wide enough for only a single car. It curves, meandering slightly uphill and then back down again, past simple residential fronts, potted plants and flowers, the tops of trees poking up from behind the tightly packed buildings now and then. The thin cloud-cover overhead, the afternoon full of calm, gray light. I take random right and left turns, losing myself in the rhythm of my stride, the momentum of my body.

I turn into a street that broadens somewhat, flat, blank facades of three and four story homes flanking the street on either side. Everything is still, my footsteps on the pavement the only sound. The road curves, almost imperceptibly, a long slow bend as I walk, continue walking along. It straightens, finally, and as it does so I see, maybe a hundred yards ahead where the street ends, the high stone wall, the trees rising behind it. I come to it, walking out from amongst the buildings, turn right and walk down the road alongside the wall; turn left at the wall's corner, continuing to follow it, walk a bit further on and come to a stop at the tall, heavy wooden gate, its doors standing open. I turn and face it, bring my feet together, my hands at my sides. I bow, slightly, and walk forward, through the gates into the exterior courtyard. I walk the twenty paces or so and stand before the main entrance. A tall, dark structure, four massive wooden pillars supporting a pagoda-style roof, over a gently arching wooden bridge. Four large paper lanterns, red with large black japanese characters, hang down from the roof, over the four corners of the bridge. I stand with my feet together again, arms at my sides. I bring my hands up, together into the position of prayer and clap, once; bow forward, more deeply this time; raise up, let my hands fall to my sides again, and walk forward across the wooden bridge, passing between the inner walls. I step off the bridge and stop, take in my surroundings.

There are several large trees, off to my left a pond. Walkways composed of large, flat individual stones wind through the grass, past small flowering shrubs, next to stone deities. The space enclosed by the ten-foot high stone walls is meandering, rambling, yet composed at the same time. Carefully tended here, left to its own devices there. A handful of buildings, structures, varying in size and degree of ornamentation. I breathe in slowly, slowly let the breath back out. Walk forward, take the branching path to the right, and stop before the small, simple wooden building. I step onto the porch, stop before the open door. Remove my shoes, place them together just outside the entrance. Breathe out as I bow down with prayerful hands, in as I raise up. I stand still for a moment, and then step inside.

The small, close room is dark, filled with flickering candlelit shadows and the smell of incense. On either side of me are seated gods, human-sized, rendered in dark wood; close enough to touch, four against the walls on either side, regarding me out of silent, impassive wooden eyes. Beyond them, directly before me on a dais raised above sits the Buddha; golden and still, meditative hands in his cross-legged lap, surrounded by candles and garlanded with flowers. I walk forward to the cushion that sits a few feet before the dais, slowly come down to my knees; lean onto my hands, bend forward, folding my body down until my forehead comes to rest on the wooden floor.

Time passes.

I raise up, come to a sitting position, my hands resting now on my upper thighs, and am still again.

The heavy-lidded golden eyes watch me, even as they watch the depths of things beyond me. I realize that the question I came here to ask is gone. That it's a question that doesn't exist, and never did.

At least, not for me.

I bring my hands together before my heart, bow my head. Then I stand, turn and walk back out the door. Outside I stop, turn and face the interior, and bow one last time. I put my shoes back on, bending to tie the laces, and I walk away.

I'm standing on the train, holding on to the strap that hangs down from the bar when the message comes. The phone trembles, with my free hand I reach into my pocket and pull it out, press the button, look at the screen:

**Tonight. Where you found me the first time, before**.

I slip the phone back into my pocket and stand, swaying slightly, watching out the window as the world rushes by.



"Why is there a line?"

"What did you expect? I told you, people call this the 'biggest club in Asia'."

"Yeah, but c'mon, can't you make us VIP's or something?"

"…We've been through this. Have to do things—"

"—The right way, I know, I know, blah blah blah," Jamie says, looking around. "Well it better be worth it."

"What are you complaining for, old man? This line is, like, fifteen people long. We'll be waiting five minutes, max," says Leandro.

"Because, I am ready, to get my groove on," Jamie says patiently, as though explaining something to a small child. He shimmies to the left, and to the right, and back again, Leandro guffaws, Jamie executes a spin move. "I'm just sayin', bro. Watch out, ladies of Japan, 'cause it's on tonight." Leandro sticks his tongue out, pronounces a loud raspberry: "pffffbbbtt."

Minutes later we're inside, ordering drinks at one of several bars. I pay, distribute the tall, ice-filled glasses of gin and tonic amongst the three of us. "Cheers," I say. "What?" says Leandro, leaning in, cupping his ear. "He

255

said 'cheers', dumbass!" shouts Jamie, his voice rising, barely, above the din.

The music thump, thumps, buzzes. I lead them on a tour, upstairs and back down again, through sweaty dancing bodies and people standing clustered around tall tables, room after room, the music changing from one to the next. We move, slowly, through the main dance floor, the ceiling high above lost in the smoky haze and blue and purple light; the music is less music than simply an all-surrounding cavern of sound, vibrating in my body, resonating in my bones. There is space between the dancers here, bodies operating according to their own responses, own resonant individual worlds.

Outside we find a spot against the railing, at the edge of the large covered wooden deck, looking out across the water.

"So what, this is like, a bay or something?...a harbor?"

"Yes, detective, it is indeed a body of water," says Leandro.

"Suuuuckk...it," Jamie replies. He turns, back against the railing, sips his drink. "This place is ginormous. And everyone's so...cool," he says, his gaze traveling across the crowd. "It's like they were born to go to clubs like this."

"You feel that marinol pill kicking in yet? I do," says Leandro, scrunching his face up and blinking several times. Jamie laughs. "I dunno man. Probably. I need another drink, and then I wanna dance." "The big sound-cave room?" "Sure, why not. You coming?" Jamie asks, I shake my head. "Go have fun," I say; and then, "You know you might have to find your own way home." "Yeah, okay. Well, good luck," he says, meeting my eyes. I watch as the two of them wend their way through the crowd, disappear.

I finish my drink, make my way to the bar at one side of the deck, order another; turn, push my way through bodies, find a spot at the end of a thin, rectangular standing table on the opposite side. I light a cigarette, sip my drink as I lean back against the table, scan the crowd of people talking, laughing, gesticulating expansively. Pretty girls, cool boys. Make-up just this side from too extravagant, t-shirts hanging off shoulders, thin belts around colorful print dresses, necklaces and earrings and fabulous shoes. Jeans and immaculate sneakers, shorts and fancy socks, vests, gelled hair with every strand in the right place, hats cocked just so. A couple of giggling girls approach; I'm polite, I smile, but don't give them much else; a third girl comes over, says something quickly, all three wander off, one of them looking back over her shoulder at me, smiling, as the crowd swallows them up.

"She's cute. Why don't you go with her."

I turn, forgetting everything else. She's standing there, on the other side of the table. Our eyes meet, for a long moment, before she breaks it, suddenly, looking away, re-assembling her composure. She sips her drink from the straw, looks past me, makes a little, half-hearted waving-off motion with her hand: "There she goes. She's going to get away if you don't follow." I stand with my hand on my drink, resting on the table, don't say anything. She meets my eyes, the resistance begins to melt, she looks quickly down and away again. "I hadn't realized there was anyone else here," I say quietly. She makes a sound that struggles to be exasperated, fails. "Why are you here?" she asks, still looking away, the emotion in her voice. "Because I never wanted to leave. Because I thought about you every day for a long,

257

long time." She looks up at me now, finally, and everything that I remember is in her eyes. "Can we please leave," she says softly, after a moment. "I don't want to be here anymore."

We make quiet electric love. Her eyes close and she sighs, her long dark hair falling across her face, her hands clenching and unclenching against my chest. My hands contain her, strong around her slim waist, pressed with force against her heart. We flow as one rhythmic body, in tune with the moon and the stars and the beautiful things in this world, she whimpers, cries out softly when she comes, and I come, and she collapses down upon me; breathing hard, her head resting in the hollow just above my chest.

I wrap my arms around her, and we lie that way together without saying anything for a long while.

"Why are you here," she says, finally. "This isn't about me. It's about her." She speaks softly, only asking, saying nothing else.

"I don't know. I'm…figuring it out as I go. I don't…I don't know what it's about, anymore."

"What do you mean," she says. She unfolds, moving to one side, nestles in against me, her head on my shoulder, her arm across my chest.

"It's changed so much, I've changed so much. When I saw you before, I was still so lost; recognized you in a way, but still didn't, couldn't really remember."

Her hand balls into a fist, raps a light admonishment on my chest. "I can't believe you made me do that; sit there with those two other women, and talk about you like that. I was furious with you."

"…I remember. I didn't know what I was doing.

That was at the very beginning, and it just happened, just came out of me. You scared me; you were so angry, and it scared me."

"Good," she says, rapping my chest again. After a moment she rises slightly, slides forward, kisses me. Her tongue touches my teeth, retreats; her mouth closes against mine, full lips moving with gentle need, feeling. She slips down, nestles against me again. "Do you remember me now," she says quietly.

"Yes. Very much so." I breathe in deeply, sigh it back out. "That's what's different. Everything else that's in there, it's like it happened to someone else. But with you, it's...it's mine. I remember."

"Mm...I'm going to get some water." She rises, with her foot fishes my pajama pants off the floor, slips them on; bends over, picks up my t-shirt, pulling it over her head as she walks across the room, I see her body silhouetted against the light as she slides open the door. Soft footsteps, the sound of running water, soft footsteps returning. She closes the door behind her, makes her way across the room in the near-darkness; sits down with her back against the wall, her legs falling across my body. "Drink?" I nod, raise up on one elbow, reach out and take the offered glass; I drink, return the glass, lie back, bunching up the pillow behind my head, twisted slightly to the right so I can see her. Dim light from the night of the city seeps into the dark of the room from the balcony behind me, tracing the contours of her face, the curve of her neck. I can feel, as much as see, that she is thinking.

"Do you remember when you would talk about her, with me?" she asks.

"No...did that happen? I don't remember that at all."

"Mm…what *do* you remember?"

"I remember when we met; kind of turning, and seeing you, and realizing that you were standing there next to me…well, but more like, this might sound weird, but more like realizing that you existed."

"No. I mean no, not weird. What else?"

"I remember you kissing me on the cheek as you got off the train later. I remember your face, like I really finally saw all of you, when we were standing on the beach. I remember sitting in the restaurant with you, next to you, making up little games and stories together while we waited for our food, feeling you at my side. I remember standing outside the train station, at night… it was raining, in a scattered kind of way; and windy, and the wind blew the raindrops across your face, and we just stood there, everyone hurrying around us…and you would look at me, and then away again, and then back…and I remember what you said, later, when we were alone together. But…I don't just remember it. It was…like I'd never heard someone speak before, almost, like I'd never heard a human voice say words until that moment. And when—when we kissed…" I look up into the dark, remembering. "It was like…like everything went away, all the lights went off. And—and something swam around, inside the darkness, and then I was—alive. And it—it shocked me…the truth of being alive. How…beautiful you were, and how I could somehow contain that beauty within my arms, within my own body. How you were you, and I was me…how we were not the same thing but still were the same thing, together…"

I stop talking, find I can't say anymore. She sits very still, doesn't say anything for awhile. Finally she reaches out, finds my hand, her fingers curl around mine. She sighs, shakes her head.    "Of course you don't remember…what happened to you? What in the world happened to you?"

"That's…that's what I'm trying to figure out."

"What…what I said before," she says slowly, "with those two other women.  I was upset, and maybe the words I used were…dramatic, I guess.  But they were also…that's what it felt like.  You would be there with me, and then you—you weren't, I don't know how else to say it.  Like you disappeared, just went away some-where."

"So that's what happened when I talked about—about her, you're saying. That I was—"

"—Gone," she finishes.  She thinks for a moment, nods her head once, emphatically.  "Yes.  It was so strange, I didn't know how to understand it. Your words changed, your voice changed.  Your eyes changed, like there was this—this cloud, that came into your eyes. That was the worst part.  You were right there, in front of me, but I…I couldn't see you anymore.  And as time went by, it was more and more like that.  That's when I started pushing you, deliberately trying to make you angry.   And it worked; it wasn't fun, but at least it worked, it made you come back.   But it also never lasted, and it wasn't…I couldn't go on like that.  If the only way I could reach you was to make you angry…I couldn't go on like that.  I couldn't figure it out…" She's silent for a bit, squeezes my hand.  "It started to feel like a dream.  And when it did, I knew I had to let it go."

I don't know what to say.   The emotion rising, welling up.  I let go of her hand, with my thumb and fingers press against my eyes.

"What is it," she says softly.   "Tell me.   Tell me what's happening inside you right now."

261

I can't say anything at first. When I speak my voice is thick, as though the words are heavy stones I am forcing out. "I don't know what to—I'm so…so upset. So—so sad, and at the same time so…angry." I press harder against my eyes, take in a deep breath and hold it until I can't hold it anymore, it comes rushing, shuddering out. "So…*angry*…and I have no idea, who or what to be angry with, and nowhere for it to go. It's this—dark fire, burning me up from the inside, but I—I can't let it out, because I'm so afraid of who it might hurt, of what it might do. I don't want to hurt someone again. I can't hurt someone again, can't go through that again…"

"Sweetheart," she says, her voice filled with feeling. She moves, kneels beside me; reaches for my hand, pulls it away from my eyes, holds it; with her other hand she cradles my face, bending over me, looking into my eyes. "Who did you hurt? What are you afraid of?"

"Her. You. Everyone. Everyone who's watched me disappear, the way you did, over and over again."

"And who do you think that hurts the most?" she asks quietly. She's staring at me, into me; the truth a light coming out of her eyes, into my body. "You can't go on like this. You can't stay here, in this place, this world any longer. Maybe it's a place you got lost in, maybe it's a place you needed to go. I don't know; those are your questions, I can't answer them for you. But you can't stay here any longer; I do know that, and I know you know it too."

Her words follow the path of her eyes, down deep inside, and unlock a door.

I look, and I see.

I remember.

She sits back as I move, sit up, facing her.

"It was you. You…you were the one, who made me

remember. Who made me realize...you said to him, 'What are you doing? Where is your life, and what are you doing?'...and I heard you. I was trapped in here, and I heard you say that. And I saw it, and I saw that I had to get out. It...it was you."

She stares back at me for a long moment, then rises, stands up slowly. The shirt comes off over her head, the pajama pants drop to the floor. She kicks the blanket off of me, steps one foot across my body; lowers herself down, her legs wrap around my waist. I reach out; my hands hold her, her arms come across my shoulders, fingers interlace across the back of my neck. Skin-on-skin, body against body...

A small, beautiful smile comes into her face. She nods, once, as she looks into my eyes. "Because I loved you," her soft voice just above a whisper. "And you loved me, too."

And as we kiss my heart speaks, and my heart is saying forever.


I blink a few times, rub my eyes. The pale light of morning. I turn my head, see the pillow next to me.

She's gone, as I knew she would be.

I throw off the blanket, stand and stretch, reaching for the ceiling. I put on a pair of sweatpants, pick up the t-shirt she wore; bring it to my face, close my eyes and breathe in, before pulling it over my head, down across my body. The phone buzzes from where it sits, on top of the wooden chest of drawers. I pick it up, press the button, look at the screen:

**Go and finish what you started. Maybe I will see you again, on the other side someday**.

I look at the words until the screen goes dark; set

263

the phone back down, walk across the room and slide open the door. "Smells like breakfast in here," I say as I walk into the kitchen, take a seat at the table. Leandro walks over, puts his hand on the top of my head, with the other sets a cup of coffee on the table in front of me. "Coffee for you, my friend...so how did your night go?" I pick up the cup of coffee, take a drink. "Mm. It went well." He pushes down slightly, squeezes before letting go. "Good," he says, walking back over to the stove. "Hope you woke up with an appetite, 'cause it's just about eatin' time."

Jamie leans over from where he's sitting next to me, sniffs my shoulder, sits back smiling. "I thought so. You smell like woman," he says. I smile, nod. "It's true, I do."

Leandro walks over, sets plates full of scrambled eggs and bacon down on the table, next to the plate already piled high with waffles and the bowl full of strawberries. He walks away, returns again with three plates and knives and forks, distributes them to each of us and takes a seat, sitting up straight. "Breakfast is served, ladies," he says politely, and reaches for the plate of eggs and starts spooning them onto his plate.

I pick up a strip of bacon, take a bite. "Mm. Yum-yum. Thank you guys, what a great thing to wake up to."

"It was mostly Leandro. I made the waffles, though."

"If by 'made the waffles' you mean 'operated the waffle-iron', then I guess yes, that statement is true."

"Hey man, we all have different talents. You see a plate full of waffles in front of you or not?"

"I do in fact see that plate, O waffle-iron master."

"Exactly. Now shut up and pass me the

strawberries, please." Leandro nods, passes the bowl over, pulls it back just as Jamie reaches for it. Jamie looks at him, shakes his head, looks at me. "What a bitch." Leandro giggles, sets the strawberries down next to Jamie. Jamie pops one in his mouth, looks at Leandro, shakes his head again.

"So whatsh nexsht?" asks Leandro, through his mouthful of waffles. He chews, swallows, reaches for the syrup. "Assuming we're done here, yeah?"

"Yes, we are," I say. I take a drink of coffee, set the cup back down. I think for a moment, then get up and walk back into the bedroom. I squat down, next to the canvas shoulder bag lying on the floor; open the flap, reach in and take out the yellow pad. I walk back into the kitchen, sit back down. I hold out the pad to Jamie, who looks back at me for a moment before he takes it. "Do you recognize this?" I ask.

He nods, slowly, as he scans the pages, flips through them. "Yeah man," he says quietly. "I got more than one letter from him on paper like this. That's...that's definitely his handwriting. Where did you get this?" he asks, passing the pad to Leandro.

"It was...it was a long time ago, now," I say; thinking, remembering. It does seem like a long time ago; a long, long time ago...I shake my head, pick up the coffee, take a drink before I continue. "It was near— near the beginning, of all—all of this, I guess. Something...frightened me, and I ran. Dark passages, tunnels, I'm not sure how to describe it. And then I found this...this room, and there was a desk, and a lamp, and this was on the desk. It was the room, that he and— and Isobel, lived in, I think. But...but the pad, I could tell it was for me. I could tell, I can't explain how, but I knew that it had been...left there, I guess you could say,

265

for me."

"So you read it, then," says Leandro. He doesn't look up at me, he's scanning the pages closely, reading.

"…Yeah. It was—it was difficult. Honestly, terrifying at first. Brought out these deep, intense emotions that I didn't understand, couldn't…couldn't hold, within myself. But I knew it was important, that was obvious; and the more I read, I started to see that it was a…a kind of story, I guess."

Leandro looks up at me, back at the pad, his eyes narrowing with focus. "Hm…that's so…" He trails off, shakes his head. "Weird. I think I know what this is," he says, looking up at me. "He…tried, once, to write it down. A long time ago now, when he was living in Colorado. But he stopped, at a certain point. Said that he couldn't do it; that it was still happening, faster than he could write it, and that it felt like it was never going to end. So, he stopped. But…I mean, I think that's what this is," he says, handing the pad back to me. I take it, look at it for a moment; get up from the table, walk back into the bedroom, slip it back into the bag. I walk back into the kitchen, sit down, pick up my fork and cut off a piece of waffle; put it in my mouth and chew, slowly, thinking. I swallow, take a drink of coffee.

"It…it did end, though, didn't it. There was—there was a final break, between them." I look at Leandro as I say it, he nods after a moment. "Yes. It took a long time, but yes, there was," he says quietly. He looks down, looks back up at me, that serious expression in his eyes. "There's one more thing that you should know. Maybe you do, already. I thought about it, sometime in the last few days. About her brother. *That* brother." He pauses, and I feel the memory, silently rising up. "Just before the accident—I mean, I think this is part of why

266

the accident happened; that it...overloaded him, I guess. Her brother killed himself. Suicide. She called him, told him. He went to see her, flew out the next day. Then he came back, a few days later, and..." He breaks off.

I close my eyes. Gently, take careful hold of the memory within myself, and put it where it belongs. Take in a long, deep breath; slowly, let it all the way back out, before I open my eyes again. I look at Leandro. "Thank you," I say, my voice clear and quiet. "You were right. To tell me."

I take a drink of coffee, set the cup down. "Now let's eat this delicious breakfast, while it's still warm. It's going to be our last meal together. It's...time." No one says anything for a bit. Jamie reaches out, his hand on my shoulder. "You sure man?" he asks. I look back at him, and I see the expression shift, change across his face. "Okay," he says, squeezing my shoulder as he looks back at me. "Okay."

Leandro smiles, picks up a piece of bacon. "Cheers. Bon Voyage Breakfast," he says. Jamie and I each pick up a piece of bacon, we touch them in the center of the table; Leandro giggles, Jamie smiles. "You dumbass," he says, and we all dig in. It's as good, in the end, as any meal I've ever had.


We're standing in a field, in the rose and soft blue light of twilight. Leandro with his broad lumberjack shoulders, Jamie with his delicate, almond eyes. They stand facing me.

"Where will you go now?" I ask.

Jamie shrugs. "Back to wherever we came from, I guess."

Leandro leans on Jamie's shoulder. "Don't worry about me and Lil Buddy here. We'll be fine." Jamie just shakes his head and smiles.

"Okay. Thank you," I say. "Thanks for everything. All of it."

"We all need help, we're all connected," says Jamie. "Nobody does anything on their own, not really. Don't forget that."

"I won't," I say.

"Good luck," says Leandro.

I nod. I look at them standing there, look for one last time. And I take a deep breath and close my eyes.

# IV

## truth and shadows

*"What are you doing?  Where is your life, and what are you doing?"*

*The worlds are merging.  Dreams being re-dreamed, words and voices emerging from forgotten places; building, making, saying until the thing is made and solid and true.*

*The world stopped and broke in half, and then came back together as though it had never broken.  But it was not the same world that it had been before.  He wrote and he wrote and he wrote, but it went on beyond him, a distance he could not travel, could not cross.  She came back and the wound opened, she came again and the blood ran from his body, gathered in a pool on the floor.*

*Something is wrong inside of me, he thought.  Something is deeply wrong, inside of me.  Why can't I let it go.  He tried many things.  He tried this thing, he tried that thing.  Each thing broke, into many pieces such that they were broken and could not be put back together again.  Finally the fire came, from nowhere; finally the fire rose up within him, and he shaped it in the form of an arrow and drew back the bowstring taut, and the arrow flew.  It ended, then. It ended, and he was finally again alone.*

*Alone with It. Alone, but not alone. The dark spirit yet within him, the shadow that covered his eyes, the dark voice that came from his mouth.*

*Why, he thought, exhausted. How, he wondered, weary in his very bones. Will it ever end, will it ever be a thing that ends, he thought, his strength fading in the depths of the night.*

*He wandered, went across the world. One night felt something old, something forgotten, move within him. Felt it awaken, as he looked into her eyes. What are you doing, she said later, with frustrated anger. Where is your life, and what are you doing.*

*She went away. The words remained, echoed. But they did not fade as echoes do. They remained, and he looked up and saw that the stars had broken free of their moorings, had been set adrift across the sea of the night sky.*

*A chance and a hope. He sat down, and picked up the pen and began to write.*

*This is crazy, he thought after a time. I am fucking crazy, he thought as he stopped, put down the pen. He sat and stared at the words on the page, shook his head, picked up the pen again. Fuck it, he thought. Bring it on, bring all the shit, empty your fucking arsenal he thought as he bent to the page. Bring it the fuck on.*

*The words began to make shapes, the swirling mass of time and memories and emotions began to distill into recognizable lines, shapes, figures.*

*Within a shadow world, a body awoke. A body, a figured body awoke; looked around itself and said, I have to get out.*

*He watched. He watched the figured body move within the shadow world; watched and wondered. He bent words into obstacles and put them in the figured body's path, led it*

271

into halls of mirrors, sent it ghosts. Who are you, he wondered, as he watched the figured body fight and struggle, gain strength and find resolve. Watched as it wandered through the landscapes of his own memories; as it found things, picked up and studied objects he himself had long forgot.

He watched, engrossed, in a kind of awe. And he began to feel something strange; something strange happening, somehow deep within him and around him at the same time.

What is in this way we tell ourselves stories, he wondered. This power inside the way we change, and grow.

This world has changed, said the figured body. This world has changed, and I am not who I was.

The worlds are merging, and time is running out.

Do you know who I am, said the figured body, softly.

He watched, almost afraid to breathe. Will it ever end, will it ever be a thing that ends.

It's time, said the figured body. And he watched, as it stood in a field in the rose and soft blue light of twilight, and closed its eyes.

# gray land

The sky is gray. Everything here is gray, blackened stone and dark, dead trees; a country of dead things and ashes. The cold wind rises, rattles through long-dead branches. I shiver, blow into my cold hands; pull the hood of my jacket up over my head, and start walking.

The only sound is my quiet footsteps. No cracking sticks or crunching leaves in the gray dirt. The forest closes in around me. Nothing moves, nothing breathes; even the wind now has disappeared, gone silent.

What is this place, I find myself wondering as I walk. What was this place. Was it ever alive. Was it ever a place where things took breath and grew, ever a place where things became other things. I stop, place my hand against the dark trunk of the nearest tree. Cold. Lifeless. If anything ever moved through this body it is long-since vanished and has left no trace of itself behind. I move on.

The forest grows thicker, dark branches cluster over-head as I wend my way through the trunks of the trees. I feel things watching, begin to glimpse movement out of the corners of my eyes. I stop, turn and look around. All is still and silent. But when I begin to walk again I feel them out there; watching, following.

I begin to hear them, now. Murmured whispers, pleas. Stop. Help me. Stay, please stay here. Please don't leave. I hear crying; something sadly, softly crying somewhere close at hand. How can you do this. How can you just go on and leave me.

I don't stop, don't turn my head. The voices begin to grow in number, to cluster closer around, a wretched multitude of whispered sadness and agony. I plunge forward, feel the icy breathing at my back, the long, despairing fingers clawing at my heart, dragging me to the ground, and I am running now; running, running, darting through the trees, leaping over fallen logs, flying across the ground. I am burning inside, it is rising, spreading out from within the core of my body, I run faster and the heat grows, faster and faster and the trees around me begin to burst forth in fire, to bloom with flames. The icy fingers retreat, the voices of despair turn to cries of fear and rage. I feel the power within surge, coil like a whip, I spring into the air and lash out, and the forest explodes all around me.

I land in a crouch, stand up slowly. Bits of debris rain down. The ground in a wide circle around me is flat, scoured clean. Thirty yards away the trees burn, madly, I am standing in the center of a towering ring of fire. I raise my hand and reach out and the flames vanish. The trees stand black, smoking.

"Your ghosts and demons, your shadow creatures are nothing to me any longer. I am coming for you," I say into the surrounding silence.

The Dark Thing's laughter booms, rolls through the air like thunder. Jagged bolts of lightning open cracks in the sky, a cold, torrential rain falls down like a curtain. The trees hiss, the water runs in rivulets down my face.

*Come*, whispers that hollow voice. *I am waiting for you.*

*Come to me.*

I pull the hood closer over my head and begin walking.

Vapor rises from the ground, tendrils of mist snake their way through the air. The rain slows, dissipates, finally altogether ceases. I walk forward through the fog. Water drips, drips from the invisible trees I can no longer see. The sound begins to fade until I hear a last, quiet drop somewhere, and then all is silence. I keep walking.

I feel it before I see it, feel it looming. The fog opens, recedes, and there it stands before me. A massive edifice of dark stone. There is no ornamentation; no towers, no battlements, no spires reaching up. There are no guards, no sentries. Only an enormous black box, sheer stone walls rising from the gray dirt.

An open doorway waits, at the base of the wall and directly in front of me, a dark tunnel. I stop, unsling the bag over my shoulder and sit down on the cold, hard ground. I take the yellow pad out, flip the pages over until I come to the last entry, scan it briefly:

*...In the end I felt collapsed by waiting; felt like I simply gave in to counting the days and the hours, checking them off in my mind, my awareness fixed on the moment when I'd see her shape walking toward me again.*

It ends as I remember. I flip the page over. As I expected, what was a blank page before is no longer blank, now filled with words.  I take a deep breath, let it back out as I begin to read.

# what we see and do not see

*Thirteen years have come, and gone.   Since that first night, the delight as he realizes that this "feeling of cooperatively-motivated   movements   is   why   people   dance   in pairs"...more than thirteen years.*

*Shed the exhaustion, rise up on the threshold.   Processes of becoming that culminate, the delicate bloom emerging from the end of the long green stem.*

*No one can see the future, this thing that we move toward with plans and hope.   No one knows.*

*But there are things within the body, secrets within the body.   In the moments that arise, it is not a process of thought that makes the choice.   Time unfolds, then, across the long years, the memories and new experiences create visions. Reveal an architecture of choices, based on reason and faith; a stunned silence at the possible implications, the unfolding panorama of plans and hope.   The view takes the breath away, the struggle to accept what is within the body, what it sees, what it knows.*

*A boy is born into light.   Into an abundance of gifts and opportunities, a world of protected joy.   Beyond that world* he senses the dark universe. He grows, feels the power within him, the power to name is the same as the power to shape, to create. Pain, in the surrounding world, darkness in the world around him. The gifts and opportunities are potential. Forgiveness, love; the power to heal, to make pain and hurt go away.

A girl is born into darkness. Into a world of sadness and pain, a darkness that fills her mouth and eyes. An enveloping, all-encompassing world of darkness and pain. Within her body It grows, nesting within her heart. A creature whose only will is to destroy, to violate. It feeds on her pain, growing stronger and stronger, the Dark Thing that lives within her.

The boy and girl meet.

He sees the Thing, staring out at him from behind her eyes.

She is drowning and she will die.

As he tries to drive away his body stops, and the world stops. Trust and belief and the secrets inside the body.

He steps forward and makes his choice.

# kiss

I read the last words, look up from the page. Gifts. The power to create. She is drowning, and she will die.

I put the pad back inside the bag, stand and sling the bag across my shoulder. I walk forward to the entrance, stop a few feet before it. The black box, looming above me, high into the gray of sky. A passage inside, a tunnel forward, into the shadowy dark. The past and the future lie within, waiting for me to find the answer, to bring it all together.

I feel my heart, beating within my chest like a wordless prayer.

I walk forward, inside, and within moments the darkness closes itself around me.

\*\*\*

The sun shines bright in the blue sky. I sit in the cool shade beneath the main platform of the wooden playset, digging in the sandbox. I hear something, I look up. Somebody is crying. Somebody small like me is crying out there somewhere.

I stand, brush the sand off my legs. I walk out of the sandbox, across the yard to the shed behind the bushes at the corner of the garden. I reach up and twist the latch, pull the door open, step inside. There is a small shape, huddled in the shadows at the back. Her head raises, turns toward me. Her eyes are wide, her dark hair is wet with tears and plastered against her cheeks.

"Don't be afraid," I say softly. I walk towards her, I reach out. Slowly, tentatively, she lifts her arm. I reach for her hand, and my hand passes right through hers as though through thin air. She looks up at me out of sad, frightened eyes as she fades away.

Something is wrong. The shadows darken, begin to creep along the floor towards me. I run out of the shed, slam the door shut, turn and run towards the house. The shadows took her, I have to help her. Mom will know, Dad will know.

They are sitting on the couch, waiting for me. I stop, stand there staring. They are so much older. Only a few streaks of brown still run through my mother's gray hair. Lines of age reach away from the corners of my father's eyes, across his forehead. Hope is seated next to them, in her arms cradling a sleeping baby.

We can't help you anymore sweetheart, says my mother. You have to do this on your own. You have to remember.

Remember what you learned, says my father. Remember when I knelt down and spoke to you, and you looked in my eyes and heard me and you saw what hate is.

Remember when I was sick with fever, and you brought me my Bambi blanket, says my sister. When

280

we were older, and I came downstairs in the morning and curled up on the couch next to you. Remember when you knew what I needed.

Remember when I came to you and said I was so sorry, says my mother. And you threw your little arms around my neck and said, Mommy it's okay. Remember what you learned about who you are. Remember the choices you made.

I look at them. My mother blows me a kiss as they disappear into the air, and I reach out and catch it. I know what to do now.

I walk down the hallway and into my bedroom. I take the little blue lamb from the pile of stuffed animals in my closet, walk back down the hall and out of the house. I cross the yard to the shed. I feel my little heart beating. I open the door and step inside.

The shadow-thing looms, reaches for me, I throw my mother's blown kiss into it. It screams in pain, and then it is gone.

The little girl looks up at me.

"Here," I say as I hold out the blue lamb. "He has a pink nose. His name is Lambert." She takes him from me, hugs him against her chest. "He's nice," she whispers.

"He's all I can give you now. But remember me. I have to leave you now, there's something I have to do. But I won't forget you, and as soon as I can, I promise I'll come find you again." She looks at me out of those wide eyes and nods, clutching the little lamb close as she fades away.

I leave the shed, feel myself growing, changing as I walk across the yard. I sit down in the swing, sheltered by the shade of the giant cottonwood. I push my toes into the cool grass. The breeze carries the sweet smell

281

of lilac, gently rustles the leaves of the tree.

I can feel him; feel that little boy within me, now. How he wanted to never leave this place, but knew that he had to; that even though that dark unknown universe scared him, there were things in it that he knew he could not find here; things that he wanted, that he needed to become.

And she is not here. I can't find her here, any longer. And I promised that I would come and find her.

I stand, look around one last time. No, you can never go home again. But you can carry it within you.

I walk back across the yard to the shed, step inside. Against the back wall, beneath where she sat all huddled up, there is a large trap-door in the floor. I grasp the handle, pull it open. Cold air rises, stone steps lead down. From the bag I take out the yellow pad, a candle, a cigarette lighter. I sit, rest the pad on my lap, flick the lighter. Candlelight blooms, illuminating the pages, and I read.

# questions and answers

*He sits, smoking. Reaches down, stubs the cigarette out against the pavement. Stands, walks back across the parking lot, onto the porch. Sits down at the table; sits still, staring at the words. He reads them over and over again, trying to hold the whole body of it within his own body, reads until the words fill him up and he can read no more. He gets up, walks back across the parking lot, sits down on the low wall, lights another cigarette.*

*What is that color, he thinks, looking past the trees into the evening sky. Thistle?…is that what periwinkle is, maybe? It isn't the color, actually the color is just chalk, pale blue. It's the light; the depth of the beauty is in the way the receding light paints the world as it says its long goodbye…*

*Beauty. The word, the idea of beauty. He wonders again, a question he has asked himself many times, what it is within the body that creates beauty. Those are just trees, that is just wind that causes the branches full of leaves to sway and bend, and that expanse beyond them is just a thing called sky. But something within the body sees those things, feels those things, and that strong feeling within the* body is what we call, what we name as something beautiful.

Is it the same as hope? He thinks back, across the course of thirteen long years; remembering how more than once, when the darkness would overtake him, from within it he would look out and see the silhouettes of trees against the pale of twilit sky, and again feel the beauty; a thing that reached within, that reached and touched something deep within him. Still there, he would think then; would notice as it came to him, with a sense of deep gratitude, of almost shocked relief, of long-abiding wonder. Somehow, still there.

Beauty is what creates faith, he thinks to himself; and faith is the engine of hope. Hope and faith are intangible, rise from the abstractions called the mind and soul; but beauty is in the world, and rises within the tangible, concrete nature of the body.

He remembers when he began to write about the body; when he began to notice, many years ago now, that the words he wrote had begun to take place within the body; said 'my body', over and over again.

He remembers the night she told him, the toneless hollow of her voice as she began to speak; the toneless hollow that told him, from the first word, what story it was that she was about to tell. The words drew the shape of what he already knew; but to know a thing exists is one experience, and to see that same thing is another. How the words drew back the curtain, as it were, and gave him to see it; to see the shape and all of it, the Dark Thing within her body.

The endless sadness of it, yes as he began to cry, as he wept it was for that deep, dark sadness. But the tears were also hope, were a thing that was also beauty.

Because he saw the truth: that it was a Dark Thing that nested in her heart, that lived inside her body. And that because it was within her body, then it could be taken out of *her body, as well.*

*A vision that changed everything. That re-wrote the basic nature of the world.*

*But how could he see it? How could he see it, when they called her the Ice Queen, when they called her Death?… alone with it. A vision he saw alone, and carried the two of them, he and Isobel together within it. The surrounding world began to recede, as he carried the two of them together further into the vision, deeper into the heart of the undiscovered country, the surrounding world began to grow dim, hazy, further beyond, further away and more remote.*

*He felt the power within him; drove it down deep within her, watched as she changed, as the Dark Thing's grasp weakened.*

*He stood alone and watched the crashing waves, the sun melting the western sky. Felt the forms becoming shadows, the world receding, becoming dreams.*

*How can I see it, he wondered. How could I not see it?*

*The question remained unanswered. A few weeks later, his heart broke into pieces as the Dark Thing struck its precise and deadly, final blow.*

*And deep, deep down within him, the rage and anger kindled, an impossibly tiny flame. And slowly, slowly, impossibly slowly, it began to grow.*

## the cold world

I put the pad of paper back in the bag; sit still, focusing my thoughts.

Isobel. I remember, almost everything now. What he did, and…why he did it.

Why he put me here.

I want to cry. I want to take something beautiful and destroy it.

But I can't. Because I'm not done. Because this is not just about me, it is also about Isobel.

I stand, pick up the bag; see the stone steps leading down from the trapdoor in the floor of the shed. I blow out the candle, put it in the bag, sling the bag over my head, across my shoulder. And I step down, descending into the dark.

\*\*\*

BZZZZT. The sound of the alarm clock yanks me out of sleep. I reach over and shut it off; sit up slowly, rub my eyes. That…that was a strange dream. Walking and walking through those dark stone corridors…where was I trying to get to? I can almost remember, but not enough, it slips back down away from me. Oh well; dreams are just dreams, anyways.

I get out of bed, open the blinds; dress in the pale, early-morning light. I feel tired, listless, like I always do when I wake up. It wasn't always this way; I remember when the world used to be different than this. I wish it was the weekend so I could just crawl back into bed, but it's not. I sigh, walk out of my room and head to the kitchen for breakfast.

Weird. There's no one here. Did I set my alarm wrong somehow? No, the clock in the kitchen says the right time. I go upstairs. There's no one in any of the rooms. I come back down, head for the garage. Both my parents' cars are sitting there. Where is everyone? I walk back to the kitchen, thinking maybe there's a note left for me somewhere, on the counter, on the table… no. Nothing.

I look around, for the first time notice the layer of dust covering everything; realize no one has been in here for years and years. I am not where I think I am. That dream. Walking and walking down those stone corridors, through those empty, hollow passages; I should've been lonely, or exhausted, or afraid. But I wasn't. I was trying to get somewhere.

I go to my room, put on a jacket, grab my car keys and leave the house. It's cold outside, a late fall day beneath a gray overcast sky. I zip up the jacket, pull the hood up over my head. No one around, no other signs of life. Wind rustles through the leaves piled along the curb on either side of the street, brings more leaves falling yellow and brown from the trees. I walk to my car, parked on the street in front of the house, put the key in the lock, and stop; realize I have no idea where I would go, where I would want to go. I pull the key out, slip it into the pocket of my jeans, walk to the front of the car and sit down on the hood, one foot on the ground, the other perched on the bumper, trying to think.

What's going on here. The last thing I remember is going to bed, but I can tell this is not the same world I fell asleep in last night. Somehow I know this isn't a dream, either; maybe because I can remember the dream I was having, just before I woke up…only that wasn't me, in the dream. Or rather, it was, but I was older, much older than I am now. But not just older… different, changed somehow.

Years. That layer of dust. It's been years and years since I was here. Those dark stone passages; like a maze, some kind of puzzle. Some reason, why I've come back here again. But why now, why here? Think, try and understand…I'm eighteen, I just graduated from high school a few days ago. Emotional, like any kind of milestone or rite of passage is, I suppose; but it's not like I'm sad. I don't hate my life, that's too strong of a word; but I've always felt lost here, essentially alone here. Funny…my thoughts are clear, in a way I don't remember them being before. That's always been the problem here; the way I think, the way I see the world…it's like, what I see, no one else around me sees. And on the one hand, I say things about what I see, and they shake their heads and call me—well, crazy, essentially—but, on the other…potential. God. I've been hearing that same, stupid word for what feels like forever now. Like it's written on my forehead: 'potential'. About what it is that they see, what is this thing they are *seeing* when they look at me. But it's just this word, this description of a vacuum, over and over again, this total displacement of who I am by this completely vague and incoherent notion of who I *could* be.

I push off the car, walk around to the passenger side door; unlock, open it, reach in and pick up my yearbook, lying on the car seat. I walk back to the front of the car, perch myself on the hood again, open the yearbook to the blank pages in the back, filled now with handwritten notes, farewell messages from my friends. Most of them are about the version of 'me' I managed to…shoehorn myself into, I guess is a way of putting it. That's the sense of 'accomplishment' I have, if you could call it that; how I managed to craft a self that could harmonize with this world. But doing so required slicing large, important parts of myself away, shutting them up inside…it let me create joy, at times, I have to acknowledge that; let me assert my vision, at times, in a way that re-shaped the world around me. But it also hurt; wounded me, in ways I don't fully understand, or recognize. I flip the page, find the message I was looking for, different from the rest: "Yeah, they voted me 'Most Intelligent', but I know it's not true, I just did all the work. I know you're the smartest in our class," it says, "but you're so damn lazy…"

There it is. Both sides of the coin. No, I wasn't lazy. I had no choice. I could've followed the steps, filled in all the blanks; sure, I had the ability. But I also couldn't. Couldn't force myself, no matter how hard I tried. Couldn't give that kind of validation, that vote of support, to a life and world I fundamentally didn't believe in. And that was the thing; every time I heard that word, 'potential', it seemed like…like what they were all saying, was that they didn't believe in this world either. That there had to be more, more than the blanks to fill

289

in, more than just boxes and boxes. And like they were nominating me, to go out and find it…

God. Do I…do I really think that?…really feel that? I'm just…just an eighteen year-old kid. But I—I remember, days ago at the graduation ceremony…it shocked me. Standing there, afterwards, everybody crying and hugging and milling around, and then suddenly I—what's that? I'm looking down at the yearbook, seeing without seeing, and I realize I'm reading something:

*…all at once he sees it, the nigh-infinite terms of the true world, the true difficulty of being alive, of existence as a sentient being. He is stunned, astonished. The panorama of the true world on whose doorstep he stands unfurls in all its complexity and strangeness and wonder, a vision that makes its place within him as it takes his breath away.*

What the…that's what happened. And that's—that's my handwriting, but I—I didn't write that. Yeah, that's it, exactly, but I—I didn't, *couldn't* have written that…

I look up, trying to gather focus; blink several times, look back down again. What in the—wait. There's—there's another new message, another message I know wasn't there before. Dark, jagged writing.

**You never came. You promised you would come and find me. But I waited and waited for you, and you never came**.

I stare at the words. The wind rises, swirls through the rustling dry leaves piled against the curb, I shiver involuntarily. On impulse I start flipping through the pages of the yearbook, looking at random photos…there. That girl, in the back of that crowd, apart; slim, dark-haired, everyone else in the photo laughing or smiling, but she's not. No smile, no trace of a smile, and…she's looking at the camera. But it—it looks like she's looking *through* the camera. Looking…at me.

I blink twice, shake my head, shiver again. It's getting colder; I look up at the sky, notice the clouds are thicker, closer overhead now. It looks like a storm is—wait. Why is it fall? If I just graduated a few days ago, it should be early summer…I look around, notice that all the trees are leafless, dark bare branches rattling in the rising wind. The leaves in the street are brown, old and dry, turning into dust…not fall. It was when I walked out of the house, but it's not fall anymore. Snowflakes are falling, drifting down to the ground around me. I look down at the photo, at the girl again. It's not just that she's not smiling; in her eyes there's something harder, something colder…

I look up as the yearbook falls from my hands to the ground.

Winter is here, the snow falling thicker, heavier now. *You never came.*

The Ice Queen.

I drop down into a crouch, breathe in deeply and shove off from the ground with power, rocketing into the air, heading west, flying towards the shadowy silhouettes of the mountains miles ahead. They grow larger and larger, the ground far below is dotted with dark trees poking up through the white blanket of snow, the mountains grow ever larger, rising into the sky, and I am soaring across the first range of foothills now, past enormous glaciated peaks and above endlessly deep, dark valleys, the snow falling fast and heavy all

291

around…

There. A shrouded figure, not half a mile away. On…no. My god, don't, please don't.

I come down, land gently on the rocky, frozen ground of the mountaintop, not more than a few yards away from her. She's facing away from me, looking down, into the depths of the ravine plunging straight down and away from the cliff edge where she's standing. The snowfall is thinner up here, flakes swirling in the gusts of wind that rise up from the abyss.

"Don't. Please don't do it," I say, my voice steady and clear.

She turns, slowly; looks back over her shoulder, heavy dark circles around her eyes. "Go away," she says tonelessly. "They called me that for a reason. This is who I am," she says, turning back away.

"No. No it isn't. What happened to you is not who you are."

I take a step towards her; she turns abruptly, faces me. "I waited for you," she says, her voice cold and laced with ice. "I waited for you, and you never came." The gusting wind swirls as she speaks, whips tiny snowflakes like shards of glass against my skin, I raise my hands to shield my eyes and face.

"I'm sorry. I'm here now. I couldn't come before; I wanted to but I couldn't, there were too many things in the way, but I—"

"Oh, things in the way? Like what. Like all your friends, your beautiful family?" She spits the words at me with cold, dark fury. "You *lied*. You promised you would come and find me. I waited for years and years, and *you…never…came*."

The sky is darkening, the freezing wind cuts like a knife, the cold sinking, seeping into my bones. I wrap my arms around myself, shivering, shaking; I take a deep breath, trying to steady myself, the frozen air burns in my lungs. "Without those friends, without that family, I wouldn't be here. Without all that, I *couldn't* be here, and you know that. And I *am* here, I have come. I told you I would find you again. I had to learn, had to grow; I didn't know enough, I wasn't strong enough. But I am here now."

For a moment the clouds in her eyes seem to part as she looks back at me. But only a moment, her face turns into stone again. "Too late," she says, her voice heavy and dull. "I can't...do it anymore. They called me Death, because that's what I am." She turns away, facing into the abyss again. Her hands, her arms come slightly away from her body, fingers trembling...

No. No, I have come too far. This is not how this ends. The anger flares, ignites, a river of fire running through my body. I feel it burning in my fists, my eyes, and I hold it, channel it, feel it flowing up and out of my mouth.

"Enough. I've had enough, and I will take no more. I kept every promise I ever made to you. I let myself break for you. I stood between you and the rest of the world, I fought for you, I bled for you, I nearly died for you. I walked into a shadow world for you, and have spent years clawing my way back out. You will not do this. I have come too far and fought through too much, to stand here any longer and act as though any of this is still true. The Ice Queen is dead, and long since buried; I know this, because I am the one who burned and destroyed her."

She is still. Her arms come down slowly, hands come to rest at her sides. The gusting wind dies away. The fire recedes from my eyes, settles into a softly burning glow.

"I remember the moment we met. The first time I looked into your eyes, and saw you. I don't know where that gift came from, the ability to see what no one else could see. I remember that moment so clearly, because it was all I needed, to realize that I loved you. I never told you what happened, later. You watched me drive away that night, and then you answered the phone when I called, and I said: Do you want to spend the night with me. But I never told you why I called, never told you what happened. I tried to drive away, but I couldn't. My body wouldn't let me, and I sat in the car on the side of the road, just sat there crying. Because it was the moment in which I had to choose the rest of my life, and what I was going to believe in."

Individual snowflakes fall slowly down, twirl to the ground. Isobel turns, facing me. Steps forward, away from the edge, until she is a couple short feet away. The dark circles around her eyes are gone, but they are still full of pain and shadows.

"But It is still in you," she says sadly. "You took It out of me, yes…but now It lives within you."

"I know. I'm not done yet," I say, looking back into her eyes. "But I've come very far, come a very long way. And I'm so close now. I believed in you," I say, my voice softening, "and I need you to wait a little longer. I need you to believe in me again, too. Yes, It is within me. But this is still within me, as well. I said it was the most beautiful thing I had ever seen, and I said that because it was true." I press my hand against my chest, drawing my focus to a tapered point; reaching deep, deep down within for the memory, drawing it up and out, and it burns through me; I clench my hand into a fist, drawing it out, and when I open my hand it hovers there, before me in the air: the shining red sphere, the burning ruby star.

I watch as the shadows and the pain in her eyes die away; displaced by hope, the vision within her face of who she became. She closes her eyes, places her hand against her own chest; pulls it away, opens it, and the ball of light, the pink rose, rises, hovers shining. She looks at me. The ruby star and the gem of rose, hovering between us. She nods, once slowly, takes a deep breath, lets it back out. "I will wait," she says, as she begins to fade, the sphere of rose light fading, disappearing with her, and a moment later she's not there anymore.

The ruby star winks out, disappears.

My knees give way and my body collapses, crumples down to the ground.

I don't even want to cry anymore.

I can't do this. Leandro was wrong, I can't do this. It's too late, thirteen years was too long. She didn't jump, she didn't fall, she didn't drown, she didn't die; she made it, made it out; she lives, with a heart full of love and light, alive. That's all that matters.

My strength is gone. I can't do this anymore. Time has run out.

I lie there on the cold, hard ground; lie still, barely breathing. The snow is no longer falling. Patches of sunlight on the far mountainside, across the abyss, shadows of clouds pass swiftly across the rocky cliff-face. There's a jagged boulder jutting from the ground a couple feet away, crusted with masses of green and yellow lichen. Dimly, as if from very far away, my mind remembers lichen. Dim, far-away thoughts. A unique thing, a kind of animal-plant, symbiotic hybrid-like organism. An animal and plant, living together on the surface of rocks. Microorganisms in a micro-world, creating micro-cities, who knows what secrets they're sharing in that micro-world together…

God, stop it, shut up, shut the fuck up! Fuck you, stupid fucking lichen. Fuck you mystery and beauty of the stupid fucking world…god, please just leave me the fuck alone, I don't…fucking…care. I don't want to do this anymore…

With an effort, I push myself up to a sitting position, arms wrapped around my legs. I close my eyes, let my head fall down, forehead resting on my knees. I sit like that for a long time. Finally I take in a deep breath, raise my head; my eyes open as I sigh the breath back out. My eyes open, and they take in all the endlessness: the ancient wonder and god-beauty of the body of mountains, the snow-capped ranging secret peaks, breaking against the sky…my eyes see it and take it all in, inside of me, and it doesn't matter whether I want them to or not.

Apparently my exhaustion is a thing that doesn't matter. Apparently the promises I gave to the world and all the people I love are more important, are stronger than what I want or don't want.

Fine. All the way to the end, then. Bring it the fuck on.

I hear footsteps, approaching from behind. I stand, turn around.

Tyler walks up and stops, stands before me.

We look at each other in silence for a long while.

Finally he nods. "Okay. You ready to go? There's a couple old friends waiting for us," he says. I start to say something but he holds up his hand. "Not yet. We'll… talk, after. But, first thing's first." I stare at him; he holds my gaze, doesn't look away. "Okay," I say quietly.

He nods again, and the world around us shifts, swirls, changes…

We're standing in a large room. Against the back wall are two beds, separated by a large wardrobe. Against the left wall and the right are two desks and shelves lined with books and various other items. Jackets, hats and scarves hang from hooks, from the backs of chairs; there are posters on the walls, the desks are strewn with papers and pieces of bric-a-brac, little trinkets. The room has a rumpled, messy-but-not-dirty, comfortable air. In the center of the room is a couch, a coffee table and two chairs; the fourth wall, behind the two chairs, is made up mostly of windows, and beyond the windows is darkness. A dark-haired, brown-skinned girl sits at one end of the couch, a blond-haired girl with glasses sits in one of the two chairs. Tyler walks to the other end of the couch, sits down, looks up at me. The two women are looking at me, also. All three of them are older now; their shapes more definite, both the tangible and intangible characteristics in who they are have been sharpened, refined. My canvas shoulder bag is on the coffee table, the yellow pad lying on top.

I walk over, pick it up, sit down in the available chair. "Your last puzzle piece," says Tyler. I look back at him for a long moment, then flip the pages over and begin to read.

# the light dawns

*He sits in front of the computer, in his isolated bubble of failure. Playing solitaire, game after game of solitaire. He picks up one of the books he's supposed to read for one of the classes, knows he's not going to read it. Still he holds it open for a minute and looks at the words; makes himself stare at the failure, at his stubborn inability to make himself do the work.*

*He throws the book down, scowls. Gets up and walks out the door, down the hall to Tyler's room, it's empty. He walks back out into the hall, up the half-flight of stairs and into Amber and Tiffany's room. Amber's sitting at her desk, Tyler and Tiffany, each with a book, are sitting on the couch. He sits down opposite them, puts his feet up on the coffee table. Tiffany glances up at him for a second or two, goes back to her reading with a maybe-audible sigh and a possibly discernible tiny frown.*

*What are you guys doing, he says.*

*Our work, like you should be doing too, says Tyler without looking up.*

*I already did it, he says.*

*No, you didn't says Tyler, eyes still on his book. That's a lie. Go and do your work.*

*Tiffany looks up at him again. Why don't you go get whatever you're supposed to be reading and come back here and sit and read with us, she says.*

*He looks back at her for a few moments and then looks away. It's okay, I'll just sit here, he says.*

*He can feel Tiffany looking at him. He remembers being in his room after christmas break, unpacking his bags, Tiffany appearing in his doorway with a funny, secret little smile. Come upstairs she said, there's someone I want you to meet. He follows her upstairs and into her room, she sits down at one end of the couch with that secret little smile, picks up a magazine. Tyler is sitting at the other end of the couch, there is no one else in the room. What, says Tyler, looking up at him; Why are you rolling your eyes? She told me there was someone up here she 'wanted me to meet,' he says as he sits down, curling his fingers into quotation marks. Tyler snorts. You silly little hussy he says to Tiffany, she giggles as she looks at her magazine.*

*Now it's months later. He can feel Tiffany looking at him. What's going to happen to you if you don't do your work? she says. Go do your work! cries Tyler.*

*Tyler, stop saying that says Amber, with irritation. She gets up from her desk, comes and sits in the other chair, next to him. Tyler and Tiffany have both set their books aside now.*

*He looks at them. Tyler's right, he says. It should be simple. But even if I could just do that, it's too late by now anyways.*

*They sit in silence. With a mixture of sadness and wonder that he can't express he feels how the three of them are cushioning the impact, how they are helping him to absorb the blow. He knows they will all be coming back here in the*

299

*fall, that all the new friends he's made here will be coming back; that he will be the only one missing, and they will keep building it without him.*

*He goes back home. Takes classes at the university, half-does the work. Moves out of his parents' house and into an apartment. But nothing changes, really. He goes up into the mountains sometimes and they are the mystery and beauty they always are, but they are otherwise silent; nothing answers his call.*

*The year goes by. He is on a plane, flying back to Portland, going back to the college for the festival, the Renn Fayre, the end-of-the-year Big Big Party. He is coming to say goodbye. Nothing has changed, a year gone by and nothing has changed; whatever it was that he thought he might've finally found here, it has remained only a question; he has decided that it's time to let it go.*

*He has told no one he is coming, for some reason he wants it to be a surprise. He arrives, he's there, wondering how it will be and then in the middle of all the people Amber sees him and her eyes go wide and suddenly somehow they are all there around him, shrieking and clapping and saying What are you doing here! with delight and dancing around him, all his friends dancing around him. The rush of feeling is strong, deep; it runs through his body, touches something inside deep down.*

*That night, with his friends and happy, a girl stares at him and speaks to him. A girl he used to dream about, who he watched from within his failure-cave; a girl who never saw him, never noticed him before. Now she is speaking to him, staring at him and turning away giggling and looking back at him. Find me again, she says as she and her friends walk away, as she looks back and smiles and laughs. Come and find me again! she shouts and waves, as she is swallowed by the night. The feeling within him deepens, branches, grows.*

*Two days later the party is over, he is supposed to leave and he cannot. Something is happening within him, he doesn't know what but that it is a Something is unmistakeable and he does not go to the airport, he does not get on the plane. He finds Tiffany in the library and says Can I borrow a pen and some paper. He finds an empty desk next to the window; looks out at the green trees in the afternoon sunlight, looks down at the empty page in front of him and he begins to write.*

*He writes about his life. He writes about the girl, the girl he once dreamed about now staring at him, talking to him, the dream suddenly become very real. He writes about this sudden, unexpected sense of flowing, of things suddenly flowing and merging together. What is happening, he asks; what is happening, he asks the words as they appear before him on the page. He has never written like this before, never anything like this. The words flow out of him, through the pen and onto the paper. With a sense of grow-ing astonishment he feels it; how this writing is not of the experience, this writing is the experience; how these words* he is writing are <u>changing</u> him. *It's time, he writes: It's time, it's time, it's time. He puts the pen down; sits still, looking out the window for a long while.*

*The week goes by. He spends time with the girl, he spends long hours talking with his friends, he writes and writes and writes; digging himself up, bringing everything within himself up into the light. It is the longest, hardest, most intense week that he has yet lived in his still-young life. Late in the last night and he tells the girl everything, he bares his soul as reads the words to her, and she looks at him with eyes full of feeling. And he feels the change as it happens, and as he looks in her eyes he is grateful to her, and he knows that it is not about this girl; it is about a change, that has finally, finally happened within him; and he knows that he has fought for it, and that he has won. He is walking now, so tired and ready to sleep, to finally sleep. Walking across the campus alone and the day is breaking, the sun is dawning after he has been up all night, the sunrise belongs to him only, there is no one else around. He is crossing a long bridge over water and it rises finally up, all the way up from within him and he is suddenly crying, and he is astonished by the voices of the tears as they fall from his eyes, as they tell him that he is full of joy. He finds himself looking up, past the green leaves of trees into the deep, rose sky of morning for God, for a thing that he has never felt before now and that he can only call God. In this moment he sees that it is a gift; that whatever else might be this thing that he has finally found within himself, that it is also a true gift that has been given, and that he will follow it wherever it leads.*

*Thank you, he says quietly. He does not know to whom he says it, but he knows he must say it. Thank you, he says as he looks up. For whatever it is, and wherever it might go, I thank you. He wipes the tears from his face and smiles, and walks away, ready to finally begin his life.*

# forgiveness

I sit for awhile, looking down at the pad in my hands; the loops and angles of the letters, the words. I lean forward, set the pad back down on top of the bag on the table. Sit back, slowly, in the chair. Look down at my hands; slowly close them into fists, clenched tight, fingernails biting against my palms. Slowly open them again, turn them over; look down at the criss-crossing lines, the vein-rivers running beneath the skin, the contours of bones. Amber's hand closes around my forearm, squeezes, fingertips transmitting care, feeling.

"How are you doing, honey?" she asks. I look up at her, she squeezes my arm again as she looks in my eyes. "You didn't know, did you, you didn't remember," she says gently.

"Of course he didn't," says Tyler. "No one remembers the moment in which they were born. Maybe a strong way of putting it, but..." His voice trails off as I look up at him, shake my head. "No," I say. "No, it's not."

"Yeah," he says, looking back at me. "Fate and des-

303

tiny are strong words, too. Words you want to be careful with. But they exist for a reason."

"Yes," I say quietly. "Yes, they do."

Tiffany sighs. "It must be…hard," she says. She cocks her head slightly as she looks at me, like she's trying to get a better view. "To not…have any—choices," she says slowly, choosing her words as she speaks. "I remember the difference, the way he… changed. He was always a person who felt things very strongly, that was one of the first things I noticed, or identified, in—who he was, I guess. But before it was so…unfocused, and afterwards it—well, it was the opposite, pretty much. Maybe he couldn't identify the right…goal, or direction. But the sense of purpose that he had, afterwards, was very, very strong; like—like a mission, almost."

I look down at my hands again. Absorbing the impact, of seeing the whole of it, finally.

"I know it's been hard, we all know it's been hard," says Amber. "But you're almost done now. You've come so far, and you're so close. I'm so proud of you!" she says, squeezes my arm again. "I know it's been hard, but aren't you…I mean, aren't you just a teeeeensy bit excited, too?" She's squinting at her thumb and forefinger, pinched together, as she says this, and I can't help but smile back at her.

"That's why you're here, now, of all places, in case you're wondering," says Tyler, dryly. "Because, believe it or not, this crappy dorm room in which these two hussies worked their hussy-magic is, to extend the birth-metaphor, the site in which you were conceived, more or less."

"If it was such a crappy room then why were you always in here?" asks Tiffany.

"Because my room was even crappier. And it didn't have a couch."

"I think you came in here because you were hoping to catch a glimpse of Tiffany's boobies since you were sweet on her," says Amber matter-of-factly.

"Yes, that's right, because that's my standard M.O. when I'm 'sweet on' somebody, I hang out in her room praying I get a chance to see her 'boobies'," says Tyler, rolling his eyes. Tiffany giggles, covering her mouth. "Oh Tyley-poo, such a trickster!" exclaims Amber. "Ok, first of all, calling me a 'trickster' in this context only vaguely makes sense, and then only to someone who is probably mildly retarded. Second of all, my name is Tyler, not 'Tyley-poo'." Tiffany bursts out laughing.

The memories are flowing. Strong, clear. Whether they are mine or not, is no longer a concern. I can feel myself within him, can feel him within myself. The worlds are merging, and I am ready. It's...time. To embrace it. It's time, it's time, it's time.

"I have a question," I say. "This is where—" I hesitate, but only for a moment; "—I failed. This is where... I attained a complete sense of failure; this room, especially, is where I spent more time than anywhere else not doing my work."

Amber shakes her head. "Sweetheart, that 'work' you weren't doing, you weren't doing because it wasn't actually *your* work. Your heart wasn't in it. Think about it; think about where your heart actually was."

I look at her, at Tiffany and Tyler. Letting the memories be mine, letting myself remember...remember when they were strangers, first; the intense curiosity I felt as I found myself saying new things, as these strangers responded in kind; became not strangers, became people I had been waiting my whole life to find.

305

The relationships I found here; the hunger that grew in me as I discovered these relationships in which I could finally let all of myself out, in which I could finally be whole.

"I think you failed out of school because you had to fail out of school," says Tiffany. "It was the only way for you to free yourself; to get off that kind of, treadmill, of the world's desires and expectations for you, and into a space in which you could start making your own choices about your life, and base those choices on the things you really cared about."

"Honestly, when you were gone that next year, it felt like something was missing," says Tyler. "I think I felt it more than the two hussies here did—" he gestures at them dismissively, Tiffany sticks her tongue out and Amber pulls her nose up, making a pig face—"because of the very specific way in which you and I connected, but I know they felt it too. I mean, this isn't just your memory, this was special to all of us."

"Look. Like I said before, you feel things very intensely," says Tiffany. "It was one of the first things I responded to in you, respected in you. I know you felt that sense of purpose I was talking about, and I also know that interpreting it was a constant difficulty for you. But I always thought…that was kind of the point, honestly; that you had chosen to live with that, that kind of difficult ambiguity, because it was the only way you could live, in order to understand that sense of purpose and figure out what you should actually be doing."

My god. I'm looking at their faces, listening to their voices, the words they are giving to me…and I remember, long ago; the night with Isobel, and Bobby and Tess, the four little white pills…the sense of danger, of possible danger, and the way these friends, these figures rose up around me that night; the feeling of angels, of a life filled with extraordinary angels…

"I have…another question," I say. They look at me, waiting; I look down at my hands again, finding the words, look back up. "A question that I—that I can answer myself, I think. But I still want to ask it. Tyler called this the place in which I was…conceived, more or less. My question is…how, or why, I guess."

Amber reaches over and takes my hand, squeezes. "Because you loved us, honey, and we loved you," she says simply.

"You have to understand what Amber means," says Tiffany. She leans forward, arms resting on her knees, looking down at her hands. "Yes, we loved you, for who you were; even if you were a major pain in our asses sometimes--"

"Annoying, rude, gross," interrupts Amber, "hyperactive, mule-headed," chimes in Tyler.

"—All of the above, pretty much," says Tiffany, smiling. "But we also loved you *because* you loved *us*; you loved us so much, and so intensely, that it was pretty much impossible not to love you in return. Not because we felt obliged, but because we couldn't help ourselves, and we didn't want to. Do you see what I mean?" she finishes quietly, looking up at me.

"You're here with us now because what you chose to do with your life was to explore and immerse yourself in these interactive, complex webs of emotion between people that we call relationships," says Tyler. "You decided that there was nothing more fundamentally important as an object of study, and at the same time that it was a body of work that most clearly articulated with your very strong and very specific gifts. With us, in this particular the-whole-is-more-than-the-sum-of-its-parts foursome, you found a depth, intensity and complexity that you had previously only been able to posit as a possible reality within the constructs of your imagination. You're here with us now because it is from within this foursome that you were first able to discern the real choices that were available to you; and because from within this foursome, you realized that you could find the depth and honesty of emotional support that you would need, in order to make the choices you needed to make."

By the time he's finished Amber and Tiffany are staring at him. Amber turns, slowly, to Tiffany. "Well," she says, in measured tones, "I would say that's all very accurate. Very well put, wouldn't you agree?" Tiffany nods, sighs noticeably. "Yes, I would agree," she says. "Especially the part about, what was it, 'depth and honesty of emotional support'…very accurate. Which is interesting, considering the speaker." She and Amber both turn to look at Tyler again. He stares back, in silence.

"I think it's time for Amber and I to go now," says Tiffany, turning to me. "Time for the two of you to have a little…chat," she says, glancing at Tyler. She and Amber both stand, walk a few feet away; turn back, looking at me, reach out and take each other's hands.

"I know you've heard me say it a million times sweetheart, but it's always worth repeating. We believe in you," says Amber. "We've always believed in you." Tiffany nods in agreement, a quiet smile on her face. And the two of them fade away.

"So that's how it works here, huh? Poof, they're gone, just like that," says Tyler, weaving his hands in the air like he's spell-casting.

"When something is necessary it's here. When it's no longer necessary it goes away."

"Hm. Straightforward, makes sense." He gets up, walks over to the windows. "Where exactly, or what exactly, is 'here', anyways? Obviously I already know the answer to that, more or less. But I want to know what *you* think it is."

"A world made up of shadows and dreams and memory. And we are in the center of it, deep inside the fortress of the Dark Thing."

"The 'fortress of the Dark Thing'. Pretty dramatic," he says, walking back over to the couch and sitting down, opposite me.

"Do you think it's inappropriate? What would you call it? How would you describe it?"

"No, I don't think it's inappropriate. Just an interesting choice of frame."

"How so?"

"Well, because this story is a true story; the events described and depicted happened in the true world, the non-magical plane of existence we call 'history', we call 'reality'. Aren't you worried that by choosing to set the story in this mythical dream realm, you will undermine the specific power that is only granted to, and wielded by, true stories?"

"You forget who you're talking to. I didn't make those choices, so I can't really answer that question."

"Okay…who did, then?"

"…he did."

"Riiiight. So a minute ago, it was 'I' this, and 'I' that…now we're back to 'he' and 'him'…yes, I noticed when it changed. Amber and Tiffany didn't, maybe; maybe they're not supposed to, or maybe they chose not to point it out. Or maybe, their job was just to affirm things. But that wouldn't be my role in all this, now would it. Amber and Tiffany: 'depth and honesty of emotional support'. Tyler: ...question mark. Hmm..."

He looks at me; when I don't say anything, he nods, stands up, begins talking again, gesturing with his hands as he walks slowly around the room.

"So the question is: why is Tyler here, what is Tyler here for...to play the bad guy?...no, I don't think so. Been there, done that, almost—what—thirteen, fourteen years ago now?...I think we're past that now. Am I supposed to beg for forgiveness, then?...no, I don't think that's it either. Because you and I, we've already been through that, too, haven't we." He stops walking, eyebrows raised slightly as he looks at me.

"Afternoon," I say quietly. "Abandoned lot next to the water, weeds and piles of broken concrete. I saw you wanted it, how badly you needed it, the deep wounds still left in your heart. I saw and I was ready and I reached out and took you in my arms; and I felt your body trembling, shaking, against mine."

He looks back at me, and nods slowly; his face is quiet, the expression in his eyes a study in the reception of grace. "Probably the worst thing I ever did to anyone. And as such, that was one of the most important gifts I've ever been given."

"And one of the most important gifts that I ever gave," I say.

We look at each other for awhile. Tyler nods again, once, and begins to walk, slowly, around the room once more.

"So that's not why we're here together either, is it. Maybe in part; but there's something more, something else...something you need from 'ol Tyley-poo." He comes to a stop, looking at me, his eyes narrowing with

310

focus.

"I think," he says, turning into his slow walk again, "that what I gave you, originally, was structure. That my original gift, or contribution, to our relationship was to help you define structures, into which your spirit could flow. Structures...of a, complexity...that you hadn't encountered before; structures into which you could place those aspects of yourself, that you had previously cut yourself off from, or hidden away, inside yourself. A creative partnership, between the two of us, in which you were able to find both definition, and at the same time the freedom and room you needed to really grow." He stops, looking out the window. Turns, circles back to the couch and sits down across from me.

"I'm not here to give you affirmation, or belief," he says quietly. "I'm here because I can see the full scope and real magnitude of what you're attempting, of what you've built and why you've built it. Because fate and destiny are inherent in their mystery. Because I, even if unknowingly, lit the fuse on the bomb that blew your life apart. Because after all these years you have finally come to the end. I'm here to bear witness; to send you on your way to finish it, once and for all."

We sit still, looking at each other for a long time. Finally Tyler nods at me, brings his hands up off his legs and back down again, exhales.

""Well, should we shake hands or something? How do I send you off here?"

"No. No, no hand-shaking. Just...just do the dumb thing we always used to do."

"Right." He smiles slightly, then composes himself, solemnly raising his hand, palm outwards. I follow suit, we move as though to exchange a high-five and just before contact our hands veer off, swoop into wild akimbo territory, arms waggling about at the elbows.

"It really doesn't make any sense, does it," I say.

"No, it doesn't. It never did. It's just a dumb thing we did. Just really, satisfyingly dumb," he says, laughing, still waggling his arm around as he fades away.

And I am alone in the quiet room. I breathe in, breathe out. It's—

*You have gone nowhere. You have gained nothing.*

The toneless, hollow shadow-voice fills the room, fills my mind. Within the space of a heartbeat I am standing, facing the windows, the darkness beyond them that roils and churns now like a living Thing.

No. I have fought for years to get to this point, and I am stronger now than I have ever been before.

*Empty. Empty as you always were, and now your dreams will finally die too.*

The darkness rocks back, rushes forward in a great wave, the windows explode and the long dark fingers wrap themselves around me. Icy and full of terror, the darkness hollowing me out, the cold seeping into my bones...

Are you afraid that if I have come this far, than I have also found the power to finally forgive you.

The fingers recoil like whips, the darkness rushes back upon itself. *Come*, It screams out in silent rage. *Come to me where I am waiting, and I will show you what you are.*

And It is gone.

I fall to my knees, gasping. Half-crawl, half-stumble forward in the darkness, feeling until my fingers find the canvas bag. I reach inside, find the candle and lighter, a moment later candlelight blooms in the darkness.

I am shaking, trembling. So close now. Everything is done but the last thing. It waits for me where It is strongest, at the center of Its power, and that is where I have to go now. With fumbling fingers I pick up the pad, flip the pages over. One last, blank page is left. As I look down at the empty page the letters begin to appear, one after another, the words writing themselves down.

# ready

*The thing is, I thought I was done.*

*And then Sumiko said, Where is your life, and what are you doing.*

*It took a while for those words to sink in. A year or two.*

*And then I looked, and saw with a kind of shock, that quickly gave way to a sense of the abundantly, profoundly obvious, that no, I wasn't done at all.*

*That it was sitting before me, and that there was no way around, no other way forward. That I would find neither the will nor the energy to do anything else in and with my life, until I went all the way through the whole entire thing, and wrote the story down.*

*It helped, in a way, to finally see that. Explained so much, all the dead ends and blind alleys I kept finding myself in, over and over again.*

*But that doesn't mean it was easy. Doesn't mean it was easy to build my life around, and stake my future on, a giant question mark. Maybe the answer is: yes. Yes, it lives and breathes, it resonates. Love and sacrifice and redemption are pretty much universal and eternal themes, as far as I can*

314

*tell.   It is not as though I don't have hope, and a certain amount of faith, that it is the thing I have struggled and worked and fought for, and dreamed: the black velvet night full of constellating stars, a wind comes up and a wind comes up in all the leaves in all the trees, and the shadows are an ornate moving gorgeousness across the ground, are shadows, cool and dark and full of wonder…*

*But also run enormous rivers of anxiety, violent storms of fear and potential despair, and also blah blah blah, what right do I have to feel any of those things, with my comfortable bed in a house and a pantry full of food.   And my amazing friends.   And my beautiful family.   All my gifts, and opportunities.*

*Hearts break all the time you whiny little bitch.   Get over it.   Get a job you lazy fuck.   You are empty, and now your dreams will finally die too.*

*Said the Dark Thing.   And I heard it.*

*But in the end, only one thing mattered.   The hopes and fears, the anxieties and dreams, all just dust on the proverbial wind.*

*It didn't matter that I didn't understand why, after all these years, I was still broken.*

*The only thing that mattered was that I wanted to be whole again.*

*Rise, now.   Rise up now, with all the strength and power and vision you have struggled and fought for and gained.   Let your eyes open and let your heart reach out.*

*Rise up, on the threshold, and finish it.*

## alone

I set the pad down on the stone floor. Stand up, let go of the candle, it hovers in the air. I push from inside, gently, and the light grows, illuminating. I'm standing in a small room, walls and floor and ceiling of stone. No windows, no doors. I squat down, reach into the bag; my fingers find the photograph, pull it out.

It's a photo that I took, many moons ago; for some reason the only picture he found himself in possession of, later. He put it in a simple silver frame, and it sat on desks and shelves in rooms I lived in, as he moved from one place to another to another. It was taken in an ordinary place on an ordinary day, when I happened to have a camera and looked at her and saw something and said, I'm going to take a picture of you. Maybe it was because she was wearing my shirt, that red t-shirt with the zebra; maybe because it was just an ordinary day, an ordinary moment. The look on her face is non-committal, slightly pouty, an I-don't-want-to-have-my-picture-taken kind of face. But the truth is in the pose: standing on one leg, the other bent at the knee behind her, parallel to the ground; the slight twist of her slim body, carelessly playful, free. I see now that it was a picture of the future; of the change that was taking place within her, of who she was becoming.

I reach into the bag, pull out a roll of tape, stand and turn around, facing the wall behind me. I tear off a strip of tape, curl it into a loop; fix it to the back of the photograph and stick the photo on the stone wall. I grasp the bottom corners and pull, gently, down and away, stretching the photograph out, widening and lengthening it, down to the floor, till it is taller than I am and nearly as wide as my spread arms. I turn around, take the candle in my hand again, walk forward to the opposite wall; turn back around, facing the photo.

The candlelight flickers, the edges of the photograph blur, blend into the stone wall. The bent leg comes down. She stands there, looking back at me. Turns and walks away, fading. I release the candle into the air again, its light guttering, dying now. I walk the few steps across the stone floor, the light dies out as my foot crosses the threshold of the door and I step into the darkness.

***

Bananabread?, he says to the girl sitting on the kitchen counter. She smiles, shakes her head No.

He falls asleep in the bed next to her and she lies awake. Her eyes wander across the room she has found herself in, at the way it is full of a color and variety of life she's never known. She looks from the room to him, and back again. Wants him to wake and also not to wake, afraid that if he does she will also wake, will find that this is nothing more than a dream that she is

317

dreaming.

Sunlight. Late-afternoon sunlight, silently shadow-stripes the room as it passes through blinds. Stop. You're gorgeous. Tear your clothes off. But not like this. I don't want it with you to be like this. He hears each word she says, painted within him like bars of shadow and sunlight.

He lies on the bed listening to the music that he has listened to many times before. But he has never heard this. How can there be secrets like this within the body. The music unlocks the bars of shadow and sunlight, unlocks the secret and it is no longer a secret, and there is no longer anything within my body that is secret. My heart is in my body, a resonance of power and beauty. The dream I have for so long dreamed is not a dream, it is me. It is I, and I alone, who will choose my destiny.

I swallow the pill that Bobby gives me. I look at her and for the first time I feel the presence of the Thing within her body. In the morning she picks at her plate of food, she looks up and behind her eyes I see It looking out at me.

When she tells me what her brother did to her I cry tears that become a river that washes everything else but the truth away. A Dark Thing that lives within her, that is not her. That she still has a heart, that she still has a hope. That within me lies a power that can make her whole again.

But the river is rising. I stand firm but the river rises, there is nothing I can do as the dark river swallows me up and carries me far, far away.


It is draining out of him. With panic he feels the love, and with it the promises he made to her, draining out of him. He cannot hide the shadows in his eyes. Where have you gone, she says. Why have you gone away from me. The anguish in her voice cuts him, and he bleeds and cannot stop the bleeding. He deserves to bleed, he thinks. Guilt fills him, as the love drains out an enormous guilt fills up the empty space.

He does not remember. He knows what she did, yes; but he does not know what it did to him. All he knows is that the love is leaving him, the love that he said was real and was hers is draining away; all he can see is that he must be a fundamentally empty creature, to have practiced such a deep and terrible self-deception. All he can see is that he can never trust himself again.

I am lost. I am nothing, I am nowhere. The Dark Thing has swallowed me whole.

She fights now. Even as she sees the light fade from him she feels it bloom within her; her love for him grows fierce and she battles, she fights to try and find a way. She pleads, she threatens, she cries. Her love is a rain of blows that bring him nothing but more guilt, more pain. She takes the book from his hand, undresses him, pushes him down. She covers his body with long, soft kisses and it is agony to him to feel nothing, to be filled with nothing. She takes him in her mouth and he comes within moments and the stars fade and he whispers Stop, please stop, please stop doing this to me...

It is gone. It is gone and he knows it is gone; that she cannot bring it back, that he cannot bring it back, that the light has gone out of him. But she still needs him; she is now fully engaged with the battle for her own life and there is no one else, she cannot do it alone. I can no longer love her but I can give my life to her, is what he realizes and decides. I made promises and my own life has become nothing, is what he sees. He becomes a net that catches her, he becomes a thing she climbs on. She looms over him, crying, her tears make lakes that he drowns in over and over again. As the months go by his bones crack and break, the pieces of his body break one by one.

The last time they have sex is in a hotel room, a trip she takes him on for his birthday. Sex that is hardedged, harsh and empty. He looks at her afterwards and says We can't do this anymore; if it is like this, then we can't do this anymore. Feels something die in him as he says it, looking into her eyes.

Within my prison I scream, pound my fists against the stone floor, cry acid tears that burn my face. There is nothing I can do.

Lost in the way things have broken, they work for the dream beneath the pain, for the quality of hope that remains. She finds a study, a group-therapy study for victims of sexual abuse. What do you think, she says. I think you should, he says. He drives her, back and forth. She talks to him, about what it's like to talk with these people, what it gives her, how she is growing. He listens, gives her the intimacy of what he knows, gives her all that he has left inside. One night he drops her off and parks, finds some way to kill the time. He returns to a car with a broken window, now missing a backpack that had her journal inside; the words she had, in recent weeks, began to give to herself, for the first time in her life. She is distraught. It registers to him as another in the long line of mistakes he makes and ways he breaks things; only, all the time now. He searches the alleys and dumpsters the next day in the drizzling rain, hopelessness growing. He turns the sodden white thing on the pavement over with his foot, it is a dirty white stuffed animal, a bear holding a red heart that says I Love You. Okay, he thinks as he gives in. Okay. He puts the bear in a plastic bag, takes it home and runs it through the washing machine. Shows it to her that night, tells her the story. She looks at him with sad, quiet eyes. Picks up the bear, looks at it; His name is Dylan, she says, softly.

She grows and she grows, rising, fighting, and he strains with everything that is left in him to push her up. He wakes one morning and she is not in the bed. He finds her in the bathroom, naked in the bath. Doesn't recognize the strange look in her face. Shortly they are leaving the house to go eat somewhere and she stumbles, he notices pubic hair where her jeans are slipping down and realizes with muted shock that she is drunk. The rest of the morning is a bad dream, becomes a nightmare when they return to the house, as the numbing effect of the alcohol wears off. She tries to drink more and he won't let her, holds her down as she screams, crying; crying because she loves him. He feels the boundary of life, somewhere not far off the boundary of is it worth it to keep living. He forces himself to find the way, the words somehow, to bring her back from the edge; she falls asleep, in the bed. He goes into the other room and collapses; curls into a ball and lies there, barely breathing.

She goes on a trip, to visit a boy who is the only real, true friend from her old life, a boy who he knows has a good heart. She comes back. Looks away; looks at him, tells him the story. I slept with him, she says, her voice soft and sad. I know, he says quietly, looking down. He knows she is filled with love and that she needs to find ways to practice it, to let it out.

I sink down against the stone wall to the stone floor

and hang my head, and shake and tremble silently in the cold darkness.

As they drive slowly across the cracked earth and sand of the desert ground, through the gates, he knows he is broken, that something is deeply wrong within him. He has never been here but he knows enough to know that this is a final attempt to find anything that is an answer. Many things happen, days of a week that push him all the way to the edge of the world. On the last night when the man burns he moves in the circle of bodies that swims around the great fire. The drugs in his system and the night in the desert carnival-city of glowing lights beneath the moon and stars, all of it opens up the world, takes it gently apart. Intensities of joy, deep wells of sadness, he moves within it, carries it along, carries his heart within his hands before him. With deep feeling he says thank you to someone, a man who built a wonderful thing, and he turns to leave and the man looks and pulls him aside and says with quiet intensity, That girl really, really loves you. He sees Isobel looking back at him as the man says it. I know, he replies softly, from within the pain of knowing. I know she does, he says. I know. As the sun rises they all write messages on the Temple of Grief and Joy. He reads what Isobel writes and he turns to her and says, Can they read it, and she nods. Tyler and Tiffany and Matthew, and the few others with them, read what she has written and they look at her in silence with wide eyes and she nods. Matthew is breaking as he realizes, sobbing, that the world can be so dark and cruel, that this person named Isobel who he has just come to know, who is so sweet and good, could ever have lived in such darkness.

And she comforts Matthew, holds him as he cries,

and she looks at me, and I awake, I rise up as I see what I have waited for, hoped against hope, waited for so long to see within her eyes. And then I write, a message on the temple, and then I turn to them and I read it aloud. I relinquish responsibility for who you are. You have risen and you are ready, I say. And for the first time in her life she steps onto the real stage of the world and there are no more chains and the world says Welcome; welcome to the world, you are free. Her smile is small and shy and the beautiful thing I have given up my life to believe in, and I see it and I breathe it, I am whole and I breathe it into my body.

It is over and I am so tired. It is over and I am so tired and it is time for me to leave. She may be ready but she is still terrified of my leaving, and I am yet worried and afraid to leave her alone, if she falls and breaks it will be the end of everything. But I have to leave, I know I have to leave. Wedged between the rock and hard place. A boy who hears music. Matthew. A lost boy with a young, unshaped heart who has entered our world now, a boy who is hungry for meaning. Come, I say in the short weeks after. Come and be with us. He feeds on what she and I have grown in our very specific garden, his lungs begin to fill with our world's air. He has begun to speak our language, to speak and understand the voice of empathic, connected love. He is ready and she is ready, and I am so tired and I have to leave. I step backwards, like children within my arms the two of them begin to come together as I step further back and away.

Alone in her new room in her new life, I kiss her goodbye, and in our lips are our hearts and the deep, sad sweetness of the last time. I don't know, I will never know, how to say what I saw in her eyes and what I felt as I said that goodbye.

I am so tired. I get into the car and leave behind a life that has broken into pieces. It is night, as I leave the city I can feel the ghosts I will carry from this life rising up in the dark night and coming into me, coming into my body as I leave the broken pieces behind. I drive for a long time and many things outside the window flash by. I sleep in a bed in a motel and get up the next morning and get into the car and keep driving. Late that night I stop, finally. I get out of the car and go into my sister's house. She is sitting on the couch and I go and lay down with my head on her lap. I'm here, she says. I know, I say.

As I lie there I know that this is the end. That I will fall asleep, and when I wake I will not awake. That I am very far away and the Dark Thing is within me. He will wake, without me, and I will be very far away within the Dark Thing's fortress and he will not know, he will not remember, and the battle will have begun.

At first he is only lost, is just nowhere. At first he is only himself with nothing and searching, searching for any single thing at all. All he finds are ghosts. He is surrounded by the features, the friends of his past life but it is now only his past life. He feels a wall between himself and everything and everyone around him. But he knows nothing, not even enough to say to himself, There is a wall.

She comes to him. I want to see you, Matthew wants to see you she says, and he cannot say No and she comes, they come. She and he go walking, and I dream that I am walking with her, I dream that I have awoken and am with her again. The feeling is so strong that I cry out in my sleep and the cry escapes my prison and echoes through him, echoes and builds and fills him up. It fills him with a pain that pushes him to the brink, that pushes him until he can no longer breathe. Answerless he looks to the heavens and the clouds part before the sun and the rays of the sun penetrate the darkness and he sees, with astonishment, that his love never left him. Sees for the first time that his heart was somehow swallowed up, swathed in darkness, but that no; no, the love for her is still there and has always been there, deep and true and strong, has been always still there within him.

It is wonderful and terrible. It has come too late. His love is ablaze and she is no longer there and out of control within him now the fires rage.

In a far-off, foreign land alone. Alone in a far-off place he sleeps, and the Dark Thing rises in his dreams. He dreams that he is awake and cannot move, cannot speak, and a dark-shadow Presence is in the corner of the room, a shapeless malevolence in the room with him. Paralyzed he pushes all of his will into a point of tremendous force and it breaks and he wakes, gasping. He dreams and re-dreams, breaks and re-wakes, over and over again. His dreams are a cascade of violence and silent power, ciphers and ghosts and god-like beings who bend to his ear and whisper secrets that he can never recall upon waking.

Again she comes. This time they are alone, and his love burns, out of control. The Dark Thing twists his loneliness and his desire together and paints this within his body, and blinded he does a thing that pushes her into the corner, sobbing. He falls to his knees on the edge of the abyss, asking aloud Is this what I truly am God, this horrible empty thing I feel, and she hears and her voice and hands come and pull him back; through her tears she sees how close he is to being truly gone and she reaches out, she will not let the Dark Thing take me.

Me. She walks into the dream and wakes me. Hours pass and the dream begins to crack and peel and wither away. Matthew picks us up at the airport and drives us. We sit in her room and Matthew looks at us and I see that she cannot speak a word and I find the strength inside somewhere because I have to, and I look at him and say, Matthew; and I tell him everything. Later I lie in the dark wondering and feel God with me, without calling it God. In the morning it is Matthew and I having coffee somewhere and God is in my heart and I say things to Matthew that I have never said to anyone before and that I will never say to anyone ever again.

And then I leave, then I leave them and I am alone with it, with everything, and I know that shortly I will fall asleep again, that I am yet in the fortress of the Dark Thing and still very far from the end.


Now is the long time in which they come together and break apart, come together and break apart, over and over and over again. His life is dominated by the memory of love and the memory of being whole, by the question of can he find a true life to live yet without her, by the dark fear that he cannot ask that question and answer yes. Now is when he fights; when he begins to see, as time passes, that he is locked in a battle, that he must fight to become alive again.

Home. It comes in stages, the return of his vision comes in stages as he unlocks the meaning of his memories slowly, slowly. Instinctively he knows that he must begin at the beginning, that he needs to go home.

The plains rush into the silence of the great mountains, the mystery that rises up, up into the night sky full of stars.

Do you want to smoke?, asks Leandro, and for some reason he says, Yes. Always before in his past life he said no, but his past life is a place in which he no longer lives, a gone thing, and Leandro asks Do you want to smoke?, and a wordlessness stirs inside his body and he says Yes. The smoke comes inside his body and is silent and then slowly and suddenly it is feeling, tumbling and rising waves of feeling, flowing and overflowing through him. Is this that?, Is that this?, No, it can't be!, and he laughs, there is magic in the world again, delight in the sound and light and he is filled with laughter. And then they walk and then they stop walking and he looks at something, he looks at nothing, and from nowhere come tears, from out of nowhere come teardrops suddenly falling and from nowhere words come tumbling out as Leandro listens, as Leandro is quiet and there, listening. And when it ends he looks at Leandro and realizes with a quiet shock and says, Two years; it has been two whole years since I kissed her goodbye and drove away that night, and I have been silent this whole time.

When they part that night they embrace, and within his friend's arms he realizes that for two years he has been living behind a wall and within a silence. This night, this initial outpouring, comes to him as a revelation; it is the beginning of seeing that there is an enormous thing trapped within him, and that he must find a way to let it out.

It becomes, quickly, an all-consuming thought: this

story of love, of how the power of love broke the chains that bound her; it has completely transformed his vision and understanding. He must tell it, he realizes; realizes that everything else in his life will be subjunctive to the mountain-like enormity of this story until he tells it, until he has put it out into the world. And yet, how can he? How can he do this, because the story itself cannot seem to end, continues now to unfold. He is still trapped within it and cannot find his way out.

Because without her, it seems, he is only a ghost. There is a gaping hole in the shape of her that he feels inside, constantly, and he can fill it with nothing else.

He goes to her. She comes to him. And it is joy, and it is madness. And neither one of them can stop, can say Enough, can say No.

I am with Matthew now she says, shrinking back. Then why are we here, he says with fury. You booked us a room with one bed. What do you think you are doing? Do you have any idea what you are doing to me? He stands in the rain in the dark and cannot think, stands in the rain and cannot feel, cannot think, cannot see. But somehow they find a way; always by the time they part it is close and tender and they see in each other's eyes that they have found each other again.

And it tears him apart, opens new wounds as well as old. He knows that when she leaves him she goes to a waiting heart, a waiting love. A thing that he precipitated, that would never have begun without his seal of blessing. And because of this a war is within him, a war that rages and rages.

Matthew is good. He is pure and he is good.

He is in my way, he is in my place. He has taken what belongs to me, has taken what is rightfully mine. Fucking christ, he is the brother of the friend who stabbed me in the heart!...and now he gets to receive the love of the beautiful creature I created? No way, no fucking way.

You blessed him for a reason. You blessed them for a reason. You have seen them, seen how they are; how they live in light, how from the way they are together they give light into the world around them.

He is the *brother* of the friend who *betrayed me*! Am I supposed to remain alone? This love within me that is so deep and strong that she cannot stay away from it, this love that is *so true,* that I cannot see within God's world how it could be that I must remain with it and apart from her. Alone. Am I supposed to live with this love and this pain, all alone? No way, no *fucking way...*

Would you be the thing that takes her away from him?

I sacrificed my life for her. She lives because I died.

And does that selflessness you practiced then entitle you to be selfish now?

Enough.

Is love a thing that wants? That wants anything beyond seeing her truly free, truly happy?

Enough, I said that's enough.

If you strive to kill what they are, then does not the truth of what you did for her die too?

ENOUGH!

Darkness. Deep, deep down in the darkness, where no one knows he goes, where no one else can see. In places he has never been before he finds true hatred, waiting. Here, It says. Here is the power you want, and all you have to do is take it. It is yours, and you can destroy everything.

He shivers. He remembers being at the edge of the abyss as he saw her in the corner, sobbing. These are not just memories, he realizes. There is something in me, he realizes, beyond sadness and ghosts. Something real and deadly.

But as he begins to see this, something happens. Something happens that lays full claim to his attention and draws him up and away.

The phone rings, and he knows it is her. He doesn't try and find a way to explain to himself, he is past trying to explain to himself, that as he reaches for the phone he knows in his bones it is her.

I'm in New York, she says. I just found out… Thomas is dead, she says. My brother killed himself, and her voice as she says it is a voice from the bottom of the world that cuts away everything.

Do you want me to come there.

Yes, she whispers.

No one understands. His mother and father, his friends; they say No, they say Don't, with a worry in their eyes that he sees is fear, is a real fear in them that they have lost him. It is an extra weight that he can do nothing but pick up, he cannot waste the energy in trying to explain.

She looks at me and I do not realize that I am awake.

The ghost of the brother who bore the darkness into her sits there, a pure sadness. I give her my hand and she takes it. She holds my hand and the strength of my love and she bends to the ghost and kisses his eyes closed, one-by-one, and the ghost of her brother fades away.

God grants me a respite, gives me a gift. In the bathroom I look up and see myself in the mirror. I'm still in there, I see with shock, and the tears well up. My god I am still in there. How can I be doing this?, and the question echoes and dies and there is no answer, only one answer that I am not ready to face, and the last of my strength dies away and my eyes close and I fall softly and the darkness takes me.

Danger.

He doesn't know he is in danger.

Hand on the bottle and he takes another drink, and another. He laughs and he drinks and drinks and does not see the surrounding darkness.

Hand on the steering wheel and he swerves and the world is chaos. Late at night, no one sees. Panic, blind panic, Holy fuck, ohmygodjesus, run, fuckfuckfuck go, go, *run*. He hides away, his breath comes fast and shallow as he crouches down in that darkness.

He blinks. Once, twice in the pale daylight. Pain inside his head as he sits up in bed, and then he remembers. Oh god. What did I...oh my god. He goes to the garage, sees the car, his mother's car, shit oh shit... his parents, gone for the weekend. No one knows, he can get it fixed, if no one has come for him yet, no one came out of the neighbor's house last night, no one has come for him yet and they won't because no one knows the car fixed get it fixed, in a fever he paces and his mind races,

and then suddenly somehow it stops.

It stops.

How I don't know, whether by God or grace or love I don't know. But his mind stops and he stops.

No. In a clear, quiet light he sees that no, he cannot hide this. The clear light grows inside and he sees the pain; sees that no, he cannot hide this, that he can no longer hide anything, that the pain that lives inside of him will kill him if he tries to hide. The clear, quiet light illuminates everything: he sees the gifts of love that surround him and he realizes that the pain is not a thing to die for and that he does not want to give up this life.

He dresses, slowly. Walks out of the house and down the street...that one. Jesus. The car with its side smashed sitting in the driveway, the splintered garage door, he winces inwardly at the visible evidence of violence, at the damage done. But he does not hesitate. He walks to the front door and knocks. Takes a deep breath and stands there, waiting. He hears footsteps from within the house and he sees that the road he has chosen will be a hard one.

Down in the darkness I wake, and lie without moving. Deep down in the darkness I feel him, searching, reaching out...

Stronger. He has to become stronger. To know the story he has to leave the story. To leave the story he has to become stronger than the pain.

He sees it now, the pain that lives inside of him. He knows its danger now and does not let it out of his sight. What is it. Where did it come from. He has to know more, he has to become stronger. He has been living in a world of ghosts and dreams and her; he must find how to bring himself back into life again.

Doors are thrown open, curtains are drawn back, light falls on rooms full of dust and cobwebs. The search is for the things within him that still have value; he cannot afford to carry around all the extra weight anymore, everything else must be let go. New tools and how to use them, and he can feel himself changing, the odd sensation of the movement within his body as he grows.

The pain is so strong. As he acts it reacts, attacks him over and over again. Sometimes he sees and is able to steel himself, at others he looks up and the wave is upon him, crashing down. The power of the pain is staggering, an icy black, crushing sadness that flattens him against the ground. It is the physical reality that floors him, the manifestation of the pain as a living entity; his body bent, curled into a ball, crying and crying until there are no more tears, until he is too exhausted to cry anymore.

He knows. He knows that it is wrong. Even when he is buried deep within the pain he knows that it is wrong, that he must keep fighting to find the way out. He becomes bolder, more ruthless in the choices he makes, as he realizes he has to be; as he sees, more and more, what he is truly aiming at and how far he has to go.

Patience becomes one of his strongest weapons. Time becomes an ally, bringing him endings, gifts. Nearly four long, long years since the night he looked at her and said No more, I can't take anymore; for the first time, nearly four years later he finds himself with a woman in his arms again. With the naked, beautiful body of a woman within his arms and he comes alive with the sweet fire and rises; like a soft rain falling within, alive in his body with light, a sense of wholeness returning and a vast, long-held sighing. Driving him to the airport later she giggles and says If you weren't leaving I'd do it with you again this afternoon, and he smiles at her and this gift she gives him. It changes something, he knows he is not the same when he returns home. And down inside the darkness I wonder, as I feel him searching; hear things moving, wonder what they are.

333

Weeks later Isobel is wrapped around him. Look at you two says someone, and he sees and he knows. His body is awake again and it draws her to him, his body is strong and alive again and it pulls her in close. Close, too close, afterwards she calls him on the phone and says I miss you and he says I know. It becomes a struggle, he knows it is too close but he is alive in his body again and strong in his love and he will not just stop, will not say no.

Two, three months go by and they are together again and it is the same only stronger, the world seems to fall away as they stand so close.

And she calls, after, and says You can't do this. But it is not the same as it was, he is not the same as he was, and he says I will not pretend for you that this is a dream only, that this is not love. And there is silence and she says Then we can't talk anymore, and he says Then we can't talk anymore, and there is silence and neither one of them can say it, it is so hard to say it. And then the silence is real, and it is over.

He sits there, in that sudden silence. Frustrated. Angry. Scared. A strong voice within him says Go there, now, before it is too late, get in the car or buy the plane ticket, whatever it takes you have no time to lose, *go there*.

He sits very still and knows he can't. This is the line, he will not cross this line. No matter how much it scares him he has to stand firm on the ground he has chosen, he has to have faith.

He sees that there is nothing here any longer; that home has left him, and so it is time to leave home. As he drives away he feels it disappear behind him. Alone in his body in the vast nature of the open world, what he is searching for is out there, somewhere.

A girl, in New Orleans. Icy streets in Chicago. In Mexico a tiny fishing village hidden along the Pacific coast. Places where no one knows him, where no one knows where he comes from; people who see only what he is in the moment he enters their lives, and what they see and what they say is what he becomes. The architecture of a life that is not her; from within it he looks out, his vision growing. He feels the Dark Thing within him and he bends to the work again and wonders Will it ever end, will it ever be a thing that ends.

It is a year later. He is in the city where she lives. He thinks, hesitates. Picks up the phone and her voice says Hello, and he says I am here.

They are having a drink, her eyes are wide and strange as she looks at him and he cannot find what he is feeling. Another drink, and another. At her apartment she lies down next to him on the couch. A key in the front door and she sits up and the door opens.

And my eyes open and I see Matthew, the once-young boy with the once-but-no-longer unshaped heart; Matthew, who I know loves me, who despite everything I have done and because of everything I have done, Matthew who I know only loves me. He is surprised and happy to see me but not only, because he knows and she knows and I know, and we three talk, talk as though we don't know and I do not like it, and in the morning when I leave I do not like it, do not like this feeling.

Days later she writes and she cuts me. I am reading her words. I don't understand and there is a darkness gathering around me and then I see, I see what she is doing, she is lying to me, these words are deadly lies that she is using to try and cut me, *to hurt me*. She is using the trust and truth I have given her, and hidden

335

within it she is trying *to cut me*.

What I feel at first is shock. And as it fades I am filled with anger. I gave up my life so that you could live again. I have walked, alone, across the world searching for a way to let you go, to find for us, one way or another, an ending. All the while you live in the love I left you with, the love I blessed you with. And now you try and take away my eyes, to tell me that I am only a dream, to take the last thing I have left away from me…no. *No.*

The anger blooms in white fire that burns away the last of the life I gave to her. She is free and her actions will generate reactions, find protection from the truth where and if you can but it is finally not my job to provide you with anything any longer. I write the anger down and the truth down and send it like an arrow and I aim for her heart.


Please don't ever contact me again.
Peace,
   Isobel


That's all she writes. That's all there is.

It tells me everything I need to know.

I am sitting in a motel room when I read these three lines and let it go. The sadness comes without regret. The ghosts rise, in the corners and the edges of the room, all around me they rise up and are still and silent.

The Dark Thing sits within me. Of course It is still within me; not her, never her, a thing within her that I took out of her, took out of her and into my body.

How?

Why?

I drift back down and away, into the shadow world. He travels onwards, still searching.

Time goes by. Time heals all wounds, reveals all monuments.

One year, two years.

Where is your life, and what are you doing, she says.

I look, see that the shadow world is closing around me, and that I must find my way out.

He begins to write the story down.

Another year, and another. And another...

And now I see.

I am here, in the heart of the fortress of the Dark Thing. I have walked through the wilderness of pain and the long, cold darkness and finally I see it all, finally I know everything.

"Am I strong enough?" I whisper.

"Of course you are," Isobel says softly, as she walks up beside me. A quiet kind of light, a garden, grows slowly up in a circle around us, amidst the surrounding darkness; a garden of vines and leaves and flowers, glowing from within, in shades of green and violet and gold.

I turn to her. She is just as I remember; the heart that I saw deep within her, so long ago, the vision that she finally became. In her face, in her dress, in the way she holds herself within her body; that self-assurance grounded in true empathy; she is as I remember her, a quiet, beautiful radiance. I take a deep breath at seeing her again, after so many years, standing now before me.

"I wondered...if I would find you here," I say. "I thought so, but I could never be sure."

She shakes her head; looks up at me, her eyes deep and full of meaning. "Just because the line has gone silent, do you think it means we aren't still tied

337

together? It's been almost seven years now, since the last time. Long enough. I wouldn't let you do this alone."

So many things. So many things go through me as I look at her. Thirteen years, since she sat there on my kitchen counter. So far away, and so many things…

"You know," I say, slowly, "it still…even though I was there, every step of the way, even though I saw you changing before my eyes, it still…it still kind of takes my breath away to see you now."

"I know," she says, looking down at herself. "As time goes by, it's less and less, obviously. But sometimes, there will be something that makes me… remember. And I'll look at my hands, or at myself in the mirror…and I still can't believe it; all over again, I still can't believe it…that I'm here, that I'm actually *here* now." Her eyes are wide as she speaks, looking down at her hands held out before her, turning them over, her voice carries her wonder; not just wonder, but deeper than that, a sense of awe. And then she looks up at me, and her face changes; and she smiles a small, sad smile. "And then I think of you," she says, and the sadness is in her eyes. "And then I think of you. I think of you out there, on the other side of that silence between us, out there somewhere. And I wonder where you are."

I bend my head, close my eyes. Letting it flow, feeling them, seeing the words as they rise up.

"You know, I…I couldn't listen to Kid A for years, afterwards," I say quietly as I raise my head, open my eyes. She takes a deep breath, gathering herself; nods once, waiting for me to go on. "Sometimes," I continue, "it would come on the stereo somewhere, some coffee shop or something. I'd be alone, or I'd be with other people, it didn't matter; whatever was going on, it would stop me in my tracks. Would touch this sadness, this deep sense of loss inside. It wasn't just Kid A, there were all kinds of things like that. Triggers, that would suddenly remind me, viscerally, all over again; take me back inside the shadow, the ghost of what I couldn't go back to, of what wasn't there anymore…when things ended, finally, between us, I didn't question the obvious fact that it was necessary. And even though in some ways, I didn't want it to be, it was a relief; more than it was anything else, it was a relief to know that it was finally over. That the story of us had finally come to an end, that I could finally…that I could finally breathe again."

I stop, feel the memory of it within me as I look at her; she looks down, and is still. She takes in a slow breath, slowly lets it back out. Looks up at me and nods, briefly.

"At first," I continue, "it was just a matter of breathing; feeling what it was like to be alone and breathing again. And finally, there was space now; for the first time, there was space between me and all those memories. But I was still just drifting, still in that shadow-world. And then I met someone. Someone who pointed out the obvious thing that I still wasn't seeing, and… woke me up. Opened my eyes up so that I could see where I was, and when I saw it I realized, clearly, that I had to get out. So I started walking, searching through all the dreams and memories. I felt the Dark Thing out there, watching, waiting for me. How?, I wondered. How did It leave your body, and enter into mine?…that was the obvious, central question. I saw the fact, of that it had happened, and the sense of it, with perfect clarity. That I had somehow engineered this transference, be-cause that was the only way. That you couldn't do it;

couldn't end It, couldn't break It down. That you had me, but only me, and that wasn't enough. But I came from a life filled with love, that had always been rooted in love. So I rolled the dice, in a way; certainly a kind of gamble, to take It into myself. But it was a calculated gamble, and I believed in myself. And I loved you, and it was the only way. In the end, it was that I loved you, with all of who I was, in a way I had never loved anyone in my entire life before; so I was going to do whatever it took, to set you free…and nothing else mattered."

I stop, as her eyes close. Watch as two tears, one after the other, break free from her eyes and roll slowly down her cheeks. She looks down, with her fingers wipes the tears away. A shudder, a small shiver runs through her. She looks back up at me, nods for me to go on.

"So," I say, my voice quieter now, "I accepted the matter of that transference, from your body into mine, as fact. But the 'how' was still something I didn't understand, couldn't see. So I kept looking, walking through the memories, searching. And what I began to see was this way in which I had…divided myself. Separated myself; different selves, with different tasks, separate selves doing separate things. Part of me that remembered everything, that built things with words… and part of me that was lost, that was lost in a world of dreams and memories and shadows….and fighting to find my way out."

I stop. I can see in her eyes that she knows, that she already knows.

"When you…told me. What you'd done. What had happened, while I'd been gone…I saw all of it, saw everything, then; one of those eternal kind of moments, the same thing, I suppose, that people mean when they talk about a whole life flashing before your eyes. I saw it: that your...betrayal...that it was your way of proving to me that you *were* the darkness. And I saw that I had to take all of it, the whole blow...in order to make you finally understand that you were wrong."

We stare at each other. The tears are running down her face.

She sighs, looks down. Slowly wipes the tears away. Makes a visible effort to collect herself; begins to speak, stops, shakes her head. Finally she looks up, looks at me for a long time. When she speaks, her voice is soft, and the words are precise and clear.

"This...thing, this thing you call the Dark Thing... that was once mine, and became yours. All It is, is the thing that hides your light. All It is, is the shadow you hide in, the place where you try and hide from who you are. You brought your light into my life. You walked in and you burned away the darkness, and you showed me love. You showed me how to love; that it wasn't a word you said, it was a thing you did. You were relentless; you burned away everything I thought I knew about life, everything I thought I knew about who I was. And then when I...when I tried to break your heart, you... you let me. You let me break your heart. And when I saw it break is when I realized everything you'd been saying to me, everything you'd shown to me, was true... too late. Too late, too late, too late. I tried so hard. It hurt so much to love you and watch you die away like that. But that was the whole point. For me to finally understand the truth of love, you had to let yourself die."

She looks at me, as the tears roll slowly down her face, looks at me in the way that only she has ever looked at me; all the way into me. I can almost not bear it, this way she looks at me, my god…it *hurts*.

"How can you do that," I say quietly. "How do you just brush it all away like it's nothing, and look straight into my heart."

She reaches out and puts her hand against my face. "Because you let me," she whispers. "Don't you see? No one had ever done that for me before. I came in because you let me." And the years fall away and the world falls away, and it is just she and I, alone together again. She kisses me, kisses my lips softly; one last time, forever and always.

"Yes, you are strong enough. Remember when I told you, that when you were ready to tell the story, you could say anything you needed to say; about me, about my family, about Thomas, about Tyler and Matthew, about anything; remember when I said that to you?"

"I remember. Of course I remember. I couldn't have done this if you hadn't said it."

"It was the one gift I could give you, in return. I knew you were strong enough. But this time you had to find the way without me. This time, you had to find your way back to love on your own."

She puts her hand against my chest and I feel it. Beneath her hand I feel it inside me; the illimitable wonder, the soft, fierce thing that burns so bright. The green vines, the tender flowers, the stars leave trails of golden sparks as they rain down.

Come to me.

Come to me, and I will show you what you are.

I take her hand in mine and I watch her eyes watch me, with so much hope, until they are gone and she is gone.

Before me stands the Dark Thing.

Come to me and I will show you what you are.

Its shadow fingers reach for me, wrap around me, they fill my eyes, fill everything with darkness.

But this is me. This is my pain, my truth. The world I choose to live in. This is love, the greatest power, the heaviest burden. And it lives within me and it is me, the strongest thing of all.

Thank you, I say to the Dark Thing as I reach for it. The light is in my hands, resting at my fingertips. I feel it within me, my body radiant with the light and alive as the Dark Thing begins to shatter, becomes brittle and shatters, a thing that has no function anymore.

Thank you.

Goodbye.

And it is gone.

There is a door. I open it.

He is sitting at the desk in the pool of lamp-light, writing.

I am sitting at the desk in the pool of lamp-light, writing. I stop, and am still for a moment. Because it is almost over, only a very last, few words left now.

I carry the light, I carry the soft fire. This is my testament.

This is love.

## Author's Note

As a self-published author, I need your help to deliver this book to a larger audience. You can provide that help by sharing the book with your friends and family, posting about it on your social networks, and writing a review on the book's page on Amazon. You can find out more about me and my work, and contact me directly at jeremyjaeger.com. Thanks for your time, and thank you for reading.

Made in the USA
Lexington, KY
10 May 2017